Readers are raving about

CURSED

By Rhianne Aile

Intriguing characterization is backed by steamy sensuality, which in turn is underscored by the theme of true fated love.

—*Rainbow Reviews*

I was enthralled from the first word until the very last. I could not put this book down.

—*Fallen Angel Reviews*
Recommended Read

Rhianne Aile delivers a wonderfully enchanting story of magic, thrill, suspense and above all else…love.

—*Joyfully Reviewed*
A Joyfully Recommended Selection

NOVELS BY
RHIANNE AILE

Betrayed
Cursed
The One That Got Away (with Madeleine Urban)
To Love a Cowboy

Betrayed
Rhianne Aile

Dreamspinner Press

Published by
Dreamspinner Press
4760 Preston Road
Suite 244-149
Frisco, TX 75034
http://www.dreamspinnerpress.com/

This is a work of fiction. Names, characters, places and incidents either are the product of the author's imagination or are used fictitiously, and any resemblance to actual persons, living or dead, business establishments, events or locales is entirely coincidental.

Betrayed
Copyright © 2010 by Rhianne Aile

Cover Art by Anne Cain annecain.art@gmail.com
Cover Design by Mara McKennen

All rights reserved. No part of this book may be reproduced or transmitted in any form or by any means, electronic or mechanical, including photocopying, recording, or by any information storage and retrieval system without the written permission of the Publisher, except where permitted by law. To request permission and all other inquiries, contact Dreamspinner Press, 4760 Preston Road, Suite 244-149, Frisco, TX 75034
http://www.dreamspinnerpress.com/

ISBN: 978-1-61581-392-6

Printed in the United States of America
First Edition
January, 2010

eBook edition available
eBook ISBN: 978-1-61581-393-3

To Cat

Prologue

THE werewolf shifted on the pallet of pillows and furs, the deep, soft nap of the furs stroking his bare skin. The room was warm; the image of an earlier fire danced along the edge of his consciousness. When he concentrated on remembering, everything faded into a fuzzy blur. He relaxed, and snatches of sensation began to get clearer.

Someone was lying next to him, the heart rate and slow, even breathing indicating the depth of sleep. He shifted closer, the tantalizing scent of his mate immediately rousing him. He concentrated on the man next to him. Even without being able to see, he knew with certainty that it was a man. He could feel the heat radiating off his body and could smell a combination of male musk and sex from their earlier lovemaking.

The body beside him shifted as his mate curled into him in search of comfort and warmth. The werewolf's arms closed around his lover, assuring him that he wasn't alone in the dark. A sure hand stroked through the hair on his chest, lingering over the tightening nubs of his nipples, knowing exactly where and how to touch to rouse him into a frenzy of desire. A low growl rumbled from his chest.

Throwing one leg over his mate's hip, the werewolf pressed his erect cock against the firm muscles of the body in his arms. He rocked back and forth, marking his mate with the scent of his desire. Extending his tongue, he tasted the skin down the side of his lover's neck, running just the tip of his tongue in patterns through the soft hair behind his ear.

A pleading whimper caused his nascent wolf to rise up, anxious to lay claim to their mate. The werewolf searched under the furs, his hand finding a hardening cock. Swallowing a howl of delight, he grasped it gently and began to stroke it to full hardness.

His mate burrowed closer, rubbing their bodies together and commingling their scents into a heady aphrodisiac. He entwined their legs, canting his hips to bring their erections into contact. Groaning, the slender man pushed himself forward so that he was lying almost on top of the broader form of the awakening werewolf.

The werewolf cradled his mate's face, straining to make out the features. He'd been denied a mate for so long, his body ached to be able to finally see the face of his beloved. Tunneling his fingers into the silk-soft hair, he pushed it back from the smooth skin, his thumbs outlining the sharp contour of cheekbones, the subtle curve of lips, and the slight rasp on the tip of his chin, but a clear image floated just out of reach. Unable to resist, he leaned forward and ran the tip of his tongue over the small patch of stubbled skin. Tilting the head in his hands, he joined their lips for a deep, slow kiss.

The familiar hands rubbed the werewolf's shoulders in widening circles and moved down his back. When they reached the base of his spine, the fingers splayed open over his ass, pulling him up from the furs and closer, increasing the friction between their cocks.

His wolf was becoming impatient, pacing and watching for a chance to break free. His mate's touch distracted him to the point where the concentration necessary to keep his wolf under control was slipping. He needed to speed things up, but this subtle buildup was so intoxicating.

The man in his arms nuzzled under his ear, nipping sharply. An involuntary shiver ran through the werewolf's body. A wet tongue replaced the warm breath and then the cool sensation of moving air caused another shiver as his lover blew softly on his neck. "I want you inside me," a husky voice whispered.

His wolf leapt forward suddenly, rolling on top of their mate and pinning him to the furs. The werewolf struggled not to relinquish control to his wolf, pinning the man under him to keep him still. Every enticing squirm fueled his wolf's strength and lessened his resolve to fight it. "Still," he ordered in a deep rumble that was a mixture of human voice and lupine growl.

The scent of arousal increased, the body pinned beneath him violently shuddering and then going completely limp. Words fell over the werewolf like a cooling rain. "Shh... easy, baby. Come back and let me love you."

His wolf pulled back with a whimper, unsatisfied at being denied release, but soothed by the calming tone. The werewolf loosened his grip, granting his lover the freedom to move again. Immediately the long, slender legs opened, circling his hips. Deft fingers moved between their bodies, coating his shaft and guiding him to the opening of his mate's body. "You need me, don't you? Come love me, so you'll both be satisfied."

The werewolf matched the head of his shaft to the small opening and pushed inside with one loud, rumbling groan. He began to move, pulling out until the head of his cock caught on the tight ring of muscle and then thrusting back in quickly. Every thrust of his hips caused a stream of whimpers and moans from his mate that spurred him to move faster, deeper, harder.

As his climax built, the connection with his mate began to fade. The werewolf struggled to pull back, desperate not to lose the link with the man he loved, but unable to stop the rush of pleasure building in his body. Clutching the man in his arms tightly to his body, he buried his face against the slender neck. Just as his body exploded with the most intense pleasure he'd ever experienced, his lover disappeared, the body... the scent... the warmth... the room fading into cool, gray mist.

Throwing back his head, he howled his pain into the dark, the gray mist absorbing his call.

Chapter 1

WILL NORTHLAND sat curled on a window seat in the library at the Sterling estate, his long, dark hair falling forward around his face as he gazed down unseeing at the book in his lap. His twin brother, Tristan, was officially mated to Benjamin Sterling, so that made Will family, but he still felt like he was intruding on Benjamin's hospitality. It had been six months since Tristan had asked him to cross the ocean from their London home to help him cast the spell that had reunited Benjamin with his wolf and saved his life.

The spell had been a success, and Benjamin had been welcomed into the local werepack: a definite change for the better when it came to his social standing. Tristan and Benjamin had been invited over for dinner tonight with the pack Rajan, Alex Hanover, and Alex's consort, Raul. Over breakfast, they had begged, pleaded, and cajoled Will into accompanying them, but he just wasn't in the mood for being the fifth wheel—something he'd been feeling a lot lately.

All the signs pointed to something major happening in his life soon, but he took that with a grain of salt. Everything happens in its time, Gran used to say. He just needed to let go and not go messing about with things best left to the Goddess.

His cell phone buzzed in his pocket. Glancing at the screen, he flipped it open. "Davie, you wanker, you haven't burned the place down, have you?" Davie Campbell and Scott Glover were his right and left hands at the small occult bookstore in London that he and Tristan had inherited from their grandmother.

"No, not that you'd care, ya wanker. Off gallivanting all over the globe," Davie retorted.

Davie was young, but reliable and efficient, and Will fully realized what a treasure he had. When Tristan had needed him, it was nothing to hand over the bookstore to Davie and Scott. The two men treated it as if it were their own, and would bend over backwards to make it successful. Will could see Davie now, hip propped on the edge of the giant, scarred desk. He'd be wearing jeans. The only time Will had ever seen Davie in anything but jeans had been at his gran's funeral. Both Davie and Scott had shown up in proper charcoal gray suits, causing Will to do a double take. The two stoners actually cleaned up pretty well. He suspected that the suits were bought for the occasion, possibly even rented, but he was touched by the effort.

"So if the store isn't on fire, why are you pestering me?" Will teased, folding his long legs and hugging his knees, the phone propped between his shoulder and ear, anxious to hear about life in the country that he'd left behind.

"Just checking in. I figured, you're the boss, and you just might like to know what is going on. Sales are up almost fifteen percent."

"You put the damn manga display in anyway, didn't you?" Will asked.

"Well, you said to run it like it was our own," Scott chimed in from the background. The terrible twosome obviously had him on speakerphone.

"And they're flying out of here, just like I told you they would," Davie added.

"Fuckers." Will shook his head, glad that they couldn't see the smile on his face.

Tristan, however, could. His twin walked into the room, spotted the phone at Will's ear, and curled into a wingback leather chair. "Davie and Scott?" he mouthed with a grin that mirrored Will's.

Will nodded, listening to the chatter on the other end of the line as the two men filled him in on sales, customers, and the gossip that ran rampant in a small metaphysical community. He'd long ago gotten used to Davie starting a sentence and Scott finishing it. Before long the two were talking more to each other than him. "Guys. Guys!" he finally broke in. "Tristan needs me for something. I'll talk to you in a few days, okay?"

They exchanged quick good-byes, and Tristan moved to curl up on the opposite side of the window seat from Will, their legs resting against each other in the middle. Tristan had always worn his thick, almost black hair shorter than Will's, but the window reflected two identical faces, framed by cascades of hair well beyond their shoulders. "Gran would say you need a haircut," Will stated, brushing Tristan's hair back from his face.

Tristan mimicked the action. "She'd be very disappointed in both of us."

"No, she wouldn't. She'd just chastise us for looking scruffy." Will chuckled. "She'd turn over in her grave if she knew that neither of us has had a haircut since she died."

Eyes gazing unfocused out the window, Tristan said, "She once told me that she harped on our hair because otherwise we were perfect and it was a grandmother's duty to complain about something."

"Ha! Now there's an expectation that's impossible to live up to."

Tristan looked back at his twin. "Not in her eyes. We could have ended up ax murderers, and she would have found a way to be proud of us. Some days I miss her so much my heart hurts."

Will scooted over to put an arm around his brother. "I didn't think there was room in your heart for anything but love these days. With Benjamin in your life, you practically walk on air." Tristan laid his head on Will's shoulder and Will rested his cheek on his twin's soft curls.

"I've never been happier. I can't describe how it feels to be with Benjamin—"

"Damn!" Will snapped his fingers in mock frustration. "I was so looking forward to some juicy details. My sex life's been a bit lacking lately."

Tristan elbowed his brother in the side, grinning when he buckled over with a sharply exhaled, "Oof."

"Don't bring up feelings if you don't want to talk about them," he scolded. "You sure you won't come to dinner with us? You know you are welcome."

"Yeah, but you guys are just too damn touchy-feely for me, and Alex and Raul are no better. I swear… you'd think werewolves would be more… I don't know… feral."

Tristan's eyes sparkled. "Oh, they're plenty wild.…" He drew out the last word and left it hanging, leaving no doubt as to what he was referring to.

"Fuckin' wanker," Will cursed, cuffing Tristan's shoulder. "Not fair gloating over your sex life when I have none and you won't share."

THE smell of grilled meat drifted in through the open windows of the farmhouse, mingling with the crisp, sweet tang of lilac. Tristan could hear the quiet rumble of his mate's laughter as Benjamin joked with Alex and Raul on the patio. The hair on the back of his neck rose and a tiny shiver traveled down his spine. He reached for the half-empty bottle of wine sitting on the kitchen counter, adding a splash to the salad dressing he was mixing and the remainder to his glass.

Something wasn't right. Tristan had been uneasy all day and had been experiencing unexpected chills since he and his mate had entered packlands. There was no safer place to be than the home of the Rajan, or King, of the local werepack, but that didn't keep the witch from sensing a pall of dread and fear. A new voice entered the mix, and Tristan headed for the open French doors, certain that the cause of his unease was about to be revealed.

Eric, the head of the Guardians—the werewolves who protected and patrolled the borders of the packlands—stood before Alex, explaining something to the Rajan. Raul, the Rajan's consort, stood beside his mate, a frown creasing his brow.

"Do you wish me to send him away?" Alex asked his mate, strong fingers reaching out to brush through his consort's thick, blond hair.

Raul shook his head, leaning into the touch, seeking comfort and reassurance. "No, it was inevitable that I'd have to face my family at some point. Grant him safe passage and we'll hear what he has to say. My father wouldn't have sent Nicolai unless it was extremely important."

Alex turned to the tall dark warrior, dressed in the silver torque of his position. "Allow him to enter, but escort him directly here. Double the normal guard on the borders and the house."

"It will be done," the Guardian replied, bowing formally before turning to leave.

"Maybe we should go," Benjamin suggested, rising from the deck chair.

Raul placed a hand on his friend's shoulder, squeezing slightly as he pressed him back into his seat. "No. You know my past. There is no reason for you and Tristan not to be present for this discussion. In fact, I'd like you here. I should like Tristan's opinion."

The slender witch walked over to the small group, perching on the arm of his mate's chair. "On what?"

"The man who is coming is one of my father's most trusted advisors, and fairly elderly. It would not be easy for him to travel. If he is here, he brings no good news. I have no idea what has transpired in my absence, but based on what was happening before I left and the circumstances surrounding my arrival here—"

"You mean the attempt to murder you?" Benjamin tossed in sarcastically. "Or rather, trick Alex into killing you legally."

Raul nodded, a slight grin tugging at the corner of his mouth. "Yeah, that...."

"You know, I still have never heard the complete version of that story—only pieces as they appear in conversation, like now," Tristan reminded the group.

"Later, I promise," Raul said, pulling a long curling lock of the witch's dark hair straight with a sharp tug.

Tristan swatted the blond man's hand away from his hair as if he were shooing away flies. "Fine, fine. What do you want my opinion on?"

"I guess the veracity of what Nicolai is coming to say. I can judge the words; I want you to judge the feeling, the intent... read between the lines for me," Raul answered.

"I can do that," Tristan agreed, taking a sip of his wine before offering the glass to his mate.

Benjamin's blue eyes glowed up at him, his hand reaching up to curve around Tristan's neck and pull him down for a kiss. His low voice rumbled against his mate's lips. "Tastes much better from you... and far more intoxicating."

Alex cleared his throat to warm them of Eric's return. All four men stood, watching as the small party made its way across the yard from the tree line.

Coming to a halt directly in front of Alex and Raul, the elderly man in the center of the approaching group struggled to kneel. Alex reached out instinctively, catching his arm. "Your neck is enough, *Adel*, ancient one."

Nicolai's eyes darted up gratefully as he bared his neck, lowering his eyes as he offered his life to the Rajan in the ritualistic show of submission. Alex lowered his mouth to the vulnerable juncture, breathing in deeply as his teeth touched the skin. He could feel the steady beat of Nicolai's heart and smell the worry wafting off the elder. Worry. Not fear.

*P*ANTING *to catch his breath, Raul ran, head down, flying around trees and leaping over brush. A pack of werewolves was closing on him. By the sound of the howls, it was a standard hunting group of six males, all in their prime. Raul was a match for their speed, agility, and stamina, but they knew the terrain, which gave them a huge advantage. It was only a matter of time before they caught him.*

Reaching the road he'd been headed toward before the Hunters had crossed his scent, he bounded straight across and into the woods on the other side. He'd been forced to change to wolf form when he'd heard the first pack call. It would have been impossible to escape them as a man, which made the road no good to him now. As a wolf, he'd either be shot or hit. If he changed back into human form, he'd be arrested for indecent exposure and with no ID, he'd be hard pressed to explain his presence without involving his family.

The trees began to thin out, allowing him to pick up speed. Focusing straight ahead, Raul put on a burst of speed that he suspected would be his last. He needed some divine intervention to escape. Breaking the tree line, he was hit squarely from the left by a dark wolf that matched him for size. The two went tumbling, each attempting to gain the superior position, growling, snapping, and biting. The dark wolf finally pinned him. He was exhausted from the run and possibly still depleted from whatever had knocked him unconscious. The attacking wolf seemed fresh and was ahead of the others. He must have heard the calls and circled ahead of him.

The dark wolf stood, his mouth remaining on Raul's neck, a low dangerous rumble issuing from his chest. Even in this vulnerable position, Raul's wolf knew it was in no danger. The dark wolf was completely in control and if it had wanted to kill, it already would have. When Raul remained passive, belly up, legs spread, limp, the victor took a step back, shaking his dark, thick ruff and shimmering into his human form. He was slightly over six feet, matching Raul in height and weight, his hair long with red highlights streaking the gold. Even in the dark, the ice-blue of his eyes glowed.

Raul was surprised. The werewolf was far more vulnerable in his human form. If he'd had his brother's instincts, he'd have lunged, but the diplomat in him recognized an offer of peace. Rolling to his feet, he changed, remaining on the ground so the other werewolf wouldn't feel threatened. Bowing his head, he ceded the fight as a man.

"Who are you?"

Raul stood, straightening to his full height, heedless of the lack of clothes on either of them. "Raul Carlisle, Beta of the Cayuga werepack."

The full listing of his title and family line were cut short by the barks and howls of the Hunters reaching the tree line. He expected them to break through and kneeled to show that he'd already been subdued. The wolf next to him was obviously Alpha in both posture and scent. The Hunters would likely surround them to protect their Alpha and carry out his orders, but they wouldn't attack until ordered by their superior.

When the wolves didn't enter the clearing, but stayed just out of sight in the trees, their barks growing more agitated, Raul looked up at the Alpha werewolf for an explanation.

"They won't enter my land," the man said simply, extending his hand to help Raul to his feet. "Benjamin Sterling," he added, introducing himself in an unexpectedly human gesture.

Raul took the offered hand, his eyes darting back to the wolves just out of sight. "Why won't they enter?"

"I am *Phelan*," Benjamin answered matter-of-factly, watching the newcomer for his reaction.

"Cursed?" Raul asked, looking at the man suspiciously. He'd never actually met a werewolf changed by a curse. All of the members of his pack were hereditary, with the exception of his twin's witch. She was an outsider who had petitioned the pack to be changed so she could mate with Richard, but the Council had yet to pass judgment. "They won't enter your home, but they let you live on packland?"

"They really don't have a choice." Benjamin shrugged. "My family has owned this land for generations. Centuries of cursed ancestors are buried there." He nodded toward a small hill.

Raul could see the headstones silhouetted in the moonlight. "Hallowed ground."

Benjamin nodded. "If you will accept my sanctuary, you are welcome in my home. Even the hospitality of a Phelan beats being killed for trespassing."

Raul silently agreed, but replied formally. Werewolves could be a ceremonious bunch. "I gratefully accept your offer of sanctuary and acknowledge that I owe you a life debt." He bowed, holding his head to the side to bare his neck, offering his life should his savior choose to take it.

Benjamin grasped Raul's shoulder, encouraging him to straighten. "Let's go up to the house and find some scotch to enjoy while we share stories. I'll tell you the history of my family if you'll share how a prince with impeccable protocol ends up running from a pack of Hunters."

"Agreed. Which way?"

"Farther east. We'll travel faster on four feet than two," Benjamin added, shimmering into the dark wolf, eyes still glowing. With a sharp yip, he turned and bounded toward the hill that held the cemetery.

Raul changed and followed, a sonorous howl answering the dark wolf's call.

A large estate appeared on the horizon as they rounded the hill. Open meadow changed to orchard and formal gardens. Raul slowed to match Benjamin's pace as they approached the house. Heading straight for the veranda, the dark wolf loped over the flagstone and pushed through a wolf-sized door into a wine cellar of cold, gray stone, with wooden racks holding hundreds of bottles.

Benjamin shimmered back to human form, indicating that Raul should do the same. Pulling boxers and jeans from a dresser in the corner, he tossed a set to his guest. "I always keep extra clothes around. It helps me keep staff."

Raul stepped into the jeans, fastening the buttons. "Do you always come in through a dog door?" he asked, his voice heavily laced with humor.

Benjamin chuckled, pulling a shirt from a hook on the wall and throwing it around his shoulders. "My grandfather had it made. My grandmother hated him coming back into the house naked after hunting. This way, he could sneak in as a wolf and dress properly before joining her in the parlor."

"Ah... well, that explains it. Now, you mentioned scotch," Raul reminded, not so subtly, rubbing his hands together.

"A man after my own heart," Benjamin exclaimed, clapping his guest on the back and letting his hand rest around the broad shoulders as they walked toward the door. "I wish it did more than taste good, but you can't have everything."

"Yeah, I remember being so disappointed as a teenager when I'd go out drinking with my friends and stay annoyingly sober while they got plastered. Drunk people can be amazingly irritating when you aren't inebriated. My twin's girlfriend has concocted a potion that seems to affect him very much like alcohol, but I don't like ingesting things I know are spelled."

Benjamin bristled slightly at the mention of potions and spells. "Your twin is mated to a witch?"

They had reached a cozy room that Raul would label a library. Most of the walls were lined with floor to ceiling bookcases, the books all looking well-read. Comfortable leather chairs and scarred wooden tables were scattered around the room. One of the tables held a crystal decanter and glasses. "Well, not mated, just dating. It is her wish to be turned, so they might mate," Raul answered as Benjamin poured them both glasses of deep amber liquid, "but the pack council has yet to vote."

It was too warm for a fire, but they sat around the fireplace nonetheless; something about fireplaces and kitchen tables draws people for discussions. "I've been married, but based on the descriptions I've heard, it wasn't a mating. Does mating only happen between two werewolves?" Benjamin mused.

"No. We have pack members that are mated to humans, but because of his position in the pack, she would have to be changed. He is in line to be Alpha, which would make her the Alpha female and bearer of children. Richard seems besotted with her, but I don't sense the kind of bond that would imply a life mating. That may just be my prejudices, though. There is something about her I don't trust."

"Oh...?"

"I suspect that she is behind my little trip," Raul said, realizing it was probably time for some explanations. "What day is it and where am I?"

"It is Friday and you are just outside of Rocky Falls, New York," Benjamin answered readily.

"Well, at least I'm still in the US," Raul snorted derisively. "On Thursday evening, I got back late from a Council meeting. I ate the dinner I assumed my housekeeper had prepared for me and that is the last thing I remember until I woke up, my head pounding, in a clearing about fifteen miles west of here."

"It's not easy to drug a werewolf. Most drugs don't work. We metabolize them too fast," Benjamin commented, staring into the cold stone fireplace as if he could read the future in the absent flames.

"Which is why I suspect Sienna, Richard's witch. She is ambitious. Richard is not enough for her as third in line to the throne. She wants to be Alpha and Mother. Within our royal line, the Alpha bears children or grants for children to be born. It cuts down on the amount of infighting for dominance." Raul ran a weary hand through his hair, dislodging a leaf. "Guess I could use a bath," he chuckled.

"I wasn't thinking." Benjamin got to his feet. "You must be hungry and exhausted."

"Actually, I ate before I ran into you, but someplace to sleep would be welcome. Can I take a rain check on the rest of our conversation?" Raul asked, not wanting to appear rude. They had talked about him and he had yet to find out anything about his host.

"Certainly, though I'm afraid my tale isn't nearly as interesting as yours. Let me take you up to a room. Mary, my housekeeper, always keeps a couple of rooms made up for guests." Benjamin led the way out of the library and up a wide staircase to the second floor. Walking down a hall of identical doors, he opened the second on the right and stepped aside.

Raul walked into a large bedroom, decorated completely in browns from the dark walnut of the wood to the light cream of the carpet. There was another unlit fireplace in the corner with a picture of a majestic looking auburn wolf above the mantle. "Family?" he asked, indicating the painting.

Benjamin laughed. "No, my family doesn't tend to celebrate its dark side. I actually started collecting wolf prints several years ago. Having my business colleagues view wolves as my 'hobby' works to my advantage."

"I can see that." Raul prowled around the room, his wolf quiet inside of him, sensing no danger. Phelan or not, he liked Benjamin Sterling.

Crossing to a connecting door, Benjamin opened it and switched on the light. "This is the bathroom. The kitchen is downstairs in the opposite direction from the library, but I'll come get you in the morning. Old houses like this can get a little confusing. We are close enough to the same size that my clothes should do until we can get to town to buy you some. Do you want a phone tonight to call your family?"

The final comment caught Raul by surprise. That should have been his first instinct, but until the other man suggested it, it had never even occurred to him. For a second, loneliness swamped him. Wolves were social creatures, yet he lived a very solitary existence. A man or wolf of his age should have a mate, someone at home who would worry about him, but no one had ever come close to stirring that level of interest in him. His mother and father would be worried, but until he figured out what was going on, it suited his purposes for his location and health to remain unknown. "No. I think for now it is best for whoever did this to think that they succeeded."

The hollow tone in the other werewolf's voice roused Benjamin's wolf. Walking to the Prince's side, he pulled him into a tight embrace. Wolves were very tactile creatures, communicating more through body contact than sound. It was the thing that he missed most, being ostracized from the pack. They stood that way for several minutes, each leaning into the strength of the other—two lone wolves brought together by sorcery.

"Get some rest," Benjamin said finally. "Tomorrow morning, we'll make a plan."

Raul nodded, watching as the door closed behind his host.

BENJAMIN was up early the next morning, taking care of business so he could spend the day helping Raul in whatever way he could. Ending a call with his assistant in New York, he sat back in his chair and propped his feet on the desk. Sensing Conrad's entrance more than hearing it, he turned, smiling at his houseman. "Good morning, Conrad. I have something I'd like you to research for me."

"Yes, sir." The stately man nodded slightly. Tall and slender, with large hands and feet, he looked like a teenager who hadn't quite grown into his body. Only the gray at his temples gave away his true age.

"We have a guest in the east wing." Benjamin didn't have to specify how he wanted him treated. His staff was first-rate and spoiled everyone equally. "I need you to find out everything you can for me about the Cayuga werepack, including what is currently going on with politics and gossip."

Conrad wasn't a werewolf, but he had incredible contacts. "Will *this afternoon be soon enough, sir?"*

Benjamin smirked. *"I think that'll do,"* he teased. *"I'm going to go wake our guest. Would you tell Mary that we'll be down for breakfast in fifteen minutes?"*

"Certainly, sir." As silently as he had entered, the houseman turned to leave.

Taking the stairs two at a time, Benjamin rapped on Raul's door, turning the knob at the response to enter. *"Good morning,"* he greeted, walking into the room.

Raul was standing by the window, looking out over the gardens toward the lake. *"You have a truly amazing estate. The dark didn't do it justice."*

"Thank you. Like many things, it can be a burden as well as a blessing."

"I'm sure. Thank you again for taking me in. I'm sure I'm not earning you any points with the local pack."

Benjamin shrugged. *"I'm not sure I have anything to lose, but we will certainly be contacted sometime today, and it would be best to stay away from the borders of the estate until an agreement has been reached. If you give me your sizes and a shopping list for anything else you might need, I can send someone to town. The estate is completely surrounded by packland, and until we have talked with the Rajan, we should stay here."*

"Rajan?"

"The Rajan—Alpha—of the Onondaga pack is Alex Hanover. He is fierce—took the pack by force from an ineffectual King about five years ago, but he's fair and a good leader. He took the title Rajan because he didn't want to be seen as the same kind of leader their King had been."

"Well, I guess we'll be seeing firsthand what kind of leader he is. It appears that whoever set me up did their homework," Raul continued as they left the room and headed down to breakfast. *"They chose a*

pack that has recently been in turmoil but been reclaimed by an absolute Alpha. Security would be strict and punishment absolute."

With a nod of agreement, Benjamin entered the kitchen. "Raul, this is my angel, Mary," he said, introducing his guest to the short, heavyset woman removing something from the oven.

"My, my," Mary tutted, wiping her hands on her apron and shuffling across the kitchen. "You've got no more meat on you than the Master." She patted Raul's flat, muscular stomach.

Benjamin grinned indulgently, rolling his eyes at Raul over her head. "Mary believes a man's wealth and well-being should show in his girth," he teased, dropping an affectionate kiss on the older woman's cheek.

She flushed, looking up at Benjamin with a grin. "With your wealth, you wouldn't fit through the door. I'd settle for your clothes not hanging on you." She swatted at him as he moved toward the table. When Raul chuckled at their antics, she swatted at him, too, shooing him after Benjamin. "Or you either, young man."

Both men laughed as they sat on opposite sides of the heavy oak table. "She's a treasure," Raul whispered as the housekeeper turned back to the stove.

"She and Conrad are my family," Benjamin said, his eyes softening.

It seemed like as good an opening as any and Raul was curious. "Tell me about the curse."

Benjamin waited until Mary had settled several large platters of breakfast meats, eggs, and a carafe of coffee on the table and moved back to the sink. Even though all of his staff knew of his condition and most knew the story of the curse, he was reticent in the telling out of habit.

"In the late 1600s, Lucas Sterling, my several-greats grandfather, got a local girl by the name of Anne Northland pregnant out of wedlock. He married a very well-connected young woman from Boston shortly after, abandoning Anne and her unborn child. Both died in childbirth."

Pausing, Benjamin lifted his coffee mug to his lips, focusing on the steam rising from the dark liquid. "Anne was a well-known hedge witch, mostly herbals and midwifery. It was not a time when witchcraft was practiced openly, so there are no official records. It is said that on the night before Lucas's wedding, Anne cursed him and his entire line. His son was the first to undergo the change. When that happened, Anne had been dead for more than a decade. Her only known relative was a twin brother, who disappeared after she died in childbirth. Since that time, the firstborn Sterling male of every generation has become a werewolf when he reached adolescence."

Raul was stunned, unsure of exactly what to say. The very thing he viewed as a gift, this man bore as a curse. "What if there are no children?"

Benjamin's mouth quirked, his eyes completely without humor. "Seems like it would be an easy out, doesn't it? But the curse seems to account for that. We seem to attract bed partners with alarming ease, something that is very hard to not take advantage of when you are young and horny. Even the men who didn't marry or set out to have a family managed to father a bastard who bore the curse."

Raul examined the man sitting across from him. Benjamin was indeed good looking. His jaw was strong and defined, his cheekbones high. His face was that of an aristocrat, and he had the tiniest hint of a cleft in his chin. He was obviously charming, noble, and more importantly, carried himself with the kind of quiet confidence that was incredibly appealing. Raul's wolf stirred at his perusal, sensing the prospect of coupling, but Raul pushed him down. That was the last complication he needed on top of everything else.

Unfortunately, Benjamin's wolf scented the waft of interest and rose, returning the scent. Raul's body was like coiled steel—all lithe, strong power. It had been a long time since he had taken anyone, man or woman, to his furs, and they were only a night away from the full moon—not a good time to test his control. He needed distraction.

"So what do we do to get me out of here, preferably in one piece and alive?" Raul asked. Nothing like talking about one's eminent death by evisceration to dampen desire.

Benjamin's wolf paced, uneasy at the abrupt change in mood and scent. Taking a deep breath, he reached inside and soothed the animal. "I'm guessing that the phone will ring shortly. It won't be Alex—probably Mark, his Beta. High enough to say, 'We aren't kidding', but letting you know that you aren't worthy of the attention of the Alpha. In the meantime, let's go back to the library and see if we can find a spell that could be used to render a lycanthrope unconscious."

"You have books on witchcraft that works on lycanthropes?" Raul asked, amazed and more than a little wary. Had he fallen from the frying pan into the fire?

"When you are a lycanthrope as a result of witchcraft, you have a tendency to want to learn all you can," Benjamin explained evenly. "My family has been researching ways to break our curse for centuries. We haven't had any success, but we have built an impressive library on the subject. If we go back to the site where you woke up, we might even be able to determine whether a spell or mechanical means got you there. That will have to wait until we see if the pack will grant you safe passage."

"Sounds good to me," Raul said, rising and stretching, the borrowed shirt riding up and exposing a strip of golden, tanned muscle.

Another purr of interest rumbled from Benjamin's wolf, but he sat on it with force.

"IT'S getting late," Benjamin interrupted Raul's story. "We should get some sleep and meet first thing in the morning."

Raul had felt his lover's agitation rise the closer he got to the part of the story where they'd first met. Knowing this part of the story as well as Raul did, Benjamin had probably sensed it too. Alex had come a long way in his acceptance of Benjamin and Raul didn't want to go back to the animosity that the two men had once shared. It was probably best not to refresh his mate's memory of the day they first met—the day he'd been wearing Benjamin's scent.

Chapter 3

"You stopped Raul there on purpose," Tristan accused, strolling into their bedroom and shooting his mate a playful glare over his shoulder. "I can't believe I finally got Raul to tell me the story of how you all met and you interrupted him. He was just getting to the best part."

Benjamin's eyes narrowed and he felt his wolf stirring. "You *wanted* to hear that we had sex and that Alex almost killed me for it when his wolf recognized Raul as his mate?" Benjamin's wolf rose inside him and started to pace, not liking Tristan being so blasé about him coupling with another.

A shiver of desire with just an edge of fear climbed Tristan's spine, his cock hardening in his jeans. He loved his mate's passionate, possessive streak and he hadn't seen enough of it since their mating. "I'm not saying I'd want to share you, but the image of you and Raul is damn hot. You can't blame me for being a little voyeuristic and wanting to hear some details."

A low rumbling started in the wolf's chest and echoed out of Benjamin's throat. With preternatural speed, he pushed Tristan back on the bed, pinning him securely. "I can't believe that you can think of me making love to someone else and find it arousing. People just casually brushing up against you on the street make me see red," he growled, rubbing his face against Tristan's cheek and neck, covering him with his scent. Releasing one of his lover's wrists, he used his free hand to work on baring more skin to his touch, ripping Tristan's clothes open and pushing them out of his way. "You are mine and mine alone. Forever."

Tristan's body shuddered again at the aggressive tone. He kicked free of his jeans, using his free hand to struggle with Benjamin's clothing. When they were both bare, he turned his head to nip at Benjamin's chest. "So did you fuck him or did he fuck you?" he asked coyly.

Benjamin saw red and then froze. "You're doing this on purpose."

A sly smile curved Tristan's lips. "Maybe… just a little. I *did* want to hear the whole story, but I think I'd better get you to tell me the rest sometime when Alex isn't around. I have no desire to watch the two of you fight, ever again." Benjamin started to relax on top of him. Arching up, Tristan nuzzled his mate's neck. "I am curious, though. I guess since Raul bottoms for Alex—"

That did it. Images of other werewolves fucking had no place in his mate's mind. If Tristan wanted him riled, it had worked.

Benjamin released his wolf.

Tristan whimpered, pressing up as his lover ground down into him. Benjamin's chest rumbled with approval as Tristan bared his neck. Lying perfectly still, Tristan submitted completely as Benjamin's tongue lapped at the exposed skin before his teeth lightly grazed the offered neck. Benjamin pressed his full weight against his mate, almost overwhelmed by the desire to howl his satisfaction when Tristan remained passive beneath him. Raising his lover's arms above his head, he rubbed their chests together, the combined scent of flesh and arousal increasing his wolf's frenzy. Forcing a knee between Tristan's thighs, Benjamin wrenched his legs apart, falling between them.

Tristan yelped as his lover's hard shaft collided with his. Planting his feet on the mattress, he bowed up, increasing the pressure. "Yes. Yes," he chanted, rubbing their erections together.

It wasn't enough. Benjamin's wolf wanted him lost to passion, unable to think… unable to think of anyone but him. "I'm going to show you who you belong to," Benjamin rasped into the skin of his shoulder. His tongue swiped the salty skin. "The only image in your mind will be me... claiming every inch of your body."

"Goddess, yes," Tristan moaned, writhing beneath his lover's possessive weight.

Benjamin's teeth traveled lower, his wolf demanding to taste flesh. Circling a flat nipple with his tongue, he sucked it to an aching peak, catching it with his teeth and tugging until Tristan cried out. Switching to the opposite nipple, he nipped at it until it was red and swollen. He could smell the bittersweet musk of his mate's fluid leaking between their bodies, but made no move to touch Tristan or relieve his need. The scent was intoxicating, and his wolf was rolling in it.

"Benjamin... please," Tristan begged, arching and twisting in an attempt to get more satisfying contact.

Pushing his lover's legs farther apart with his knees, the werewolf sank his shaft into the tight crease of Tristan's ass. A needy whimper caused his wolf to surge forward, anxious to bury himself in the tight body of his mate—to join them. Benjamin held back, restraining the eager wolf. "What do you see?"

Tristan opened his eyes, blinking up at his mate, eyes unfocused with desire. "What?"

"Tell me what you see. When you close your eyes, what do you see?" Benjamin asked again, thrusting forward until the blunt tip of his cock pressed enticingly against the entrance of his mate's body.

Another pained whimper and Tristan's legs fell open wider. "Please... please fuck me."

Benjamin rocked forward, letting the clenching muscle massage the moist head of his cock. "Tell me. Close your eyes and tell me what you see."

"You! Inside of me!" Tristan snapped, his hips lifting off the bed in frustration, his hands still restrained above his head. "Pounding into me so hard that I come screaming."

With a quick thrust of his hips, the werewolf breached the tight muscle, fluid from his body the only lubrication. Slowly he worked in and out, Tristan tilting his hips and meeting him on every stroke.

"More," Tristan pleaded, muscles trembling.

Benjamin's wolf was buzzing on the mixture of sweat and need hanging thick in the air. He vibrated with unsatisfied hunger. The pounding that his mate had described was quickly becoming inevitable. Finally releasing Tristan's hands, he reached to the side table for lubricant. He wouldn't hurt his mate.

Rising to his knees, the werewolf pulled Tristan's thighs over his own, trickling a cool stream of liquid onto the point where their bodies joined. Tristan gasped as it seeped over super-heated flesh. He squirmed, his struggles further enflaming Benjamin's wolf. The werewolf moved in and out in long, even strokes, every push carrying more lubricant into the tight channel and easing his thrusts.

Tristan gasped, his muscles clenching as Benjamin stroked directly over his prostate. The werewolf could smell his lover's climax; it was close. Shifting his weight to his arms, he snapped his hips forward, pummeling the receptive body beneath him. Tristan arched, his legs rising to rest on Benjamin's shoulders. "Fuck me. Fuck me harder," he demanded.

Folding his lover in half, Benjamin swooped down to claim his mouth. He plunged his tongue deep, the motion mimicking the rhythm of their bodies. Burying himself deep inside his mate, he threw back his head and howled as his release was torn from his body.

Lowering his feet to the bed, Tristan pushed against the dead weight of his lover, trying to achieve the extra bit of friction that would bring him release. Hands grasped his hips in a steel grip, stilling his movements. He thrashed, frustrated and yearning, his climax just barely out of reach, needy sounds spilling from his lips. Pulling gently out of Tristan's body, Benjamin pushed the damp, dark curls back from his lover's face, crooning soft words of love in his ear.

"Benjamin... Benjamin, please," Tristan rasped, unable to form the words to ask for more.

"Shhh..." the werewolf soothed. Pulling even farther away from Tristan's trembling body, he firmly held his lover's grasping hands away as he flipped him over. Tristan moaned, lifting his hips from the mattress to relieve the pressure on his aching cock. Spreading the creamy ass cheeks, Benjamin lowered his mouth to the rosy pucker, lapping at the heady combination of his seed flavored with Tristan's taste.

Tristan screamed, bucking wildly as Benjamin's tongue probed his sensitive hole. "Oh fuck... fuck!"

Slipping his hand under Tristan's body, the werewolf grasped the leaking shaft. With every stroke, he licked, fucked, and sucked the clenching hole until it was taking all his strength to keep his lover from jerking out of his touch. He gripped him harder, his touch unrelenting.

"Oh Goddess... Benjamin!" Tristan screamed, his hips rocking between the mouth on his ass and the hand around his cock.

Flipping his incoherent lover onto his back, Benjamin closed his mouth over the throbbing shaft just as it released a stream of creamy fluid. Humming his pleasure, he suckled the shaft until it slipped from his lips, limp and clean. His lover lay in a boneless sprawl across the bed. Benjamin lifted and positioned him until they were both under the covers.

"You were supposed to fuck me until I came screaming," Tristan protested sleepily.

Benjamin spooned up against Tristan's back, cradling his precious mate in his arms. "Oh no... you manipulated me, incorrigible whelp. I'm not going to reward that kind of behavior."

Tristan drifted off to sleep, a smile on his lips. Was first thing tomorrow too early to try it again?

BENJAMIN was already up and gone from bed when Tristan woke the next morning. Slipping on a pair of worn sweat pants, he padded barefoot down the stairs in hopes of luring his lover back to bed.

Stepping into the kitchen, he gave up his fantasies of a leisurely morning lie-in. Will and Benjamin were bent over the kitchen table, obviously in the middle of a serious discussion. With a sigh, he filled a cup with coffee and went to join them, snagging one of Mary's scones on the way.

"Isn't it too early for serious discussions?" Tristan complained, pulling out a chair, collapsing into it and settling his feet in Benjamin's lap.

"Raul answered Nicolai at dawn," Benjamin reminded his mate. "He's decided to return home with him to help find Richard. I was just talking with Will about the possibility of Will going along with him. I don't trust Sienna, and Raul knows next to nothing about magic."

"Will? Wouldn't it be better if I went?" Tristan asked, pulling his feet back and sitting up at the table, suddenly alert. "Raul said last night that he'd need my help."

"Yes, Raul knows he needs a witch's help dealing with Sienna. I just thought Will might be the better choice," Benjamin explained.

Will chimed in. "I'm willing to go and I don't have anything holding me here. It might be fun to get to see a little more of the United States before heading home."

"See a little more and maybe get killed! This isn't a sightseeing trip. Based on what Raul said last night, this witch is dangerous and not at all worried about what is ethical," Tristan argued.

"So it's better for you to get killed?" Will shot back. "You have Benjamin. I have Davie and Scott, and they seem to be able to get along without me just fine."

Tristan's face grew serious. "Benjamin, will you let me and Will talk alone for a minute?" he asked, his eyes softening as they shifted to his lover. He gave the werewolf's knee a reassuring squeeze under the table.

"Okay," Benjamin agreed, although somewhat reluctantly, "but we need to be at Raul's by noon. That's when he and Nicolai plan to leave."

Tristan nodded, watching his lover until he disappeared through the door. His eyes remained focused on the empty doorway as he spoke. "I don't want you to do this. I feel like I'm going to lose you."

"Lose me how?"

"I don't know." Tristan turned a worried look on his twin. "It isn't a premonition or anything that specific. It is just a general feeling of unease and loss and it definitely is focused on you. Let me go with Raul."

Will reached over and picked up Tristan's hand, threading their fingers together and squeezing. "I know you're worried about me, but I have an equally strong feeling that this is what I am meant to do. Maybe even the reason that I'm over here. You didn't really need me to help Benjamin. Your power was more than enough to bring him back. This...."

Will paused, his eyes losing focus as he stared just to the right of Tristan. "I need to do this. Not just for Raul... but for me."

Hooking his brother's neck, Tristan pulled him into a tight hug despite the intrusion of the corner of the table between them. "Are you sure?" he asked, his voice choked. "Because if I lose you—"

"I'm not that easy to lose."

"Okay, let's go tell Benjamin."

Will winked at his twin, looking over at the clock. "Why don't *you* go tell Benjamin? There should be just enough time for him to express his *appreciation* to you while I pack. Just keep it down to a dull roar, huh? You two kept me up all night."

Tristan grinned, but wasted no time sprinting up the stairs, Will's laughter chasing him.

ALEX'S face showed his surprise at seeing both Northland brothers with Benjamin. "Benjamin. Tristan. Will," he greeted, his voice rising just slightly on the last name, indicating his surprise. "Raul's in the kitchen."

The four men walked silently to the back of the house. Once there, Will took the initiative, explaining why he wanted to accompany Raul.

Raul sat down next to Alex. "It makes little difference to me. From everything I know, the two of you have almost identical skills and knowledge. I just need someone to help me combat Sienna's knowledge and use of magic."

"I like that Tristan is staying here. He and Benjamin are still recently mated and shouldn't be separated," Alex put in, leaning close to his own mate. "It is never easy to be separated from your mate, but it is even harder for a newly mated pair."

Raul turned into his lover's arms, kissing him tenderly. "I've not found that it gets any better with time."

Will's eyes darted away, feeling like he was intruding on an intimate moment, only to find Benjamin cradling Tristan's face and staring into his eyes with a look that would melt glass. The ache that had taken up permanent residence in his stomach increased tenfold, a lump filling his throat. He coughed to clear the tightness, bringing the others' attention back to the room.

"Sorry." Raul's flush had more to do with the kiss than embarrassment. "Nicolai has gone ahead, so if you are ready, we can leave."

"I'll go get my bag out of Benjamin's truck," Will offered, giving the werewolf couple a chance to say good-bye in private.

Benjamin picked up a cooler from the kitchen counter. "Is this going?"

"Yeah, and my bag is lying in the hall, if you want to toss it in the trunk," Raul answered. He and Alex had gotten to their feet and were standing with their arms securely around each other. They'd been through every option exhaustively and both knew this was the best choice. Raul's family and pack needed him. Alex couldn't leave his own responsibilities to go with him. Neither of them would enjoy it, but they'd survive until Raul found Richard and could return.

Stepping around the side of the house, Benjamin pointed out Raul's car. Will climbed into the passenger side of the older Mercedes, relaxing in the wide leather seat. "I could get used to this," he sighed, closing his eyes.

"Just don't offer to drive," Tristan teased, leaning in through the window. "Last time you tried driving on the right side of the road, you ran that poor bicyclist into the ditch."

Will glared at his twin. "I still say that wasn't my fault. Bloody wanker was in the middle of the road."

"What's this about running people off the road?" Raul asked, flashing a grin that didn't reach his eyes as he slid into the opposite side of the car. Alex didn't come out and Will wasn't surprised. He couldn't imagine how hard it must be to watch your mate drive away, knowing you were sending him into a dangerous situation.

Ignoring the question, the witch reached over and laid a hand on Raul's leg. "I really admire your commitment to your pack, after everything that happened to you." At Raul's quizzical look, Will jerked his head toward Tristan. "He filled me in on the way over."

Raul looked at the two almost identical faces: Will's next to him and Tristan's framed by the window. "You know exactly why I can't ignore this. He's the other half of me. I won't let her hurt him."

Tristan nodded. "We do understand. Take care of *my* other half for me." Reaching in, he hugged Will one last time before stepping back from the car to stand next to Benjamin.

Will waved as the car pulled away, catching a glimpse of Alex watching from an upstairs window. As Raul pulled out on the road, Will turned in his seat, leaning against the door. "So tell me about Sienna."

Chapter 4

"Well, you remember the Wicked Witch of the West from *The Wizard of Oz*?"

Will snickered. "So... long nose with warts, greasy hair, and gnarled fingers?"

Raul joined in the laughter. "Unfortunately, no. She's beautiful. Petite. Perfect figure. Curly blonde hair that falls in ringlets past her shoulders. Bright blue eyes. She resembles a china doll."

Will wondered briefly if she was using some sort of glamour. Very few people possessed the perfect beauty that Raul seemed to be describing. "How'd Richard meet her?"

"She opened a metaphysical bookstore in a neighboring town... carried books, occult supplies."

"I take it Richard doesn't have your aversion to magic."

"Actually, she reached out to us. She called because she had a customer requesting some specific herbs and other supplies that in combination could be harmful to lycans. Richard went over to talk with her and didn't come home for three days. The rest is, as they say, history."

Will could see Raul's knuckles turning white as they gripped the steering wheel. "Was there really someone out to harm pack members, or was it just a ruse to get close to your brother or someone from your pack?"

Raul took a deep breath, releasing each hand in turn and flexing his fingers before settling them on the wheel in a new location. Turning his head briefly, he looked at the man sitting next to him. A year ago, he'd have predicted that he'd never voluntarily have a relationship with a witch, but the respect he held for the Northland twins had grown into sincere affection.

"Actually, there really was a threat. With her help, we tracked him down and dispensed with him. She won her way into the pack's good graces with that gesture."

"I'm sure," Will agreed, wondering if she had set up an innocent patsy to take the fall.

"Richard moved into the apartment she kept above the shop less than three weeks later."

"He moved in with her? Didn't he need to stay on packlands?"

Raul shook his head. "Not really. Her apartment was well warded and at the time, I was heir apparent. I'm sure they moved onto packlands when I disappeared. In fact, I'm sure she had the U-Haul packed before anyone even noticed that I was missing."

"Did you always mistrust her?"

Pursing his lips, Raul examined his memories. "No, I can't say I did. When I first met her, Richard was so blissfully happy—as his twin, I couldn't help but respond to that." Will nodded his understanding. "It was only later when his behavior started to change…."

Will waited for Raul to continue the story. When he didn't, he prompted, "What exactly did you see that caused you to worry?"

"It never was anything major. Certainly, not enough to raise formal suspicions with the elders or my father, but Richard seemed to lose all his motivation to do anything except to be with her. He went from never missing council meetings to barely making one in four. He always listened to petitions alongside my father and me, but once he met her, he stopped. Usually meticulous about his appearance, he quit cutting his hair, wore the same clothes until they were almost threadbare with repeated washings."

"You have to understand, pack... position... meant everything to Richard. He was the one who *wanted* the crown—who had the drive to claim it and fight to keep it. I was firstborn, but I was *Fridolf*, peacekeeper. I didn't have the drive to rule that he had. I never intended to lead our pack. I always knew that Richard, someday, would take my father's place, and I would support him. After he met Sienna, he became... almost lazy. Sort of like the spoiled younger children of royal or wealthy families who have no motivation or purpose. He spent days just sampling concoctions she brewed to try and imitate the intoxicating effects of alcohol for a lycan."

Will had never heard the term *Fridolf* before and tucked it away to ask about later. He was more interested in learning everything he could about Sienna first. "She was drugging him regularly?"

Raul nodded sadly. "With his approval and encouragement. He tried several times to get me to sample some potion she had brewed, but I didn't trust her. I'm sure Tristan told you that we suspect one of her creations of knocking me out so I could be deposited in the middle of foreign packlands."

"He mentioned it. It would take powerful magic and extensive knowledge of lycans to brew such a potion."

"She was obsessed with lycanthropy. They were together less than six weeks when she made her first petition to be turned. That one was easily refused, since they had been together such a short period of time," Raul explained. His voice was calm, but his hand betrayed his growing tension by reaching up repeatedly to rub at the muscles on the back of his neck.

"Are there other witches in your pack?" Will asked, turning his back against the car door and pulling one of his legs up beneath him. "I've never read anything about witch lycans."

"My pack is now Alex's, but to answer your question, no, we had never heard of a witch being turned or a hereditary lycan exhibiting a propensity for traditional witchcraft. For all we knew, turning her would've destroyed her powers. I almost wish we had tried it, but I was scared of her acquiring even greater powers. I still am. We have shamans, but they are more priests who are acutely attuned with the earth and lead our rituals."

"I've met Ian. He's powerful, but you are right, his interaction with the power of the earth is different. Did she continue to push to be accepted?" Will asked.

"No, she seemed to back off. Always present… helpful, almost to the point of being intrusive, but just when you thought 'enough is enough', she'd jump back, and we wouldn't see her for a while."

Will nodded. He was going to have to meet Sienna, but he suspected that in addition to a glamour to alter her physical appearance, she was using some form of a shield to filter her intentions. It would take a very powerful witch to pull it all off at once over an extended period. He hoped that he hadn't gotten in over his head. Changing the subject slightly, he asked, "So do you have a plan for finding your brother?"

"I've got a house about twenty miles east of packlands that my maternal grandmother left me. A local church uses it as a temporary loaner to help families get back on their feet. It is empty at the moment, but someone moving in won't raise any eyebrows and it stays furnished. I figured it would make a good home base. If we can find Richard, we can bring him to the house first while we figure out what is going on with Sienna."

Will stared out the window. The landscape was changing slightly, opening up into more farmland. It wasn't so different than the countryside he was used to in England. "Do you miss home?" he asked, thinking about Tristan's decision to stay here in the states with Benjamin.

"Yeah, I miss the people, but I can't imagine being anywhere Alex isn't. He's my home."

Will sighed as the hollow feeling returned to his chest.

THE sun was high in the sky as they slowed at a school zone marking the beginning of a small town. Raul turned off the state highway, easily navigating the twisting back roads until he pulled into a long drive shaded by elm trees. Coming to a halt in front of a two-story, white farmhouse with hunter green shutters, Raul put the car in park.

"It's beautiful," Will said, reaching over the seat for his backpack and opening his door.

"I spent many summer days playing in this yard," Raul answered, his eyes scanning the house and field. "It never seems to change. There is something comforting in that."

Will walked to the back to retrieve their bags. "Not all change is bad."

"No, but when too much changes, it is hard to keep your balance," Raul said, climbing out of the car.

Will followed Raul up the stairs to the porch, pressing their shoulders together as Raul paused to flip through his keys for the one to unlock the door. "That's what family and friends are for—they remain the constant that keeps you steady."

Raul smiled down at the slender man at his side, unsure if Will just shared Tristan's touchy-feely nature or if he had learned enough about lycans to know that the physical contact would be comforting. A jab of longing for his mate stirred his wolf, making the hair on his arms stand up and his skin feel hypersensitive. Once they were settled, he'd call Alex and soothe himself by listening to the tenor of his mate's voice.

Will watched as the werewolf's mind drifted far away, surmising correctly that he was missing his mate. "Speaking of family," he gently pulled Raul back to the present. "I have an idea of how to start our search for your brother. Do you have a map of the local area?"

Raul flipped on the ceiling fan to circulate the stale air in the closed-up house. "I've got a road map out in the car, and there used to be a rubber-banded stack of hiking maps in the pantry off the kitchen."

"Let's start with the road map, but we might have to switch to the hiking maps if he is in a more rural area." Walking across the well-worn hardwood floor, Will pushed back white eyelet curtains and opened a window, multiple layers of paint making it squeak and protest as he lifted it. Looking around at the mismatched furniture, he asked, "Was the furniture your grandmother's or did the church furnish the house?"

"Most of it was Nanna's, pieced together from local estate sales and junk shops. She loved to poke around in dusty, hole-in-the-wall stores, looking for her next treasure. She found a few too. I have a Tiffany lamp beside my bed that she said cost her six dollars. The shade was so caked with dust when she bought it that you couldn't tell it was stained glass. She spent a week cleaning it with a toothbrush."

"Sounds like your grandmother was as special as mine. Did Richard spend time here as a kid too?"

"Sure. We were rarely apart growing up. Why?"

"It'll help the energy. I'm going to scry for his location and anything that holds his energy will help," Will explained. The rise of Raul's eyebrow told Will exactly how the werewolf felt about his idea, but Will had confidence in his ability. Finding Richard would quiet Raul's doubts.

"I'll go get the map and the cooler."

Will almost laughed as the older man turned and walked out the front door, but a quick thought of Sienna sobered him. Raul was going to have to learn to trust magic if they were going to expose Sienna and break whatever control she had on his twin. He raised his voice so it would reach Raul. "I'm going to unpack and get a feel for the energy of the house and land. Does it matter which room I use?"

Raul's voice floated back through the open window. "Not really. We removed all the personal stuff from the bedrooms when we turned it over to the church. Richard and I shared the sleeping porch when we were kids."

Not quite sure what a "sleeping porch" was, Will assumed he could figure it out. Slinging his backpack over his shoulder and picking up his bag, he headed up the stairs, enjoying the feel of the worn oak banister as his hand slid up the smooth surface. The landing at the top of the stairs led to three doors—one bathroom and two bedrooms. The first bedroom overlooked the front of the house and connected through a second door to the bathroom. The other bedroom spanned the back of the house.

Walking into the back bedroom, Will trailed his fingers over the well-used desk. This had been the room the twins had used growing up; he was sure of it. He opened a door on the opposite wall, finding a long, screened-in porch. The "sleeping porch." He imagined the two adolescent werewolves sleeping on the narrow twin beds as the ceiling fans made the summer heat bearable, sharing secrets and dreams.

This was where he needed to scry for Richard. The energy in the room was so palpable he could practically close his eyes and picture them, lying in bed, staring at the ceiling while they discussed life and love. He wondered if they had ever competed for the same lover, like he and Tristan had. Raul was obviously gay and it appeared that Richard preferred women, so maybe that hadn't been an issue.

Lost in his thoughts, Will jumped as Raul's voice sounded from the doorway. "I see you found it."

Will grinned. "Yeah, I can feel you in this room. You and Richard. I can almost hear you talking."

Raul laughed self-consciously. "Goddess, I hope not."

"Did you find the map?" Will asked, excited to get on with the scrying while he could still feel Richard's energy so acutely.

"Right here." Raul slapped the folded map against his hand.

Looking around the room, Will picked up a lamp and set it gently on the floor, pulling the bedside table into the center of the room. "Sit there," he instructed, nodding at the bed, "and think about Richard in as much detail as possible. How he looked. How he smelled. The sound of his voice. Think about times he made you angry or proud. What is your best memory of him? Lose yourself in that moment."

Raul lowered himself slowly to the polyester bedspread. "Oh... kay."

"The clearer we can get Richard's energy, the better the chance we'll find him."

A determined look settled on Raul's rugged features, the werewolf obviously struggling with his mistrust of magic to help his brother. "Okay." He closed his eyes, focusing on his twin. Will watched as his energy changed from cool blue-gray to a reddish-orange. Love. Anger. He could see them all in the werewolf's aura, but that was fine. That was good. Strong emotions would help. It mattered not if they were positive or negative emotions.

"May I have a few strands of your hair?"

Raul's green eyes opened; puzzled, he tilted his head. "I guess."

With a quick yank, Will plucked several white-blond hairs from the werewolf, an idea forming. "Would you mind changing so I could get a couple strands of wolf fur?"

"Are you kidding?"

Will shook his head solemnly. "The more ties the better and Richard has a wolf side as well."

Without saying a word, Raul leaned forward, shaking his head. In the blink of an eye, an enormous tawny wolf was standing on the floor at Will's feet. A shiver ran up the witch's spine. Falling to his knees, he stroked the thick, soft fur. "Thank you for sharing of yourself for your brother," he whispered. Just his hands combing through the coarse fur were enough to free a handful of hairs. "I have what I need. May Artemis guide your hunt and watch over you always."

The wolf nudged at him, rubbing the side of his face against Will. Hugging the wolf's head to his chest, Will buried his face in the deep fur. A strange feeling stirred in his chest. Before he could identify it,

Raul's wolf was pulling back and changing into his human form—familiar, other than its nakedness.

"Be right back," Raul mumbled hastily, retreating quickly from the room.

Will averted his eyes, catching only the barest glimpse of the werewolf's muscular back and tight ass. He had no desire to incite Alex's wrath. Sitting on the side of the bed, he dug through his backpack and pulled out the things he would need. He spread the map on the small table, efficiently braiding the strands of Raul's blond hair and the wolf's fur with cotton thread to form a single strand. Digging through a small black silk bag, he pulled a teardrop-shaped crystal from its depths, securing it to one end of the length.

Raul returned to the room, dressed in jeans and a T-shirt, still barefoot.

"Go back to thinking about Richard," Will said as Raul sat down on the bed next to him. Holding his creation in his left hand, Will closed his eyes and concentrated, taking deep, even breaths. Without opening his eyes, he held his hand over the top of the map, muttering a string of words that Raul didn't understand.

The crystal circled.

Once.

Twice.

Raul watched as the course abruptly changed, snapping like a magnet to a spot on the map. Amazed by what he'd seen, he stared, mouth open, as Will read off the name of an intersection in the next town.

"Raul. Raul!" Will raised his voice to get the werewolf's attention. "How well do you know Clear Creek? Do you know what is on Caldwell and Main?"

"The county jail."

Chapter 5

THE hollow, empty feeling Will had been experiencing for months was gone. He felt warm… safe… protected in a way he had never experienced. Drawing his knee up in front of his body, he moaned as the soft nap of fur stroked his bare skin. He shifted, wanting to feel more of the decadent sensation. His movements brought his body into contact with a muscular body curled behind him.

The witch looked over his shoulder, curious about the identity of his unknown bed partner. A chill immediately dissipated the warm, protected feeling. The room began to spin and fade. Closing his eyes, he rubbed his body against the man behind him, feeling his lover stir, an arm curling around his waist and pulling him tight. Possessive. Intimate.

His mind warred with his body. One wanted to drift back to sleep, wrapped in a cocoon of love like he'd never experienced; the other, more interested in the spiraling desire building as he rocked back and forth between the silky soft fur and the rougher texture of the hair on his lover's chest and thighs. The feeling was familiar. He knew this body intimately and wanted nothing more than to experience as much pleasure as he could.

Twisting his torso, he rolled over, his hands running from broad, muscular shoulders down into thick chest hair. Grazing a hard nipple, he circled his fingers around the smooth disk, pinching and twisting it until his lover's hips canted. The chest beneath his hands rumbled with a low growl that caused his cock to jump between their bodies.

A strong thigh crossed his hips, controlling the motion of their bodies, the hard lengths caught between them smearing fluid against their bellies. A rough tongue swiped up his neck, making him shudder and whimper. A sure hand circled his erection, callused fingers teasing every sensitive spot.

Will burrowed closer, any space between them too great. He slid his thigh between his lover's, moaning at the increased pressure on his shaft and balls. Rolling into the contact, he thrust his hips forward forcefully.

Strong fingers cradled his face, tracing his features the same way a blind man would memorize a face he wanted never to forget. He willingly let his head be tilted up until their lips touched for a slow, deep kiss. The taste of his lover's lips rushed straight to his cock. He had to have more contact… more friction… just… *more*. His hands tunneled under the furs, stroking the flexing muscles of his lover's back and ass while his mouth and lips explored his neck.

Feeling like he would explode if he didn't come soon, he rasped, "I want you inside me."

His lover rolled him under his body, the warm weight spiking his desire. Planting his feet in the furs, Will arched up in a silent plea to be entered.

Unyielding hands gripped his hips, halting his motion. "Still."

Will shivered at the barely constrained threat in the quiet order, the edge of danger amplifying his desire. Without knowing why, he completely relaxed, falling limp and baring his neck to the man over him. "Shh… easy, baby. Come back and let me love you," he coaxed, knowing his words would ease his lover's distress.

It wasn't the first time he'd done this. It was a dance well practiced between the two of them. One that he had no doubt would end in mind-searing pleasure. Opening his legs, he pulled his lover between them, his ankles locking around his waist. "You need me, don't you? Come love me, so you'll both be satisfied."

Both.

His lover was a werewolf. The rightness of the realization pushed Will even closer to his climax. As his lover pushed inside of him, he moaned, his hands clutching at his lover's back and ass, encouraging him to move faster... deeper... harder.

Will could feel his climax building, but as it rushed toward him, the feeling of connection with his lover began to fade. "No. No!" he screamed as his body succumbed to the inevitable and the feel of his lover slipped completely beyond his grasp.

Desolate and awake, Will turned in the narrow twin bed, the cold sheets that had felt so good when he first crawled between them now irritating his skin. He was sticky with evidence of the greatest pleasure he'd ever felt, but the suffocating loneliness left in its wake prevented him from moving to relieve the discomfort.

"Damn," he whispered into the dark night. He wasn't sure he wanted to be in love with a werewolf. Maybe he should have let Tristan come.

WILL walked down the hallway, uneasy surrounded by iron-enforced concrete, cut off from the energy of the earth. With surprisingly little investigation, he and Raul had found Richard in the county jail, held on a series of little charges that hadn't been cleared because they didn't know who he was. Apparently, Raul's twin had not only gotten himself arrested but had no recollection of who he was. Will had managed to drive himself into town without incident thanks to Raul's clear directions, light mid-morning traffic, and an absence of bicyclists. After a brief conversation with the local sheriff, he was headed to face Richard for the first time.

Turning a corner, Will found Raul's twin standing at the bars three cells from the door, staring at him like he'd been expecting someone to show up at any minute. His face was the same as Raul's, but harder—all chiseled lines and angles. Dressed in worn jeans and a thin cotton shirt open halfway down his chest and with rolled-back sleeves, he was an enticing sight, even standing in a jail cell. His blond hair hung well past his shoulders, but his eyes shone with the same blue-green intensity as his twin's and seemed to look right through Will. The blatantly hungry look made the young witch shiver. He tried to adopt the casual teasing tone of a long-time friend. "Richard, what the fuck did you get into this time?"

Richard's brow wrinkled. "I know you," he said.

Will's steps faltered. Was their ruse about to be blown? Had Richard's memory come back or had his amnesia been a lie told to the local law enforcement? Will took a deep breath. Richard's words hadn't been a question. It was a statement made with complete surety. Since they didn't really know each other, the memory loss must be real. Sticking to the story he and Raul had agreed on, he answered, "Yeah, mate. Why didn't you call when they threw you in here? What are friends for if they can't post bail for a mate now and again?"

Richard shook his head like he was trying to clear an unwanted thought, his long blond hair curling over his shoulders. "I... I didn't... I know I know you. I can feel it. But I can't remember your name or where I know you from."

Will's heart raced as Richard rested his elbows on the bars, cradling his head in his hands. "So the sheriff was serious. You really do have amnesia." Internally, he sighed in relief and prayed that the ruse would last long enough to get them away from the jail.

"Yep, can't remember shit and every time I try, I get a splitting headache. They found me on the side of the road, thrown from a car that had plowed through several telephone poles. They say I was drunk and have me in here on driving under the influence, destruction of public property, driving without a license, and vagrancy. Apparently, I didn't have a wallet on me and I can't remember my name for them to look it up." Richard's breathing was quick and shallow. "They can't seem to track down an owner of the car. It must not have been stolen or they'd have added that to the charges."

Worried, Will laid his hand on Richard's muscular forearm. Raul had warned him that if Richard really had amnesia, he might not remember that he was a lycan and the feelings he'd be experiencing would be confusing and scary. They also had no idea how long it had been since Richard had changed. The witch had intended to try a simple calming spell just to get them out of the jail, but he hadn't anticipated the explosion when his fingers touched the werewolf's skin. The simple contact lit up his body. It was like an electrical charge, raising the hair on his arms and making him feel uncomfortably warm.

Richard's eyes locked with Will's. "Who are you?" he rasped.

Will took a step back. "I'm your best friend. Who else would drive all the way down here to bail out your ass?" he teased, trying to hide his reaction to the simple touch.

"Friend?" Richard asked, obviously unsure.

Deciding that he could explore his reaction on his own time, after they were safely away from the jail, Will gave the werewolf his most convincing smile. "Yeah. Friends. Now let's blow this popsicle stand before they trump up some new charges. The paperwork should be done by now. I'll go wait up front." He backed away, unable to take his eyes off Richard. The tension in the werewolf's muscles revealed his agitation.

RICHARD stepped into the warm sunlight, heat reflecting up from the sidewalk. His eyes closed as he took a deep breath of air not tainted with the stale scent of suffering, urine, and blood. The smell that permeated every niche of the jail had been driving him to distraction. Reaching up, he smoothed Will's hair away from his face, staring intently into the dark eyes. Will lifted his head and looked at him questioningly. Richard didn't know what he was doing or why he was doing it. All he knew was that something inside of him was demanding he kiss the man by his side… immediately. He leaned closer and brushed their lips together, almost scared of what was going to happen after his reaction to the friendly touch on his arm.

Will started at the unexpected move, but the attraction that had been building from his first sight of the blond werewolf clouded his judgment. Rising onto his toes, he pressed up into the kiss and parted his lips so Richard's tongue could have free access to his mouth. If their first touch electrified him, their first kiss was going to melt him to a puddle on the sidewalk.

Richard's tongue brushed against Will's, sending tingles through his body. His hands seemed to take that as a signal to move, because his right hand roamed under the hem of Will's shirt and began tracing every bump and valley of his spine while the other cupped the back of the witch's head and tangled in his hair. His world felt right for the first time since he'd woken up in that godforsaken cell. He took a deep breath of fresh air. He could smell Will's arousal and that feeling deep inside of him approved, demanding more. An obnoxious burst of horn in the distance shattered the moment and Richard broke the kiss, spinning Will away from the road, sheltering him between his body and the wall, every sense on alert in an effort to protect his—. He shook his head, the pain beginning to build behind his eyes.

Immediately sensing the tension in the werewolf, Will opened his hands on the warm chest. "It's okay. I'm safe." He wasn't sure why those words had come out of his mouth. He had intended to make a joke about teenage drivers.

Relaxing slightly, Richard leaned his forehead against Will's, not releasing his hair or moving the hand that now rested under Will's shirt at the small of his back. "I need to be somewhere alone with you." Richard's voice was low and shaky, almost pleading.

"Yes." Will's voice was just as uncertain but still silky and seductive, answering the question exactly as Richard had hoped.

"I need to kiss you like that again," Richard said breathlessly, still fighting the internal voice that was telling him to push the younger man up against the closest wall and claim his body in the most intimate of ways.

"You better not until we get back to the house."

"But you'll let me?"

"I'll hurt you if you don't." Will bit his tongue. Seducing Raul's brother was *so* not a part of the plan. Raul had felt it would be better for Will to retrieve Richard under the guise of being his friend, since Raul would be so easily recognized as Richard's twin and it was possible Sienna was watching. After sunset, Raul would return to the house from the side bordering the woods, away from the road, and they would decide what to do next.

Richard nodded his agreement, moving away reluctantly, feeling an almost physical pain as their bodies lost contact. Will repeatedly had to take his foot off the gas on the way back to the farmhouse to keep from speeding and landing them both back in jail… or a ditch. Pulling up in front of the house, he killed the engine, getting out and racing up the front stairs, Richard matching his long strides.

"Is this your house?" Richard asked, reminding Will that he was taking advantage of a man with no memory.

Unlocking the door, Will shook his head, trying to reinforce his resistance to the sexy werewolf. They needed to unlock Richard's memory and secure Raul's birth pack, not fall into bed. His cock twitched in his jeans as an image of them both naked and sweaty inevitably followed, melting his rational intentions.

Richard touched his shoulder and within seconds, they were kissing again. Breathless, hungry kisses that consumed them, blocking out all rational thought. Richard deftly unbuttoned Will's shirt as they kissed, his hands running over the newly exposed skin. He finally released Will's lips and moved down his throat, placing open-mouth kisses in a line to Will's Adam's apple, where he stopped and sucked until Will moaned. "Sweet Goddess, Richard… we shouldn't…."

The sound of Will's moan made something in Richard jump and surge forward. "Yes," he purred as he moved from Will's neck to trace the lines of his collarbone with his tongue, and then lower to worry a nipple gently between his teeth. "Just like that."

"Like what?" Will finally managed to question between whimpers.

"I want you to say my name just like that when you come for me." Richard's mouth moved down as he spoke, his tongue tracing the edge of Will's navel before flicking in and out, his hot breath on the wetness sending chills radiating out in all directions.

"Please," Will gasped, his body arching wantonly.

Richard chuckled softly against wet skin and more chills spread over Will's body. "Just like that, *conchure*." His lips moved back up Will's chest, nipping at the other nipple and making Will gasp.

"Yes." *Conchure*. He had heard Benjamin use that term for Tristan, but couldn't remember what it meant.

Richard walked slowly around Will, pulling the shirt off his shoulders, feasting on the sight of his naked skin. He nibbled the back of Will's neck as he wrapped his arms around his waist and began to unbuckle his belt. "I want to taste every inch of you," he whispered in Will's ear as he nibbled it and artfully unbuttoned the moaning man's jeans, being careful not to touch the obvious erection.

Will gasped as his clothes fell to the ground, cool air hitting his cock as it sprang free from his jeans, his boxers damp where they stretched over the leaking head. "Please," Will released a ragged groan, trying desperately to stay in control and not rip Richard's clothes off and throw him to the floor.

"My beautiful *conchure*," Richard whispered into Will's ear as he nuzzled the satin skin hidden behind dark curls.

Will toed off his shoes and stepped out of his trousers as he turned to face Richard, his eyes clouded with desire. "You have entirely too many clothes still on," Will complained, attempting to fix the problem as quickly as possible.

Richard wasn't sure how they got to the bed, but once they were there he couldn't stop. He craved Will's taste... Will's scent, and for some reason he didn't think one night would be enough. For all the familiarity he felt, he was sure they hadn't done this before. Will arched up to him, a string of nonsense words and expletives coming from swollen lips. He looked so beautiful and vulnerable lying beneath him, digging fingers into his hips.

Will writhed beneath him and Richard growled, his cock moving faster against Will's stomach, covering it with slick wetness, their scents mixing. He was trying hard to keep his focus, but his hips were moving to a rhythm all their own. His head was spinning from lack of oxygen, but he couldn't force himself to let go of Will's lips to breathe. Then Will was coming, a low moan issuing from his lips, his cock spasming between them. "Richard!"

The sound of Will's voice forced Richard's orgasm from him, sharp spikes shooting through his body that lasted for an eternity before he collapsed on top of Will.

Will wrapped his legs around Richard's hips to keep him from moving away. "Oh damn... don't move... don't leave."

The last thing Richard remembered before sleep overtook him was Will kissing his forehead, his temples, his eyes, anything he could reach from the odd angle he was wedged into underneath him. His own voice, almost unrecognizable it was so thick with emotion, rasped in response, "Mine."

WATCHING from the shadows, Raul frowned. Had he rescued Richard from one witch only to deliver him into the hands of another? He might not have the gift of foresight when it came to mated pairs that the king or shaman of a pack possessed, but he could recognize the scent of a mated pair. Had he made a great mistake bringing Will with him?

Chapter 6

Will woke, thinking at first that he was having another dream. The warmth. The strong arms holding him close. Opening his eyes, he focused on the relaxed features of the werewolf in front of him.

Richard.

Even as his body began to respond to the werewolf's proximity, Will cursed himself. What had he been thinking? This was Raul's brother, his twin, the one with no memory. A condition most likely caused by a less than scrupulous witch, and here he was taking advantage of him.

It seemed pretty mutual, the little voice in his head rationalized. *He wanted you just as much as you wanted him.*

Richard shifted in his sleep, pulling Will closer. The witch let himself be cuddled, justifying his actions with the excuse of not wanting to wake the sleeping werewolf. He'd obviously been through so much; he deserved a good nap.

The sound of plates clinking together in the kitchen interrupted Will's descent back into sleep, bringing him fully awake and allowing his conscience to kick in fully. Carefully extricating himself from Richard's arms, he backed off the bed, trying not to jostle the mattress. Grabbing a set of clean clothes from his duffle, he headed to the bathroom to clean up. Facing Raul wearing his twin's scent didn't strike the witch as the best of ideas.

"That isn't... I don't... fuck!" Will's fingers ran through his hair. Looking up at Raul, brown eyes begging the other man to understand, he admitted, "Maybe."

Raul chuckled. Oh yeah, Will had it bad. This was not a complication they needed, but he knew better than most that the mating instinct didn't always appear when it was easy or planned. "Go on. Be careful, though. He's got a wolf inside him that he isn't aware of and may not have any control over. We have no idea how long it has been since he's hunted."

Will shivered again. Nodding in agreement, he left the kitchen, his mind already picturing Richard as he'd left him, sprawled across the white sheets, golden skin covered with a light dusting of matching hair. He took the stairs two at a time.

Bursting into the room, he paused, letting his eyes roam over the werewolf's sleeping form. His memory hadn't done it justice. Even in sleep the muscles were clearly defined, and Will felt his cock twitch, beginning to swell.

Richard shifted restlessly, the smell of Will's rising arousal stirring him. Opening his eyes, his intense gaze immediately captured Will's. "Come here," he ordered, his voice a rough growl.

Torn, the witch approached the bed. "There is someone downstairs who wants to see you," he said, trying to distract the werewolf from his obvious purpose.

"It's not you and you are the only person I want to see," Richard answered, reaching up and grasping Will's hand, pulling him onto the bed. "You took a shower," he accused, rubbing his face against Will's abdomen.

"Well... ahhh... yeah." Will's voice cracked as Richard positioned him. He straddled the werewolf's hips, nothing but a thin cotton sheet and his blue jeans separating their cocks. "I couldn't go down... I think you'll want to see...."

With a pitiful whimper, Will braced his arms on either side of Richard's head. His body undulated, rubbing the zipper of his jeans against the hard ridge extending up onto Richard's stomach. Liquid from the tip of Richard's erection seeped through the sheet, and Will couldn't resist. Shifting back so he was sitting on the werewolf's legs, he curled forward, taking the blunt head into his mouth through the sheet, sucking the unique taste from the cotton.

"Ah, fuck!" Richard cursed, his hips lifting off the mattress. His fingers sank deep into Will's dark curls, his hands easily guiding his motions. "Suck me."

"I am." Will ran a teasing tongue up the covered length, his teeth just barely grazing the head. So much for good intentions.

Richard pawed at Will's shirt. "Whyinthefuck'd you get dressed again?" he complained, pulling the offending garment over Will's head.

"Because Alex wouldn't take kindly to me walking around in front of his mate naked and smelling of sex," Will quipped back before thinking.

"You're mine!" Richard roared, rolling Will onto his back and looming over him. "No one… no one but me sees you… touches you… tastes you."

Will anticipated the chill that shuddered up his spine this time. Apparently he had a possessive werewolf kink. He owed Tristan an apology. If being with Benjamin felt like this, it was amazing his twin ever got out of bed. "Well, the seeing part might be hard—" He tried to lighten the mood with the gentle tease.

Richard cut off the words with his mouth, his hips thrusting into the juncture of Will's body insistently. "Mine," he said again, his eyes burning into Will's as he pulled back, his body continuing to rock against him.

"Yours," Will agreed, sucked into the sensual spell. The energy flowing off the werewolf was warm and heavy, surrounding him… shielding him… protecting him. He melted into it, their auras blending as the hard ridge of Richard's cock stroked against his repeatedly. "Fuck! I'm going to come."

"Yes," Richard urged. "Come for me. Come so I can lick you clean."

Will's fingers twisted in the sheet. "Ahhh ... damnit!" His hips bucked up, desperately seeking the last increment of stimulation that would push him over the edge. "Fuck me," he pleaded, his hands moving to Richard's ass, carelessly pushing the sheet out of the way so his fingers could knead his lover's bare ass. "Oh Blessed Goddess, I want to feel you inside me."

"I will. Again. And again," Richard purred, watching the waves of sensation wash over his lover as he thrust against him, punctuating each word with a snap of his hips.

Legs splayed wide, Will lifted up into the glorious pressure. "Now. Want you inside me now."

Richard growled, his mouth falling to Will's bared neck, his teeth grazing the flesh, his mouth sucking a purple bruise to the surface. A pained noise of primal need escaped Will's lips as he came inside his jeans, his hips rising erratically until Richard's entire body tensed. The warmth of Richard's release seeped through the layers of cloth, but neither man felt the discomfort.

When Will's head cleared enough for rational thinking to return, he said, "I was supposed to bring you downstairs."

"This was more fun."

Will laughed. "Can't argue with that, but I think your brother might object to sitting downstairs alone while we fool around."

"Brother?" Richard sat up, alert and obviously curious.

Will propped his head up with his elbow. "Yeah, your brother, Raul, is downstairs." He watched as the man next to him processed the information. He could see him search his memory... and fail. He reached out to comfort his lover. "He knows that you've lost your memory. We were kind of hoping that seeing him might help. Come downstairs with me."

Richard's head spiked with pain. He pulled Will tight to his chest. Finding out he had a brother reminded him that there was so much he didn't know, but somehow holding Will made it better. "I can't seem to keep my hands off you. When you picked me up, you said we were friends. Is this how you define friends?" he asked, voice tight.

"No," Will answered honestly. "We've never done this before, but it was obviously way past time."

Richard pulled back to look into his eyes. "I'm not sure I want to remember if I'm going to remember things that will change this."

Will melted into the loving embrace, his mouth getting ahead of his brain. "Nothing will change this. Can't you feel that?" Inside, he cringed. Once Richard knew the truth, would it ruin any chance of having something more?

The werewolf stilled his body, the complete stillness of a predator waiting for his prey. "I can." Running his fingers in a gentle stroke down Will's cheek, he whispered, "Let's go see my brother."

Grimacing, Will started to roll away. "I think I need another shower."

The thought of Will washing off his scent made the voice in Richard's head howl. Pinning the younger man to the bed, he tugged at the opening of his jeans with his teeth. "Oh, no... I promised to clean you."

Will whimpered, his body bowing from the bed as Richard's tongue swept from hipbone to hipbone. By the time he was clean to Richard's satisfaction, he was completely hard again, the tip of his erection leaking onto the freshly licked skin, his soiled jeans discarded in a heap at the side of the bed. A noise from downstairs reminded him that Raul was waiting. "We really should go downstairs," he protested feebly.

"Is that what you want to do?" Richard purred, his mouth poised over the head of Will's cock, the warmth of his breath teasing the surface.

Moaning, Will arched until the soft lips grazed his foreskin. The contact was both too much and not enough. "No... yes... *yes!*" Forcing himself to move, he rolled away from the addicting touch.

Richard sat up on the bed, his arm draped casually over his bent knee, perfectly at ease with his nudity. He didn't like that Will seemed capable of walking away from him, but the protesting voice in his head was too sated and sleepy to make much of a fuss. With a satisfied growl, he watched as Will pulled on clean clothes without bothering to wash.

"Are you going to get dressed and come down or should I go get Raul and bring him up here?" Will teased, throwing Richard's jeans and shirt at the lounging man.

Reluctantly, Richard dressed and followed Will down the stairs. Catching sight of the man pacing restlessly, he froze. It was like staring in the mirror—or would have been if he'd visited a barber in the last couple of years.

Will hesitated. Would Raul want him to stay or leave them alone? Moving to an inconspicuous corner of the room, he watched as the two men walked silently toward each other. It was obvious that Raul wanted to embrace his brother, but was restraining the impulse. Will realized how hard that must be. Richard just seemed stunned.

"I guess there is no doubt that you're my brother," Richard muttered ruefully, smiling at the other man. "Are we twins?"

Raul nodded, at a loss for what to say. Secretly, he'd held out hope that Richard's memory would return when he saw him. He could feel their bond, his own wolf responding to the satisfied happiness of his brother's. The need to hug his brother close was almost overwhelming, but he didn't want to scare him away.

"Don't talk much, do ya?" Richard said, choosing to sit in the oak rocking chair and pulling one leg up to tuck underneath him.

Clearing his throat, Raul sat in the corner of the sofa. "I'm not sure what to say. I've been so worried about you."

"Why didn't *you* come bail me out?" Richard asked. It wasn't an accusation, just a curious query.

Raul glanced nervously at Will. It didn't take long for Richard to get right to the heart of the matter. Could they have a conversation about Sienna while his brother still had no memory? Deciding it would be ill advised, Raul said, "I just got here. Will was closer. We didn't figure you'd want to lounge around in jail any longer than absolutely necessary."

Raul's comment brought Richard's attention back to the man he'd spent most of the day ravishing. He realized that, even without paying attention, he knew exactly where Will was and what he was doing. "And you'd have been right." Silently he added, *and if you'd gotten here earlier, I would have missed out on spending the afternoon in bed with Will.*

The smile he sent Will was intimate and secretive. The hair on Will's body rose, his cock twitching in his jeans. Fuck, his libido knew no bounds when it came to this man.

"So is this your house?" Richard asked, gesturing around.

"It is actually our house. It belonged to our grandmother. She left it to us," Raul explained.

Richard pondered that for a moment. "I feel very at home here and comfortable with you, but I just can't remember any details." His brow furrowed, his hands coming up to rub at his temples. "Every time I try and think about the past, I get a splitting headache. Just about doesn't make it worth it."

Raul and Will shared a meaningful look over Richard's bent head. "Let me get you something to drink," Will offered, heading toward the kitchen. "You want tea or soda?"

"Soda," Richard answered, smiling at him again. Turning to Raul, he said, "Well, tell me about myself," and chuckled.

Deciding the safest place to start was the beginning, Raul began to reminisce. Will delivered the drink, adding a glass of the iced tea Raul had been drinking ever since they'd arrived, and returned to his corner. The brothers seemed oblivious to his presence, but he was as curious about their past as Richard was. During the conversation, they adjourned to the kitchen, eating the dinner Raul had prepared. If Richard found the amount of steak and lack of side items unusual, he kept it to himself.

"Sure beats the swill served at the jail," Richard sighed, pushing back from the table and rubbing the back of his neck. The headache that had been present almost constantly from the moment he woke up in the jail cell had been getting worse throughout the evening. He'd hoped food would make it better, but it hadn't. "I think I'm gonna take a shower and go to bed. A full night's sleep in a real bed sounds like heaven."

Getting up from the table, he looked pointedly at Will, leaving the younger man no doubt that he'd be welcome for either the shower, the bed, or both. "I'll come up and find something for you to sleep in as soon as I help Raul clean the kitchen."

Richard nodded, looking at Will standing next to his brother and feeling a pang of jealousy. He didn't like that Will would choose Raul's company over his. Was there something between them? It didn't feel like it, but he had no memories to support his conclusion. A sharp pain struck behind his eyes as he tried to force himself to remember past relationships.

Raul watched his brother go. Turning to Will, he said, "Use the spell. Something is controlling him. I can feel it."

"Me too," Will agreed. "I could see it color his aura as the two of you were talking. It seems only to activate when he tries to remember the past. Earlier when… uhm…."

"When the two of you were in bed?" Raul supplied.

"Ahh… yeah." Will cleared the lump in his throat. "There wasn't any sign of it."

"I think it can only affect his human side and I suspect your earlier interlude was primarily driven by his wolf."

Will's skin prickled. Damn, he was going to have to get over this visceral reaction to wolves if he was going to continue to live among werewolves. *You didn't have this reaction until you met Richard*, the voice in his head reminded. Will frowned. His inner voice was beginning to sound remarkably like Tristan—a real smart-ass.

"There'll be fewer questions if I do it tonight while he's asleep."

"If he's anything like he was growing up, he can sleep through a tornado."

Will grinned. "Well, that's handy."

"Of course, something to help tire him out before bed couldn't hurt." Raul pulled Will away from the sink and pushed him playfully toward the door. He was growing used to the idea of his brother with Will, and it didn't bother him as much as he thought it should. It had a lot to do with the immense feelings of happiness and satisfaction that he'd felt radiating from his brother every time Richard had been anywhere near the young witch. Plus, he trusted Will; something he'd never been able to say about Sienna.

Will paused in the doorway and shot Raul an incredulous look over his shoulder. "You sure?"

"Yes, but I'm leaving the dishes in the sink for you to do in the morning, so don't stay up too late."

Chapter 7

WILL grinned all the way up the stairs, amazed at the warm feeling Raul's acceptance gave him. Reaching the top of the stairs, the warmth was replaced by a completely different feeling as he caught a glimpse of Richard through the steam billowing out of the bathroom. The rogue had left the door wide open, and the clear shower curtain didn't hide one inch of his incredible body. The water fell from the showerhead, running over the werewolf's body in streams that traced the hollows defining his muscles.

"Am I to infer that you'd like company?" Will drawled, leaning a shoulder against the doorjamb.

Richard looked up, the innocent expression on his face completely ruined by the soapy hand stroking his cock to complete hardness. "A man can hope."

He grinned, and Will was lost. Pulling his shirt over his head and stepping out of his jeans, the witch closed the door behind him. "You're incorrigible," he teased, stepping into the tub beside the werewolf.

Pinning Will to the tile wall, Richard licked at the water running down his smooth chest. "Hey, what do you expect? I just got out of jail."

Will laughed, his fingers tangling in his lover's long, wet hair, pulling him closer as Richard's mouth closed over his nipple. "Ahh…

fuck, yeah," he sighed. "That argument might persuade me if you'd been in prison for years, but you were in the county lockup for less than a week."

"Details, details...." Richard hummed, sinking to his knees as his mouth worked its way lower on Will's torso.

"Ahh... fuck. Don't tease," Will swore as Richard's tongue swiped from hipbone to hipbone and into the crease where his thigh met his body.

"Tease? What is it you want, lover?" Richard purred, his tongue dancing in patterns over the twitching muscles of Will's lower abdomen.

Will's entire body trembled. "Your mouth," he pleaded. "Put your mouth on me." The annoying "Tristan-like" voice was back, reminding him that he was supposed to be wearing Richard out, not the other way around, but frankly at the moment, he didn't give a damn. Thrusting his hips forward, he groaned, "Suck me."

Running his tongue up the bottom of Will's shaft, Richard mouthed the rosy-pink head, his tongue flicking rapidly against the pulse at the base. They both moaned as the distended shaft pressed between the willing lips.

"Fuck. Fuck. Fuck," Will chanted, his hips snapping forward as Richard sucked more and more of his prick past his lips.

Unable to do more than hum and moan his approval, Richard's hand stroked up the back of Will's muscular thigh to knead the clenching ass, his fingers dipping ever so slightly into the tempting cleft. He wanted to taste... take... claim... every inch of this man.

Will felt the probing fingers and his knees threatened to give out. "Oh Gods... yes..." he moaned, widening his stance. His movements changed, driving forward into Richard's mouth and then back onto his fingers. "In... put them in me," he panted.

The broken plea almost made Richard come. Pressing against the tight opening, he began to pulse the tip of his finger just inside the muscle until it relaxed enough to let him in easily. Sucking harder, he sank his finger deep into the clenching channel, coordinating his attack until Will was writhing and cursing, his hands clenching the fixtures, his eyes tightly closed.

"Gonna come," Will warned just moments before streams of hot liquid shot down Richard's throat.

The warning didn't matter. Richard wanted nothing more than to taste his lover's passion. His hand fell to his own erection and in less than a dozen pulls, he was spilling his own load over his fist. "Damn… fuck.…" he panted, his forehead resting on Will's hip.

Will slipped down the wall and both of them sat on the bottom of the tub, the shower raining water on their heads as they leisurely soaped and cleaned each other's bodies.

"Time for bed?" Richard rasped, his lips pressed tight to Will's damp neck.

"Oh yeah.…" Will whispered. He just wasn't sure how he was going to stay awake long enough to cast the spell.

WILL'S eyelids felt like they were made of lead. They wanted to close so badly he could taste the sleep. His cheek pressed to the warmth of Richard's chest, he pinched his thigh to keep from succumbing to the overwhelming drowsiness.

Just a few more minutes.

Just long enough to assure himself that Richard was deeply asleep before he moved away to gather the things he needed to cast the spell. He heard a shuffling in the hall. Looking up, he spotted Raul pacing in front of the doorway. Carefully, he eased himself away from his lover's body. Pulling on a pair of boxers he'd left on a chair, he tiptoed to the door.

"What are you doing?" he hissed.

"Have you done it yet?" Raul asked, pulling Will out into the hall.

"No. I was waiting for him to be deeply asleep."

"Can I… do you need my help?"

Will stared at Raul. The last thing he'd ever thought he'd hear come from Raul's mouth was an offer to help perform a spell. "You might. No one has as strong a connection with him as you do."

Raul started to say something about the bond building between Will and Richard being much stronger, but bit his lip. Who knew what would happen when, or if, Richard regained his memory? "What can I do?"

Efficiently, Will gathered the necessary herbs, starting them burning in a censer beside the bed. "I'm going to cast a spell that should allow us to see visible traces of any magic affecting your brother. If we know what spell she used, it'll be easier to banish it."

Raul nodded, shifting uncomfortably, obviously out of his element.

"Just relax," Will instructed soothingly. "Take a deep breath and focus on your brother like you did when we were scrying for him."

Holding his hands over the sleeping werewolf, Will began a low chant. The air around Richard began to glow and pulse with color, strands of light coalescing in a rainbow of hues. The brightest by far, a pure golden band that ran directly from Richard's chest to Will's, surprised the witch to the point that he almost lost his rhythm. Taking a deep breath and pushing his doubts away, he fell deeper into the trance until a rope of ritualistic knots of binding appeared. Focusing on the restrictive bands, he channeled more energy into the chant until the bands remained clear even when his voice paused.

Looking up at Raul, he motioned toward the bands with his eyes. "We can loosen them just like you would a corporeal rope. Focus on the knots," he instructed evenly. "See them loosening and unwinding. The knots hold the power."

Raul looked panicked, but Will watched as the werewolf, through sheer determination, calmed his fears and focused on the task at hand. The bands slackened around Richard's body, the rope of energy pulsing and the knots loosening until the band appeared simply wound around itself instead of knotted.

While Raul focused on the visible rope, Will worked on determining its origin, looking at the design and power stamp on the spell. It wasn't one he had ever encountered before, so he learned everything he could about it in the hopes that he could find a spell to counter it. Finally, his energy began to drain, the colors beginning to fade.

Raul looked up, worry and an edge of panic clear in his eyes.

Will smiled reassuringly, slowing his chant until the energy in the room returned to normal. Laying hands on the sleeping werewolf, he closed the spell with an incantation to ensure that Richard would sleep deeply and awake strong and refreshed. Pushing a little extra energy into the spell, he eased it through the bonds open between Richard and Raul so that Raul would reap some of the benefits as well.

Thanking the Goddess, Will bowed his head, breathing deeply of Richard's scent, opening his hands flat on the bed and allowing his excess energy to flow through the antique wood into the ground. "Blessed be," he whispered.

Overcome by exhaustion, he stretched along Richard's side, unable even to say "good night" to Raul. The best he could do was a weak smile as the werewolf left the room.

RAUL prowled down the stairs, restless and not the least bit sleepy. The strands that he had seen binding his twin disturbed him. He couldn't fight a magical battle, but he could damn well tear out Sienna's throat. *Fridolf* or not, he would gladly end that nefarious witch's life. The problem was, he wasn't sure if killing Sienna would end her magic. What if once cast, the spell remained, and she was the only one capable of undoing it?

Running a weary hand through his hair, he mechanically went through the motions of getting ready for bed: making a last trip around the house, checking windows and doors and turning off lights before heading up to his room. Stripping off his clothes and draping them over the armchair in the corner, he brushed his teeth and crawled between the cool sheets. Flipping open the cell phone he'd laid on the nightstand, he looked at the time and debated calling Alex.

It was late, but his lover wouldn't mind. Hitting the speed dial button, he waited for the soothing sounds of his mate's voice.

"'Bout time you called me," Alex purred, his voice deep and rough from sleep.

Raul opened his mouth to answer the gentle teasing, but no words came out. He could feel their mating bond, even over the distance, but instead of comforting him as it always did, he felt lost and alone.

"I miss you too." Alex's voice was still hushed, whispering to his lover in the dark, responding to the unspoken emotion. "I got the message you left, that you'd found Richard. How is he?"

Raul swallowed, turning on his side and closing his eyes so he could pretend he was lying next to his mate, instead of hundreds of miles away. "Physically, he looks fine. A little thinner than I'm used to seeing him and his hair's as long as Will's." He forced out a choked laugh. "But he has no memory. Not even after he saw me. He recognized the resemblance, but… but nothing more. He doesn't know me at all. I haven't even broached the subject of our father or the pack."

"Oh baby, I'm so sorry. I wish I could be there to hold you. I might be able—"

"No," Raul cut Alex off. "It would be no better with you here. You are needed at home. I'm a big boy. I can handle this."

"It isn't a matter of you being *able* to handle it, lover," Alex crooned. "It is a matter of wanting to be there for you. I wasn't blessed with a sibling, but I know how much he means to you—even after everything that's happened. Have you found anything to indicate if he was involved in your abduction?"

"Not a thing. I mean, he doesn't remember his name, let alone what he did years ago. Will has found evidence of magic currently at work on him. He thinks it may be responsible for his memory loss."

"How are you and Will getting along?"

Raul smiled at just the touch of jealousy in his mate's voice. If things had been different, he might have even teased just a little, but the last thing he needed was more strife between the people in his life. "Okay, I guess. He's easy to talk to and seems to know what he's doing, but what do I know about magic? He could be casting spells he got off the back of a cereal box."

A fleeting doubt passed through Raul's mind. Maybe Richard's reaction to Will was a result of a spell. He'd seen evidence of a spell binding his twin, but he had no way of knowing if that spell had been cast by Sienna or Will. He took a shaky breath, trying to calm his paranoia. He had no reason to distrust Will and he knew that the mating instinct couldn't be recreated by any spell. If it could, Sienna would have used it long ago.

"We've had one interesting and unexpected development," Raul said.

"Oh…."

Raul could hear his lover shifting in their bed and his wolf stirred. Reining him back, he rubbed at the physical symptom of his wolf's interest, not sure if he was trying to make it grow or subside.

"Will and Richard?" Alex asked, his voice dripping with implication.

"What do you know?" Raul asked. His lover sounded far too sure of himself. He could almost hear Alex's shrug.

"Just a vision Ian had when we were working to turn Benjamin."

"Why didn't you tell me?"

"You know that visions of the future aren't cast in stone. The fewer people privy to the information, the less chance that expectations could influence the outcome. Besides, I wanted Will to go with you, and I was afraid if you knew, you wouldn't take him."

"I'm not sure I would have. I'm still not sure it was a good idea. I've got a werewolf with no idea he's a werewolf under the effects of a mating instinct. This could get bad quickly."

"You can't control the drive of the instinct. You'll just have to focus on restoring Richard's memory so he can control his wolf. How does Will feel about all this?"

"Ravished." Raul snorted, feeling a little of his worry and tension disappearing, just sharing this with his mate. Alex joined him with a chuckle. The initial needs of a newly mated wolf could be a little demanding. "He's not unwilling, just a little confused. He obviously returns Richard's feelings, though not being lycan, he doesn't recognize the actual mating instinct."

"You might want to either tell him or make sure you're around to guide him. Richard can't warn him about the commitment involved in completing their bond and Will should know before things go too far," Alex cautioned, his role as Rajan showing even though he wasn't the leader of Richard's pack. "It hasn't gone too far already, has it?"

Raul sighed; the last thing he needed was more complications. "I'm not sure, but if it has, there is nothing to do about it now. I'll talk with him first thing in the morning. Richard and the spell took everything out of him. I don't think they'll be getting up to anything more tonight and I doubt I could wake either of them if I tried."

"Well then..." Alex drawled, "it sounds like I have you all to myself and the children are sound asleep."

Raul's wolf immediately perked up, causing Raul to feel the overwhelming urge for a languorous stretch. Since there was no immediate need to deny them both what they wanted, he pressed the button for speakerphone and laid the handset on the pillow next to his head. Indulging in the stretch, he ran his hand down his chest and into the curls at the base of his semi-hard cock. "Why do I have the feeling that you aren't about to suggest that we join them?" he teased.

"That would be incest," Alex squawked in protest.

Raul laughed. "You know perfectly well that I meant join them in sleep. Besides, I like my men a little taller and broader than Will. Someone who can pin me to the furs and take what he wants."

Alex's moan vibrated through the phone and across Raul's nerve endings, straight to his growing erection. "You know what I want...."

His hand circling the base of his shaft, Raul squeezed, biting his lip at the surge of pleasure. "What?"

"I want to hear you come."

Raul whimpered, his hips lifting from the mattress as he started to stroke his cock. His wolf continued to demand more. He didn't understand the concept of phones and wanted to be physically joined with his mate.

"That's it," Alex crooned, his voice pitched so low that Raul had to strain to hear it. "I know your cock better than you do, the way the skin slides over the steel of the shaft, the feel of the velvet-soft head under my tongue...."

Raul cursed, already on the brink of exploding. "Ah, fuck! Tell me you're close."

"Oh, I'm close. If you were here, I'd barely make it inside you. The first grip of your muscles around my cock and I'd be coming... filling you as I bit into your shoulder."

"Fuck, yes. Alex!" Raul screamed. Perversely, he stilled his hand, riding the crest of his peak, waiting to hear the growl of his lover's climax. The anticipated sound was followed closely by his name. Two quick strokes sent him careening into his own orgasm. Warm liquid covered his hand and stomach as every muscle in his body contracted and trembled. Digging his heels into the mattress, he strained up into his hand, his eyes tightly shut as he listened to his mate's pleasure. "Damn... fuck... I... I...." he stuttered as the aftershocks wracked his body.

A sated, sleepy chuckle filled his ear. "You love me?"

"Yeah… I love you." Raul turned on his side, wiping his stomach with the sheet and then kicking it to the floor. Head resting on his outstretched arm, his wolf satisfied and sleepy, he listened to the familiar rumble of his lover's voice.

"I love you too. Now sleep. Leave the phone on so I can hear you."

Raul nodded, too sleepy to realize Alex couldn't see him. In his mind, his mate was beside him, just like he'd been every other night since their mating. "Night…."

Chapter 8

A STRONG hand traced a path along Will's side, making him shift in his sleep as it brushed over his ticklish spots. Grasping the wandering hand, he pinned it to his chest, sleep immediately beginning to reclaim him when a muscular thigh pressed between his own. With a sleepy sigh, he moved closer, the hair covering the thigh sweeping against his balls. His eyes fluttered open and he looked up into the amused face of his werewolf lover.

"Rise and shine, sleepyhead."

"It can't be morning," Will grumbled, burying his face against Richard's chest.

"'Fraid so." The hand that had been teasing his side moved to trace random patterns on his back, down over his hip and the top of his thigh.

"Can't we do something about that? Maybe close the shutters and pretend that it's still the middle of the night?" Will suggested, still refusing to open his eyes, but pressing his body close in response to Richard's touches nonetheless.

Richard's mouth sucked gently on the side of Will's neck, working its way down onto his shoulder. "Your body seems to be waking up...." He rocked his full erection forward to stroke against Will's.

With a grumpy look on his face, Will looked down at his prick, rising up along his stomach. "Traitor," he snapped.

Richard laughed, rolling Will onto his back and settling on top of him. "Tell me you don't want me and I'll get up and let you go back to sleep." His mouth dropped persuasive kisses across Will's chest as he talked.

"Ahhh...." Will gasped as teeth grazed a sensitive nipple, "sure you would."

Richard froze, his mouth poised over the dark nub. "I would if you asked me."

"Fuck!" Will capitulated, lifting his chest to meet his lover's lips. "Don't stop." He was rewarded with warm, wet suction that made him squirm—the sensation almost too much.

Will's legs wrapped around the werewolf's hips, increasing their intimate contact. "I don't understand this. I've never... we shouldn't...."

"Shhh...." Richard soothed, his hips rocking rhythmically. "Don't think so much. I feel it. You feel it. Nothing that feels this good can be wrong. I know deep inside me that if I don't make love to you—right now—I'm going to explode. Let me... take me inside you... let me love you," he cajoled.

Will whimpered as Richard's hard shaft slid against his opening. He *did* want this, and he could sense nothing evil or wrong. Lycans didn't contract STDs, so they didn't need condoms. He was out of excuses. "I didn't pack lube," he said, which could have been either a "yes" or a "no." "You better take your time," he added, changing the first statement into a definite "yes."

"Oh, I will," Richard promised, his rich, deep voice alone going a long way toward making Will ready. Flipping Will onto his stomach, he rested his full weight along his back, every part of their bodies aligned, his prick nestled into the crack of Will's ass and their legs tangled together. "You were made to fit me."

Gasping, Will bucked into the strong body over him. Richard's strength and size were an incredible turn-on. He'd always been attracted to older men, but most of them had been about his size. Richard made him feel protected, controlled, dominated. "Fuck me," he whispered.

"I'm going to claim every part of you," Richard mouthed against Will's skin, grazing his teeth along his shoulder blade and trailing his tongue down the impression of his spine. "Until you know that you belong to me."

Normally, words like that would have set warning bells off in Will's mind. He didn't like possessive boyfriends, but coming from Richard's mouth, the words sounded right and true. A niggling worry danced at the edge of Will's consciousness. Something Tristan had said about… the thought disappeared as Will reached out for it, Richard's sensual onslaught destroying his ability to think rationally and leaving only raw need in its place. "Take me. Make me yours."

Richard's soft hair trailed against Will's skin, raising bumps as his mouth worked its way down his body. "Oh, yes…." Will breathed as Richard's mouth sucked on the dimple at the base of his spine, his hands pushing his thighs farther apart. Will lifted his ass, offering all of himself.

"You look so beautiful like this," Richard growled, his teeth nipping at the back of Will's thigh, moving down to the sensitive back of his knee. "Open and begging me with your body."

His hands swept up the smooth muscles, cupping Will's ass, kneading and spreading it open. The flat of his tongue passed over the wrinkled opening and Will fell apart. Fingers twisting in the pillow, he rubbed his dripping cock against the sheets. "Oh fuck, fuck, fuck!"

A million pulses of pleasure ran along his nerves directly to his prick. It was too much and not enough. He felt like he was going to come. He could feel it. He could taste it. But the moment just went on and on. Richard held all the control. His world narrowed to Richard's tongue as it lapped, sucked, and probed his opening. "Put… oh, fuck…

put something in me," he wailed, not caring if it was his lover's tongue, fingers, or cock.

Richard's fingers tightened on Will's hips, holding him down, ending the friction of his erection against the mattress. His tongue pushed past the tight muscle, fucking the wet hole with fast, hard, short thrusts. Will pushed up, trying to get more of Richard deeper into his body. Stopping long enough to nip at the ticklish lower curve of Will's ass, Richard rasped, "I love the feel of you pushing up to get more of my tongue in your ass."

Will whimpered as Richard's tongue returned, a wet finger sliding into the opening beside it and working his hole wider. "More!"

A second finger joined the first, Richard's tongue lapping at the clenching rim while his fingers drove Will crazy. Will lifted his hips, pulling his knees beneath him and offering his body to the werewolf. "Please... please, Richard."

Richard growled, gripping the slender hips roughly, rising to his knees and pulling Will back against his groin. "Say it again. Say my name."

"Richard. Richard," Will choked as the blunt head of a cock pushed against his hole. Grabbing the painted iron headboard, he pushed back, feeling his body give as Richard slipped inside him. Both men yelled as their bodies joined.

Will could feel the power rising around them, warm and red. With every push of Richard into his body, it grew stronger until it glowed, pulsing and growing. The small part of him not lost to passion recognized the incredible power they were raising. Deep inside, he knew nothing could stand against it, but did he want to dissolve the magic that bound Richard? He had promised Raul, but if Richard regained his memory, Will might lose him. He couldn't bear... but he couldn't not. If Richard chose to return to Sienna, that was his decision. Will wanted this to be more than just sexual chemistry, but he'd forever doubt a relationship based on magical influence.

Focusing his mind on the feeling of the werewolf moving inside his body, Will channeled their sexual energy into a sphere of cleansing white light, starting at their skin and burning out in a flash so bright he worried it might set the room on fire. He felt the bonds fall away, the evil they released retreating in a whoosh from the purity of the energy they were generating. The connection between them was so strong; he could feel the moment when the blocks fell in Richard's mind.

Surprisingly, the werewolf didn't falter... didn't pull away. Wrapping his body completely around Will's, he whispered in his ear as his cock continued to plunder his body. "Mine. Mine. Mine," he chanted as Will's orgasm ripped through him, sending every bit of his remaining energy out through his cock.

Richard followed him down as he collapsed to the bed. "So beautiful. So beautiful when you surrender to me," he rasped, turning Will's chin so their lips could meet in a long, clinging kiss. He released an almost pained howl into Will's mouth as he came, filling his body. His arms gave way and he fell to his elbows, his forehead resting against Will's sweaty back as he tried to catch his breath.

Falling to the side, he pulled Will into his arms. "I remember."

"I know." Will cuddled closer, wondering if it would be the last time he'd be held in Richard's strong arms.

RICHARD lay in bed, content to hold his mate close to his body and feel the gentle rise and fall of his chest. A part of him was anxious to see his brother, greet him properly, and find out exactly who Will was, but the feeling didn't supersede the desire to hold onto his mate for just a moment longer. It didn't matter where Will had come from or how he had come to be with Raul. Will was his mate, and his physical presence calmed Richard and allowed him to wade through some painful emotions.

His mind was spinning with images as he tried to piece together the past few weeks: fighting with his father, fighting with Sienna, feeling so lost when he couldn't remember his past, and the overwhelming feeling of homecoming when he'd laid eyes on Will. That part hadn't changed. He identified it for what it was the second he regained his memory—the recognition of the other half of his soul. It was as if a curtain had parted, and the first sensation he experienced was joining with his true mate.

He'd have to deal with Sienna as soon as he returned to the pack, and he harbored no illusions that it would be easy or civilized. Holding Will, his erotic dreams of the past few months made a lot more sense. He should have paid more attention. He could have already been rid of Sienna and free to join his life as well as his soul with his chosen mate. A memory danced just out of reach and his brow furrowed as he tried to bring it closer.

"My, what a frown for such a beautiful morning," Will's sleepy voice teased, stretching his body to relieve the aches of their vigorous lovemaking. "Wanna share?"

Richard rolled onto his side. Looming over Will, he stole a quick kiss. "No, not particularly."

It was Will's turn to pull a worried frown, unsure of where he stood now that Richard had his memory back. "I'm sorry I misled you. I didn't—"

Another hard kiss stopped the apology. "It's okay. If Raul trusts you, so do I. The details can wait for a while. I'd like to think the chemistry wasn't an act, though," he drawled casually. Covering Will's body and pinning him to the bed with his weight, he held his breath, waiting for the answer.

Will lifted his hips, pressing his obvious erection into Richard's belly. "I think you can tell it wasn't an act."

Burying his nose into his lover's neck and inhaling deeply, Richard soothed his wolf with the scent of his mate. The light-hearted reply was less of a declaration than he'd been hoping for, but it would have to do for now.

"Well, I hope you still feel that way because you've done something that can't be undone. Now you have to woo him or you are going to be one unhappy wolf," Raul warned. "I'm not sure how much you care about my opinion any more, but he's a worthy mate. What are you going to do about Sienna? I understand you married her."

Richard lifted himself up to sit on the railing, his eyes focusing on his feet. "Not technically. She did some sort of handfasting ritual, but we didn't get a marriage license or anything."

"You bound yourself to her in a magical ritual!" Raul shouted before remembering that he was trying *not* to wake Will.

"It's not legal."

"No, but did it never occur to you how much power you were handing her with her potions and rituals? How much control over your mind, body and spirit?" Raul asked.

Richard shrugged. "I guess not. What difference did it make what I did? You were going to lead the pack, carry on the family line, and you were so blasted good at everything, I could afford to mess up. Even after you left, everyone was constantly quoting you. 'Raul would do it this way'. 'Raul would make this decision'. 'When Raul gets back, he'll fix this'."

"Is that why you tried to get rid of me?" Raul blurted before he could bite it back. He hadn't intended to bring up the transportation that had almost gotten him killed so soon, but Richard's comment brought back all the feelings of betrayal and hurt. "I told you hundreds of times that I didn't want the throne. I would have been happy to step aside so you could lead."

Richard stood and started pacing, his human body needing to release his wolf's agitation at the acrimony between him and his twin. "I know you kept saying that, but you were a much better leader than I was. It all came so naturally to you. You always knew exactly what to say to settle a dispute or motivate the guard."

"That is nothing but the *Fridolf* in me. It is a bred instinct. Just like your desire to lead and care for our pack. I not only didn't want to lead our pack, but I couldn't do it. It is not in me to fight to take and keep the throne. You didn't have to try and kill me."

Raul's words fell like a dropped book in a silent library, reverberating in the suddenly quiet morning.

"Kill you? What in the fuck are you talking about?" Richard asked. Piercing green wolf eyes locked on Raul's.

"I'm talking about waking up in the middle of foreign packlands with no idea where I was, how I got there, or a chance to petition for safe travel!" Raul knew he was yelling, but didn't really care. If Will was going to bind himself to Richard, he needed to know exactly what he was getting into.

Richard's voice calmed, coming out almost completely void of emotion. "I don't have any idea what you are talking about. You left a detailed note when you left, explaining that you had an opportunity to mentor with an elder *Fridolf* of the Cumberland pack. We've had update letters from you every two to three months...." Only an almost imperceptible tremble in Richard's voice gave away his distress.

With a roar, Raul struck out at Richard. They had always been physically matched, but Richard's weight loss and the unexpected attack put him at a disadvantage.

Richard went down hard on his back. Tipping his head to the side, he bared his neck to Raul, offering his life if his twin demanded it. He would get to the bottom of this betrayal, but he had little doubt that Sienna was behind it, which meant ultimately he was at fault.

Pinning Richard's legs with his weight, Raul sniffed up his brother's torso, letting his teeth graze the tender flesh of his neck. It was an honest offer of submission, not just a ruse to cover up his crime. Raul could scent no deception, only distress and the lingering smell of Richard's mating. Surprisingly, it was the scent of Will that calmed both Raul's human rage and his wolf. Rocking back on his heels, he rose with powerful grace, grabbing his coffee mug and heading into the kitchen to refill it.

Richard got to his feet, brushing himself off, his eyes following Raul. He knew that their conversation was far from over, but he'd felt the anger leave his twin and hoped that their relationship wasn't forever damaged. When Raul returned to the porch, Richard pulled a chair to the railing and sat, purposefully keeping his head lower than his twin's. "I didn't know."

Raul's hand combed through his hair, rubbing at his neck. "No, but you brought her into our lives."

The younger twin nodded. "And I will get rid of her."

Pulling a chair forward to face Richard's, Raul sat facing his twin, their knees touching, the act speaking more clearly than any words that he forgave Richard. "How do you plan to do that? She is more powerful than either of us know."

Giving into long habit, Richard laid his chest and head in Raul's lap as he had when they were children. His twin completed the ritual by stroking his hair. "I go back and face this head on like I should have from the beginning. Like the leader I'm supposed to be. I never should have kept her around when I knew she wasn't my mate. It was just easier to let it flow than face the confrontation."

"It will be dangerous. She won't go willingly. She's invested too much time and effort."

Richard sat up, meeting Raul's eyes. "Which is why I need to go back alone."

"But—" Raul objected.

"No," Richard stated firmly, "I need you safe in case something happens to me and I won't risk Will. She'll sense that we are mated. He'll be a greater threat to her than you ever were."

Raul shook his head. "He's not going to just let you walk out of here. I may not know Will as well as I know Tristan, his twin, but they both have heads hard enough to be carved of granite."

Richard chuckled. "Then he'll fit right in, won't he? I need to know he's safe, and I can't properly court him until she is gone. I'll leave right now, before he is even up. Give me three days and then follow me."

Raul's mouth twisted into a wry smile. "That sounds incredibly selfless of you, but I suspect you are just leaving me to deal with his tantrum. He came south with me to help overcome Sienna's magic. He won't be happy to be left behind. Especially now that he has feelings for you."

Richard couldn't help the warmth that spread through his heart at Raul's comment. It made his face glow with love and satisfaction. "Which is precisely why he needs to stay here."

"Okay, but if he kills me, you have to tell my mate," Raul agreed reluctantly.

Grasping his brother in a tight hug, Richard buried his nose against his neck, inhaling the familiar scent. "There is so much we still need to talk about, but I can't see him or my resolve will falter. For the pack, I must go back. Keep him safe for me."

Raul stood, pulling Richard up with him. "You have my word. Take the car. I can arrange to have a rental delivered and not having a way for Will to chase you might work to my advantage… or detriment." He glanced at the stairs and shivered. He'd never seen Will angry, but he'd watched Tristan fight for his mate. He wasn't looking forward to the coming confrontation.

Chapter 9

WILL woke slowly, surprised at how bright the room appeared. He rarely slept late. Gran had frequently joked that Will had gotten all the early-riser genes. Tristan could sleep past noon and would whenever he had the chance. The twinge of over-exerted muscles reminded him of why he'd slept past his usual rising time. Pulling a pillow tight to his chest, he inhaled Richard's scent deep into his lungs and felt an unfamiliar ache that his lover wasn't still beside him. He could hear the deep rumble of voices from the back of the house and was glad Raul and Richard were talking. As much as he wanted to hurry to Richard's side, the brothers needed some time alone.

Once awake, however, it was almost physically impossible for Will to stay in bed. Sitting up, he winced at the pressure. He'd definitely used some muscles that hadn't been used in a while. Pulling on a soft pair of sleep pants, he moved a throw rug into the sunbeam next to the window. He'd been incorporating yoga moves into his own daily rituals for almost a decade, but the simplicity and flowing movements of the *Surya Namaskar*, or sun salutation, were still his favorite way to start the day.

Taking a deep breath, he folded his hands in front of his chest, centering himself and thanking the goddess for another day. Raising his hands over his head, he released the muscles in his shoulders, allowing the energy to shift and flow down his legs and into the floor like roots sinking into the earth. Exhaling, he rolled forward from his hips until his hands rested next to his feet, completing the circuit of earth energy. His mind flitted to Richard coming in and finding him in this position and his cock twitched in interest. Scolding his lack of focus, he took two conscious breaths, coming up slightly with each inhale, relaxing and re-centering with each exhale.

Focusing his mind, he lunged forward with his left foot, feeling the stretch in his legs and groin. Concentrating on the fluidity of his movements, he moved his feet together and pushed his ass into the air, forming a mountain and thanking the spirits of the earth. Straightening his body, he moved steadily through sequential positions, holding each as he thanked air, fire, and water. At the pinnacle of the series, he held the *Urdhva Mukha Svanasana*. Eyes raised to the sky, he reached out, connecting his power with the energies of the world before moving backwards through the positions until he was once again standing with his hands folded in front of his chest.

A pleasant hum of energy flowing through his body, Will draped a towel over his shoulder and headed for the shower. His morning ritual complete, he allowed his mind to wander back to Richard. The connection he felt with the werewolf was unlike anything he'd ever experienced. He wondered if it had anything to do with the lycan's preternatural nature. He could sense the power flowing through Richard, and it resonated with his own on an elemental level.

Stepping into the shower, he reached out in much the same way he communicated with his twin. Only this time, his mind was searching for Richard. Sensing his lover's energy, he allowed his desire to flow along the bond. A warm wave of tender emotion came flowing back, but then the connection was abruptly gone, like a door had slammed shut. Worried that he'd overstepped the boundaries of a new relationship, he hurried through the rest of his shower, anxious to get downstairs and see Richard.

RAUL paced, already on his fourth cup of coffee. The caffeine had little effect on him, but the ritual of fixing it soothed his nerves. He could hear Will moving around upstairs and knew it was only a matter of time before he had to face a pissed-off witch. Not the way he'd choose to spend his morning. Though not much had been of his choosing since Nicolai had showed up at the farm.

Right after Richard left, Raul had considered calling Tristan and enlisting his aid in reasoning with Will, but he'd been afraid that Tristan would side with his twin. The only thing worse than one pissed-off witch would be two. He'd dragged Will all the way down here with him to help, and now he was preventing him from doing just that.

"Raul, where is Richard?"

The werewolf jumped at Will's question. He'd been so distracted by his worries that he hadn't scented the witch's approach. Turning to face the younger man, he tried to draw up a reassuring smile. The frown on Will's face told him he failed. All his carefully rehearsed speeches fled at the look of worry in the dark eyes. "He's gone back home."

"Home?" Will asked, stepping out onto the porch. "Why would he go alone?"

"He needs to… there are things he has to do," Raul finished lamely.

"But Sienna is there."

"She is what he needs to take care of."

"Raul, you brought me all the way down here because you didn't think you could face Sienna without magical help, and then you sent him to face her without either one of us? He doesn't exactly have a sterling track record when it comes to resisting her spells."

Raul knew he was messing this up, but he couldn't find words to explain the situation to Will without revealing too much. "I didn't send him. He decided that he needed to go and he asked me to stay here with you."

"I'm not the one who needs help! How could you do this to him? I know you are angry with him for trying to kill you, but—"

That Will would think he'd sent Richard into danger as payback for Sienna's attempt to kill him had never even occurred to Raul, and the shock of the accusation loosed his tongue. "It wasn't *my* decision. Richard doesn't want to see you hurt!"

"Me? I'm not the one in danger."

"You would be if she sensed your bon—"

"If she sensed what? Are you worried that she'd know I'm a witch? I never had any intention of hiding what I am from her. Richard loves you. Richard has always loved you and the pack. If she was capable of subverting that once, she can do it again. We have to catch up with him. She's failed to get rid of him once. She'll try again."

Raul slumped against the handrail. Letting Richard go had made sense that morning, when his twin's feelings for Will had been thrumming along their bond, but Will's argument made sense in a much more objective way. "Fuck!" How many times could he screw up the same situation? "Richard took the car. I'll have to get a rental sent out to us."

"Raul!" Will took a deep breath. There was no sense in wasting energy on something that couldn't be changed. The important thing was to catch up with Richard as soon as possible. *And never let him out of your sight again,* the little voice inside him tacked on. "You call the rental car company. I'm going to see if I can reach Richard."

"He doesn't have a cell phone." Something else Raul should have thought of—he could have sent his phone with Richard. They would have still had Will's, giving them a way to stay in contact.

Will jumped over the railing, his bare feet landing in the soft grass. "I'm not planning on using a phone."

"Oh...." Raul could feel Alex's emotions through their mating bond, but it wasn't a way to communicate anything specific. "Can you do that?" he asked, but Will was already halfway to the lake.

Striding purposefully, Will focused on the blue water of the lake and the slightly lighter shade of the sky. With each step, he attempted to release the emotions that were clogging his mind. If he was going to reach Richard, he needed to recapture the clear, focused connection with the earth he'd had that morning.

Slowing his steps, he concentrated on the feel of the earth beneath his feet. At the lake's edge, he stopped with his toes just touching the cool water. He closed his eyes and pulled up his memories of Richard: the feel of his skin, the taste of his mouth, the deep vibration of his voice, and the unique scent that belonged exclusively to him.

Will felt his cock begin to harden. Instead of blocking the flow of sexual energy, he encouraged it, amplifying the sparks of electricity radiating out through his body. He made himself recall in minute detail the rasp of Richard's day-old whiskers scraping across the sensitive skin in the hollow of his hipbone. Shifting in hope of allowing his erection more room, he swore he'd turn the lake water to steam if this kept up.

Richard firmly in his mind and senses, Will opened the channel he'd followed earlier that morning. This time he encountered neither the warm rush of feeling nor the complete absence that he'd experienced after Richard had closed the link. As he drew closer to Richard's energy, he felt lethargic and tired, like he was slogging through setting cement. He could see Richard's energy aura, but it was muted and dull, not the sparkling hues it had displayed as they'd made love.

He tried calling out, but there was no response. He could sense Richard, but even though the link was open, the werewolf seemed completely oblivious to him. A cold chill of foreboding ran down his spine. They needed a car. Now. It was going to be impossible to wait the hour or more he estimated it would take to get a car to them.

Turning back to the house, Will reached out to his twin. Having already done the prep work, it was easy to refocus his energy on his brother's familiar signature. Successfully establishing a link, he grinned at Tristan's sleepy grumbling. Sitting on the edge of the king-sized bed, he poked his brother, allowing himself a moment of normalcy to calm his nerves. "Jeesh... and I thought I slept half the day away. Benjamin keep you up late last night?"

Tristan rolled over, stretching lazily with a grin on his face. "Yes, he did, and it was worth every lost minute of sleep."

Will let himself rest in the comfortable flow of banter. Raul wouldn't have a car yet. "You seem to have made up for it. Do you have any idea what time it is?"

"Don't know and don't care. Ben went over to help Alex with something and won't be back until dinnertime." Sitting up against the headboard, Tristan looked at his twin. "So spill it. I haven't felt you this agitated since Gran died."

Will paused, his physical body sitting down under the thick umbrella of an old maple tree. "Well, I told you when I called that we had found Richard. The thing I might not have mentioned was there seemed to be an instant and explosive chemistry between us."

"Oooo...." Tristan squirmed against the pillows, burrowing into the down to create a comfortable niche. "Now this sounds like a much more interesting conversation. Go on."

Will rolled his eyes. His twin could be such a queen when it came to love. "Raul and I did a revealing charm and the spell binding Richard's memory was one of the most intricate I've ever seen. If Sienna cast it, she is stronger than either of us guessed. I didn't plan it, but I used sex magic to break it."

"Stop." Tristan held up a hand. "I think we skipped a couple of key plot points in this story. How did you get Richard to agree to have sex with you? Sex magic takes a pretty intimate bond to be effective."

"Well, I didn't exactly get him to agree to the sex magic. We were just making love and—"

"*Just* making love? We obviously need to go back over this again."

Will sighed. There was no hiding anything from a nosy twin. "Fine. The first time I saw him... the first time I touched him, sparks flew unlike anything I've ever felt. He kissed me on the sidewalk outside of the jail, and it felt like I had waited forever for that moment. Have you ever had that instantaneous a response to someone?"

"Yeah, Benjamin. He wrapped his coat around me and I swear my insides melted."

"I think it might be something to do with the nature of werewolves. The magic in us responding to the magic in them."

"I didn't have that reaction to any other werewolf—only Benjamin."

"Yeah, but by the time you met any other werewolves, you were already mated."

"*You* met wolves from Alex's pack and didn't have that reaction. At least not until you met Richard," Tristan reminded. "Don't downplay this. It could be something very special."

"Provided he isn't dead when we get to him," Will muttered, anger over Richard and Raul's rash decision resurfacing.

"Dead? How'd we get from sparks and sex magic to dead?"

"Well, that first kiss just seemed to snowball. Every touch just made me want more and Richard was just as bad. I swear we've spent more time in bed than out of it since I brought him back from the jail, but we hadn't actually made love until this morning. The energy we raised was overwhelming and it occurred to me that if I could channel it—"

"You could break the binding spell," Tristan finished. "I guess it worked."

"Yeah, I was a little worn out, between the revealing charm the night before and breaking the spell—"

"Multiple orgasms and probably little sleep," Tristan added helpfully.

Will glared at his twin. "And that… anyway, I slept in." He held up a hand to stall the comment coming from his brother. "Yes, *I* slept in. Not as long as you did, I might add, but significantly later than I usually sleep. When I got downstairs, Raul and Richard had dreamed up some harebrained scheme and Richard had headed back to the pack to face Sienna without us."

"What!"

"That was what I said. The only reason I'm down here is because everyone was so worried about how dangerous Sienna was and, based on her spellwork, I'd say it was completely deserved. Now Richard is headed back into her clutches and I'm sitting on my arse waiting for a rental car to show up so Raul and I can follow him."

Tristan shot his brother a narrow-eyed look. "Clutches? That's a bit dramatic, don't you think?"

"Maybe a little bit, but I tried to contact him just before I contacted you."

"You can use mind-contact with him?" Tristan interjected, his voice conveying his surprise.

"That isn't the point. I got the weirdest response. I could see him, sense him, but I couldn't get to him. There didn't seem to be anything in my way, but it was like moving through cold oatmeal and there was a feeling of—I don't know how to describe it—thick negativity. Not evil exactly, but whatever it was gave me the chills."

"Not good. You and Raul need to get to him fast."

"Right on top of things as usual," Will drawled.

Tristan sat forward, his body tense. "No, I mean really fast. I experienced something similar with Benjamin when the curse was trying to kill him. I thought at the time that it was because he was already being pulled through the veil between life and death."

"Shit. I'll get back to the house. Hopefully, the car will be here any minute."

Breaking the connection with his twin, Will sprinted toward the farmhouse.

Chapter 10

RICHARD walked into the main house of the rambling old estate where he and Raul had grown up. The three-story building had been run as an inn at one point, the upper level separated off for the owner's living quarters, with the middle level housing stand-alone suites. The first floor held offices, a large common area with couches, and a commercial kitchen. A sweeping staircase connected them all, creating a soaring atrium as you walked in the front door. Sprawled into the side of a hill, all the north-facing rooms opened on to large balconies. It made the perfect setup for the pack.

A county highway ran about a mile to the south of the house with the other three sides bordered by woods and farmland. A barn, several guesthouses, a greenhouse, and various other structures surrounded the central building, connected by a spider web of paths and gardens. Richard's mother had been a master gardener, any plant thriving under her care. He missed the bouquets of flowers that had adorned every room in the house when she'd been alive. Each morning, she had walked the gardens and greenhouse, selecting new blossoms so that the arrangements had seemed perpetually fresh.

Richard and Sienna lived in one of the guesthouses, but he needed to see his father before facing his wife. Just thinking the word put a bad taste in his mouth. How had he let himself be so deceived? Sienna was a beautiful woman, but he couldn't help but compare her to Will's carved features, sparkling eyes, and passionate spirit and find her lacking. The ache in his chest throbbed. His wolf pulled, wanting to return to their mate. The entire drive home had been one long battle of wills, and he was getting tired of resisting when he longed for Will just as much as his wolf did.

Stopping in the large foyer, Richard's eyes darted between the hallway that led to the offices and up the curving staircase that rose to the private quarters on the second and third floors. Normally, at this time in the afternoon, his father would have been in the offices dealing with pack business, but lately his health had been keeping him in bed later into the day. Some days he never even ventured out of his quarters, the elders coming to him with important issues. Before his unplanned trip, Richard had been picking up the slack in the offices and, according to Raul, Sienna had been doing it in his absence. Another twinge of unease crept up his spine. Something else was wrong. The building smelled off... sickness and anger. He couldn't remember it smelling that way before, even after his father got sick. Was it possible that he'd been so drugged it had muted his wolf's senses to that extent? He shook off his sense of foreboding and started up the stairs.

Father first, then Sienna.

Taking the stairs two at a time, Richard climbed to the third floor without passing anyone, which added to his sense of unease. Someone should have been stationed at the door, and he shouldn't have been able to approach the royal quarters with no one to stop him. Punching his code into the keypad by the door, he entered the dark sitting room. All of the shades were drawn against the bright afternoon sun and the air smelled stale—the scent of sickness and death almost overwhelming. Walking immediately to the French doors leading to the balcony, he pulled them open wide, letting in the sun and breeze. He could smell the fresh-turned earth of the fields being prepared for planting.

Still no sound. No sign of life from any of the rooms. Where was his father? Meg, their housekeeper? Someone should be around.

Crossing the room, Richard tapped on the door to his father's bedroom. "Apa?" he called softly. If his father was asleep, he'd wake him. Sleeping this late in the day couldn't be healthy, even for someone needing rest. He turned the knob with trepidation, peering around the door. A mound of blankets covered a sleeping body on the bed. Richard released his breath. A part of him had been hoping to find the room empty, his father out engaged in the normal activities of leadership. His wolf whined in his head, pacing, his agitation and fear almost overshadowing the ache of missing his mate.

The bedroom was in the same condition as the sitting room, every curtain drawn against the light, the air hot and stale to the point of being stifling. Still his father was covered with what appeared to be multiple blankets. Everything was wrong. Lycans had a higher than normal body temperature, especially as they slept. Rarely did Richard use covers and not even on the coldest nights did he require heavy blankets.

Sitting gently on the side of the bed so he didn't startle his father, Richard laid a hand on his shoulder and whispered again, "Apa?" Somewhere in the early stumbling of speech, the twins had used the shortened term to refer to their father. No one could remember if had been him or Raul. Few had the ability to tell them apart at that age, but it didn't really matter. The term had stuck.

Lethargically, the large man stirred under the covers, turning to face his son. "Richard?"

"Yes, Apa, it's me. Are you not feeling well?"

A weak smile turned up the corners of the werewolf king's mouth. "Much better now that you are home. I was afraid I had lost both my sons."

Richard leaned down and hugged his father, the heat radiating off the older man scaring him. "Never, Apa. I'll always be here for you, and I've been with Raul. He'll be here in just a few days. We'll be together again."

"Ah, that *is* good news—" The words broke off as Randolf Carlisle broke into a violent coughing fit. Richard helped him struggle to sit, the ragged hacking finally subsiding.

Richard began to push the covers back. "You need to get up out of this bed, Apa. It can't be good for you to be lying down with a cough like that. Let me help you to a chair in the sitting room and get you something to eat and drink. Where is Meg?"

"Meg?"

Richard didn't like the confusion that clouded his father's eyes.

"Meg... I'm not sure... I haven't...."

"Don't worry about it, Apa. I'll go down to the kitchen myself and bring you some soup and tea." If his father didn't know Meg's whereabouts, it was no use asking him about the other noticeable absences around the house. Richard would take care of his father and then go searching for some answers.

He was halfway down the stairs when another concern made Richard hesitate. His father hadn't asked about Will. As the leader of their pack, the scent of a newly mated wolf, especially his own son, should have immediately drawn his attention. More was wrong with Randolf Carlisle than just a cough.

BURSTING through the back door, Will came to a sliding halt in front of Raul, who was sitting at the kitchen table working on his second pot of coffee.

"When can we leave?" Will asked, breathless.

Raul didn't meet his eyes, keeping them focused on the magazine in his hand. "They can't get here until tomorrow between ten and twelve, but the dispatcher promised to make it as close to ten as he could."

"Tomorrow! You've got to be fuckin' kidding me!" Will exploded.

Raul closed the magazine he wasn't really reading anyway and faced the angry witch. "'Fraid not. The closest rental places are more than two hours away at the regional airport. I had to bribe someone to get a car delivered at all, and they don't have staff available this afternoon to bring one."

"That isn't… we can't… tomorrow is too late."

"Why? I know we need to get there, but I don't think she's going to kill him the second he shows up. The pack will be so glad to see him, he won't be alone much. Werewolves are nosy creatures; he'll be mercilessly pumped for information by everyone from my father down."

Will collapsed into the chair next to Raul, his fingers sinking into his curls as he rested his head in his hands. "Something isn't right, Raul. I can see Richard, feel him, but I can't get to him. He is surrounded by a thick, negative energy. We've got to get there as quickly as possible."

"You got any better ideas?" Raul asked, alarmed by Will's description.

"Cab?"

"Not in a town of this size. Anything else?"

Shaking his head, Will stood, helping himself to a cup of coffee. "Not really, but I don't like waiting. If I thought I could get anywhere, I'd walk. Don't you know someone in this area? We could borrow their car or they could drive us to the airport to pick one up."

"Nope. Not anymore. Everyone has grown up and moved on. It is the way with small towns."

"How about someone from the pack? If Richard can drive home, someone could come get us?"

"I tried that, but I think we just need to calm down and trust Richard," Raul assured, silently praying that he was right.

"You tried that? What aren't you telling me?"

"I couldn't get an answer on any of the lines I called. I didn't even get answering machines or voicemail."

Will muttered a prayer of protection to the goddess. "There has to be a way."

"I'm out of ideas. He wasn't going back unarmed this time. He knows how treacherous Sienna can be. He'll be fine."

"I hope so. I really do hope so." Will got to his feet. "I'm going to go upstairs and pack. Then I'll probably try and contact Richard again. I'll be on the sleeping porch if you need me." Maybe if he kept the connection open all night, he could keep Richard safe, or at least monitor if the danger to the werewolf prince became grave enough to call the police. Richard and Raul wouldn't thank him for involving others in pack business, but if it came down to Richard's life, he would.

LOST in his own thoughts, Richard ran into a tall, lanky man as he turned into the kitchen, almost knocking him to the ground. Catching his elbow, he helped the werewolf to his feet with a smile. "Arthur! I was beginning to wonder if everyone had left on vacation."

Surprise passed through the crystal blue eyes of the dark-haired werewolf. "Richard! I didn't know you were home. How was the conference? Has Sienna seen you yet?"

Richard's smile evaporated, the rush of happiness at seeing his old friend drying up with it. Conference? If Sienna had used a cover story, his disappearance had obviously been planned. "No, I went up to see Dad. What in the world is going on around here? Where is everybody?"

"Out. Busy doing something. Sienna's had a list a mile long."

Richard fired a stream of questions at his old friend. "What's going on with Dad? I couldn't find Meg. Has Hugo been treating him?"

Arthur shrugged. "I don't know. Sienna's been spending most of her time in the apartment, taking care of him. I saw Hugo and the other healers going up and down a lot early last week, but I haven't seen him lately. I guess he's busy somewhere else and has been telling Sienna what to do."

"Nicolai? The elders? Surely someone should be sitting with him when he is this sick!"

"Is he really that bad? Sienna said he was getting better." A worried look passed over Arthur's features, and Richard's wolf growled softly, raising the hairs on the back of his neck with the low vibration. Arthur should have been able to scent the seriousness of the illness on Richard, him having just come from the king's chambers.

A pall of fear darkened Richard's eyes. Arthur obviously had no clue what was going on. Richard would have to track down Nicolai himself, and Artemis only knew what Sienna had been feeding his father under the guise of making him well. He was convinced she'd been controlling him through potions hidden in his food and drink, and it would be even easier to slip something to his father as medicine. She wouldn't have to mask the taste or smell. "Who's in the kitchen? I need to get some broth and juice for Dad."

"Wendy," Arthur said, his cheeks flushing as he grinned. "I'll tag along."

"Sure you will." Richard smiled. He'd suspected that Arthur had a crush on Wendy for some time, but it was hard to tell since the skinny werewolf was a bottomless pit and had a habit of hanging out in the kitchen anyway.

Wendy quickly prepared a mug of rich beef broth and a chilled glass of fresh grape juice, adding one of the king's favorite sweet rolls in an attempt to bribe him into eating everything else. While the young cook was preparing the tray, Arthur browbeat Richard into eating a few mouthfuls of a ham sandwich.

Standing at the bottom of the stairs with the tray, Richard turned to Arthur. He needed an excuse not to have dinner with Sienna on his first night back, a situation that would be unavoidable unless he had already eaten. "I didn't have a chance to hunt safely while I was away. You want to go out with me at dusk?" He could linger afterwards and pump Arthur for more information of what had been going on while Richard had been gone.

"That sounds great. I'd better finish up my list if I hope to be free by dusk," Arthur agreed. With a smile and wave, he headed out the front door, already lifting his cell phone to his ear.

Richard headed up the stairs. He'd sent Wendy to find Meg and he would try and reach Hugo from the apartment phone. He needed to know what was going on with his father.

RAUL paced the worn kitchen floor of his grandmother's farmhouse. How had things disintegrated so quickly? A week ago, he'd been happy and blissfully ignorant of the intrigue and machinations of his birth pack. Lifting the coffeepot, he poured the remaining dark liquid down the sink. If they did find a way to leave earlier, he'd have to stop every half hour to go to the bathroom. He cleaned the rest of the kitchen until the counters shone, moving randomly through the rest of the house, straightening until he found himself readjusting things back into the position he'd moved them from only minutes before.

Picking up the magazine he'd been using to distract himself earlier, he considered taking it out on the porch to read, but the worry flowing through his veins made him edgy. He'd never be able to settle and be still. Aimlessly wandering outside, he picked a path headed around the nearby field. He had his cell phone. If Will needed him, he could call.

The farmer was harrowing the dark earth, turning up moist smells of the cycle of growth and decay. His wolf wanted out to run, to roll in the freshly turned dirt, to chase the birds attracted to the seed being unearthed, but he pulled him back. Hunting tonight before their trip tomorrow wouldn't be a bad idea, but letting his wolf out to frolic in broad daylight definitely wasn't a smart thing to do. The last thing he needed was a bullet wound courtesy of an overzealous farmer protecting his livestock.

Reaching into his pocket, Raul pulled out his cell phone. He'd distract himself by calling Alex. If Alex was busy, maybe he'd be able to reach Benjamin. Hell, he'd even talk to Tristan if it got his mind off Richard.

Alex answered the phone on the first ring. "What's wrong?"

Raul sighed. Apparently he was projecting. "I'm okay," he reassured his mate, knowing that would be Alex's first concern.

"I'd say that's a debatable statement, but I'm glad you aren't lying in a ditch somewhere, broken and bruised. So what *is* wrong? Is Will all right? Tristan will kill both of us if he gets hurt."

Trust his lover to cut right to the heart of the matter. An admirable trait in a leader. Slightly less so in a lover. Sometimes Raul wanted a chance to approach things in his own slightly circuitous way. "I didn't get to Will in time."

"They mated."

"This morning. It broke the spell blocking Richard's memory."

"A first mating is a powerful thing," Alex agreed. "Does Will know? Did Richard tell him?"

Raul couldn't help but snort. "I hardly think Will wouldn't notice Richard making love to him, but no, the idiot didn't tell him anything about the mating. In his defense, it was the actual act that broke the spell and up until that point, Richard didn't know he was a werewolf, but he didn't say anything afterwards either and then he left."

"Left?"

Alex—King of the leading questions. Raul rolled his eyes, stopping to lean against a fencepost and watch the orderly rows of turned earth appear from behind the tractor. "Richard's gone back to face Sienna."

"Without you?"

"It seemed like a good idea at the time," Raul said. "Richard wanted to keep Will safe."

"I can see that. Nothing would be as important to him, so newly bonded—not even his own safety."

"I could see it, too, until Will woke up and pointed out all the reasons Richard needed our help. Now we are stuck here, waiting on a rental car. Richard took ours."

"I'd help if I could, but I'm sure the car will get there before I could," Alex offered.

Giving in to a moment of weakness, Raul muttered, "Yeah, but you could hold me."

"Aw, baby, I'd love to be able to do that. You go help Richard. I'll see what I can do."

Raul straightened up. He hadn't meant to dump all this on Alex. His lover felt far too much responsibility as it was. "You don't have to do anything. I can handle it. I'm just feeling sorry for myself. Too many pheromones flying around Richard and Will. It makes me miss you."

"I miss you too. And I love you. Letting you go without me was a mistake that we are never repeating again. You belong by my side."

Raul felt the deep rumble of Alex's voice wrap around him like a blanket. "I love you too." Silently he added, *now I just have to straighten out this mess so I can come home to you.*

Chapter 11

THE shadows of twilight extended across the lawn from the woods as Richard and Arthur walked out the front door. Richard had entrusted his father to Meg's capable hands, leaving the housekeeper with strict instructions to stay by the king's side and not to let anything past his lips unless it came from Richard's hand or had been prepared by Meg herself. The housekeeper's scent was the first normal thing he had run across since returning, and Richard knew he could entrust her with his father's care.

Meg was a formidable opponent now that she had the prince's order to back her up. She had never liked Sienna, and Richard had almost laughed aloud at the glint that lit her eye in anticipation of the coming conflict with the beautiful witch. The king seemed much more alert after his meal and had even joked with his son. The laughter had prompted another coughing fit, but Richard left his father's side with far fewer worries than he'd had earlier in the afternoon.

"Are you sure you don't want to wait for Sienna to return?" Arthur asked as they walked away from the house. "She said that she'd be home just after dark."

Richard shook his head. "I need to reconnect to the land and she has a habit of being late. We'll probably beat her back." He wasn't feeling the intense distaste of facing Sienna that he had been, but he still wasn't looking forward to it.

Approaching the tree line, Richard grinned at his friend. "First kill?" he challenged, already beginning to strip away his clothes, laying them over a fallen tree.

Arthur grinned, his wolf rising, vibrating with the anticipation of the hunt and the competition. "You're on," he accepted, stripping his T-shirt over his head.

Richard's head swiveled, his ears catching a rustling in the underbrush. In two steps, he had shimmered into a large auburn wolf, his yellow-green eyes glowing in the low light as he loped toward the smell of prey. A rabbit darted from a bush to his left. He could hear the pounding of its heart and the staccato beat of its feet as they hit the ground. Tightening his powerful haunches, he surged forward, watching Arthur's pale gray wolf keeping pace with his strides out of his peripheral vision. Pushing his nose to the ground, he nudged at the terrified rabbit, pulling to the right and tumbling into Arthur, letting the rabbit disappear into the safety of her hole. This was far too much fun to let it end so soon.

Throwing back his head, Richard howled out the pure joy of the hunt. Arthur's slightly less jubilant tones joined his as the two raced off in a different direction. The woods reeked of deer, quail, rabbit and the familiar traces of pack wolves. Richard yipped excitedly. It was good to be home. He couldn't wait to teach Will the joys of hunting.

Arthur sped up, catching the fresh scent of a yearling deer. Head down, he dove into the underbrush. Richard debated following, but it would put him a pace or two behind. Taking the clearer path, he circled in front of the running deer. It was a buck, which meant its path would be straight. Does zigzagged to lose a predator, not wanting to leave familiar territory. Bucks picked a direction and ran, sometimes covering miles in a single chase.

Richard's blood pounded in his ears as he put on a burst of speed, scenting the air and listening for the progress of the prey. His pack kept a field full of domesticated animals, but nothing matched the rush of the wild hunt. Arthur howled, only a stone's throw behind him to the left. Leaping a fallen log, Richard launched himself at the young buck as it appeared in front of him, knocking it to the ground while his powerful jaws closed on its neck. Only a single stride behind him, Arthur helped him with the kill, but first blood had been Richard's, and the deer tasted sweeter for the victory.

After eating their fill, Richard and Arthur dozed sated as the moon rose to shine brightly between the high branches. Nudging the gray wolf to break his post-hunt stupor, Richard trotted toward the lake, wanting a swim before he returned to his clothes. Bounding into chilly spring waters, the two wolves barked and tumbled like pups. The feel of this place, the scents of the pack, they meant more to Richard than his life. An unfamiliar ache spread through his chest.

He needed Will.

He needed to share this with his mate.

Subdued, Richard walked out of the water, shaking the excess from his fur before walking to the log where they'd left their clothes. Shimmering back to human form, he dressed quickly to prevent the night from chilling his skin.

"You want to stop at my place for a beer?" Arthur offered, slipping his feet into his sneakers.

With the alternative being returning home to Sienna, Richard agreed. "Sounds good." He'd share a beer or two with Arthur and go back to check on his dad. After that, he really couldn't put off facing his wife. Walking back up to the house beside his friend, he looked up at the moon and sighed. What was Will doing right now?

WILL watched the gibbous moon rise over the lake, his legs pulled up to his chest. Richard was out there somewhere without him and he wasn't happy about it. He hadn't gone down to the kitchen for dinner. He knew he was being childish. It wasn't Raul's fault, but he just felt so helpless that he really didn't have an appetite.

A giant yawn snuck up on him and he stretched to relieve the kinks in his muscles. He'd been maintaining an open connection for hours, hoping to reconnect with Richard, and it took an extraordinary amount of energy. He glanced at his watch. Ten-thirty. Another few minutes and he'd allow himself to go to bed, knowing that he'd be up at dawn. Not that it would make the car arrive any faster.

Closing his eyes, Will fixed his mind on the feeling of lying in Richard's arms this morning and broadcast it down the channel toward his lover. "Be safe, Richard," he whispered. "I love you."

Downstairs on the porch, Raul's acute hearing picked up the almost silent blessing, his conscience pricking. He shouldn't have dragged Will into this mess.

RICHARD woke to bright sunshine. It was obviously late in the morning and the intense rays made his head hurt. Lifting a hand to shield his eyes, he looked around the room. He was lying on the couch in the house he shared with Sienna. He had a pillow from the bed, but no blanket and was still wearing his clothes from last night. How had he gotten here and why was he on the couch?

Rubbing his forehead and keeping his eyes tightly shut, he tried to sit up, the room tilting horribly and making his stomach revolt. He felt awful. His head pounded and his eyes watered every time he tried to open them fully. If he'd been human, he'd call it a hangover, but even humans were capable of drinking two beers without suffering this way. Had Arthur brought him home?

He cracked open one eye. He was definitely in his house. Where was Sienna? He called out her name. No answer. She was due home last night; surely she would have woken him. Struggling to his feet, he searched the rest of the house, finding it empty. A growing unease was filling his chest, compelling him to dress quickly and head for the main house at a jog.

He was anxious to see Sienna, to make sure she was safe, and the intensity of the emotion felt wrong and right all at the same time. They'd always been close, but he didn't remember ever missing her this way or worrying about her safety. Sienna could take care of herself. Maybe it was his father. He had been in terrible shape yesterday, but had improved by evening. That didn't explain the panic that was running through his veins.

Will's face popped into his head and he flushed. What had he been thinking, telling Raul that Will was his mate? Now that he was away from Will and back home, it was obvious that his feelings had been mainly lust. He'd had no memory of Sienna and Will had been alluring and available. It was a good thing he had only had that conversation with his twin and not Will.

Richard's mind swirled with emotions and memories and he was having a hard time sorting through them. He was obviously still suffering the effects of the accident that had damaged his memory. It was the only thing that explained the disjointed recollections and irrational behavior. He'd come home to get rid of Sienna. Raul's explanations had sounded so rational, but Richard knew that Raul had never liked Sienna. No, he needed to make a decision on his own, now that he was away from the influence of Will and Raul. They didn't know her. Not like he did.

Richard's wolf rose inside him, forcing the prince to slow to a walk so he could concentrate on controlling his rebelling beast. He couldn't remember the last time his wolf had fought him so hard. Seeing Sienna would fix it. He just needed to get to Sienna. She had always been able to calm his wolf. When he was with her, he rarely even felt his wolf's presence. The urgency to reach the house and find his wife increased.

A sharp pain almost sent Richard to his knees. Clutching his head, he stumbled up to the back of the house, climbed the low steps and collapsed on a cement bench.

"Richard!" Sienna's worried voice carried across the flagstone terrace.

Richard's wolf snarled, but the witch's slender arms were around him and he was feeling better already. She was whispering calming nonsense against his neck and he could feel his wolf retreating, just as he knew he would. For the first time since he'd gotten up that morning, he felt calm and at peace.

"Can't you drive any faster?"

Raul rolled his eyes, shooting Will a dirty look. "Sure, and we'll end up in jail, have to call someone to come bail us out, and be restricted from leaving the county. That'll get us there a lot faster."

Will shifted impatiently in his seat. "Something is wrong, Raul. I can feel it. It was bad last night, but it is ten times worse now. He's farther away than he was when he had no memory."

Raul frowned, but pushed slightly harder on the gas pedal. "Nothing to be done about it now. We broke her spell once; we can do it again."

"Not if she kills him. I can't fix death, Raul."

"She won't kill him. She needs him."

"Exactly how badly did she need him when she set up the little accident and locked his memory?" Will asked.

Raul took a deep breath. He was as worried as Will, but one of them needed to stay levelheaded. "Which is why she can't do that again. Once looks like an accident. A second disappearance would be highly suspicious. She's never been turned. By our laws, she can't rule on her own. She needs him."

Will deflated, pulling his feet up onto the seat and hugging his knees. "If she thinks she has nothing to lose, she'll react like a cornered animal. I'm not sure we can count on her being rational."

Reaching across the seat, Raul stroked Will's arm. "I know, and we'll be there in less than an hour. Then he won't be alone."

Will closed his eyes and worked on calming his body and focusing his mind. He was no good to Richard like this. He wasn't sure he had the skills to beat Sienna in a head-to-head fight. Everything he'd seen of her magic told him that she was a formidable opponent and not one concerned with morals. "Can't you just go a little faster?" he muttered.

RICHARD frowned, standing up suddenly. Sienna's hand fell from his thigh to the couch where they'd been sitting and talking with his father.

"It sounds like someone has released a gaggle of geese into the foyer," the king commented.

Meg chuckled from her corner, scowling at Sienna before returning her attention to the knitting in her lap.

"I'll go see what it is," Richard said on the way to the door. Sienna stood up to go with him. "It's okay. You stay with Dad," he told her.

"Nonsense. You've been away for weeks and he's doing just fine. You may as well get used to me by your side because I'm not leaving it," Sienna warned with a smile, looping her arm through Richard's to anchor her position.

Meg clucked, raising her hand to shield a fake cough to hide her obvious disapproval. The second the two stepped out of the room, she got to her feet. "I can't believe this," she fretted, removing the mug from the table beside the king and pouring it down the sink. "The second that witch—and I mean that in *all* its connotations—gets near him, his brain disengages. He was perfectly clear about keeping her away from you yesterday, and this morning they dance in here all chummy. He even pulled me aside to say that he overreacted about your food. Well, I don't care what he says. You and I know better, and she'll not be feeding you anytime soon."

Randolf accepted the fresh mug from his housekeeper. "Don't you fret, Meg. We saw him yesterday and he was my son in a way I haven't seen him in years. It gives me hope. Richard is still in there. She can only control the outer behavior. He said Raul was coming home, and I could smell the mate on Richard's skin even though he didn't mention it. He was cognizant enough to place you at my side and rallied the Guardians back to their normal duty. Sienna may think she's won this round, but she's never faced a mated werewolf denied his chosen."

RICHARD reached the top of the stairs, looking down at a madhouse of pack members. In the middle of it all was Raul. Richard's wolf stirred, his eyes immediately searching for Will, knowing the young man was there somewhere. He could smell him. Just as his eyes spotted the familiar long, dark curls, Sienna squeezed his arm.

"Raul's home. Isn't that wonderful? Look at how many people have come out to welcome him back. Did you create such a stir when you got home yesterday?" she asked. "I'm so sorry that I wasn't here."

"No... no, I couldn't find a soul," Richard muttered, his eyes drifting back to his twin. Raul was surrounded by chattering pack members, everyone pushing forward for a chance to touch him... to welcome him home. A familiar tight knot of jealousy twisted in his gut. Sienna was whispering something to him again, but he couldn't hear what she was saying over the excited voices rising from below.

Richard's gaze was so focused on Raul that he jumped when Will stepped into his line of sight, capturing his twin's attention and pointing to where he stood with Sienna. He had an irrational urge to run, but a gentle squeeze from Sienna's hand quelled it. Taking a deep breath, he headed down the stairs, a smile on his face.

"Welcome home, brother," he called in greeting from halfway down the stairs. "As you can see, you've been missed." Sienna was

"That is what he said, but Ohio used to recognize common law marriage. I don't know where they fall in relation to that. Better safe than sorry."

"I guess so," Will conceded, dropping wearily into a well-cushioned arm chair. Their arrival had been anticlimactic. He'd been braced for a fight and looking forward to an impassioned reunion with Richard, and he had gotten a formal greeting and an invitation to be presented to the king. He sighed. The unreleased energy was making him jittery.

Sitting down next to the witch, Raul pulled the slender man against his chest and hugged him. "It'll be okay. He's safe, at least."

"I'm withholding judgment until we get a chance to talk with him without her around."

"Well then, let's get this over with," Raul said, getting to his feet. Pulling off his T-shirt, he slipped his arms in the dressier shirt. "Ready to go meet dear old dad?"

"As ready as I'll ever be." Will got to his feet. He was actually looking forward to meeting Randolf Carlisle. Any man who could produce two sons like Raul and Richard had to be interesting.

They walked down the hall and up a narrow flight of stairs, obviously built for servants to move between floors inconspicuously. Will examined the pictures on the walls, noticing several of the same beautiful woman. "Is that your mother?" he asked, pointed to a portrait of the woman on her knees tending a garden.

"Yes," Raul answered with a melancholy smile. "She loved her flowers."

"How old were you when she died?"

"Eighteen. Dad was almost nonfunctional with grief for more than a year. I presided over the council."

Will reached out and squeezed Raul's hand. "You were awfully young to take that on, and must have been missing her just as much."

Another half smile twisted at Raul's lips. "In a different way. He was her mate and I had Richard. We did everything together that year. I don't think we've ever been closer, before or since. We—" He stopped as a Guardian stepped out of the shadows.

"Prince Raul," the heavily muscled werewolf said with a courteous bow. "Welcome home."

"Well met, Tim. He's expecting us," Raul said, nodding toward the entrance to the king's chambers.

"Our heir, Prince Richard, said to expect you," the Guardian said, opening the door and stepping to the side for them to pass.

"You guys are a lot more formal than Alex's pack," Will whispered, leaning close to Raul's ear.

"We might be slightly more old-fashioned," the elderly man on the couch laughed, struggling slightly to get to his feet. An older woman hurried forward to help steady him. "Something my sons will no doubt remedy when they take over. You must be Raul's friend. I've been looking forward to meeting you, young man."

Will flushed slightly. When would he get used to werewolf hearing? He met the king halfway across the room, taking his arm to help steady him. He was surprised that Randolf Carlisle headed for him and not Raul.

"I'm honored to be welcomed into your home." Surprisingly strong arms encircled him and Will was pulled into a tight hug. His eyes flickered briefly around the room. Feeling overwhelmed by an unexpected feeling of love and belonging, he purposefully avoided looking at Richard.

"Let my home be yours," the king said, smiling and nodding slightly as he pulled back from the embrace. Turning to his oldest son, he opened his arms in silent invitation.

Raul flew forward. "Apa."

Will looked away, giving the men a moment of privacy. He noticed the woman who had helped the king earlier standing in the corner, watching the reunion with unabashed delight, tears in her eyes. Unable to avoid it any longer, his gaze sought out Richard, the hair on his neck standing up and his nipples tightening into almost painful buds as his body responded to the werewolf's presence. Richard and Sienna were on their feet in front of a love seat, giving the impression that they had risen as Raul and Will entered, but not joined in the greeting.

"Come. Come. Everybody sit," Randolf encouraged, walking back to his chair on Raul's arm. "We have much to talk about."

Raul took the seat next to his father and Will looked around for a safe location. Sitting too close to the king seemed presumptuous and too close to Richard was dangerous. Just being in the same room with him made his heart race, something he knew wouldn't go unnoticed in a room full of werewolves.

"I have both my boys home. We should celebrate," the king continued. Turning to Sienna, he extended his hand. "Come, daughter, I have a task for you. Go marshal the kitchen staff. I want tables of food by evening."

Sienna clasped the king's hand, kneeling to be at eye-level out of respect. "Wouldn't Meg—"

"Nonsense. No one motivates the staff like you do and I still feel the need of Meg here," Randolf chided gently.

Sienna obviously wished to argue further but couldn't come up with a respectful way to disregard the king's request. "It shall be done, Father." With a lingering look between Richard, Raul, and Will, she left the room.

Will was glad to see her go, even though he knew that she'd work like the devil to get back to Richard's side and run interference. For the first time since they'd arrived, he looked at his lover with an unguarded expression. The total lack of response in Richard's eyes chilled him. He needed to get Richard alone.

Looking around the room, Will found Raul, Meg, and Randolf in conversation. Taking a deep breath, he shifted to the loveseat beside

Richard, letting his hand settle on the werewolf's thigh. "Are you okay?"

Richard's fingers circled Will's wrist, gently but firmly moving it away from his body. "I'm just fine. I'm afraid I might have given you the wrong impression at Nanna's. I really appreciate you helping Raul find me, but what we had can't continue here. I have a position, responsibilities, duties that now include siring heirs. You are welcome here always. As Raul's friend," he ended firmly.

Each word felt like a physical blow, leaving Will silent, stunned, and furious. He just wasn't sure if he should direct his anger at Richard or Sienna. In a handful of words, Richard had discounted everything that had passed between them.

Standing, Richard walked to his father's side, whispering something in his ear, something Will couldn't hear with his human ears. Squeezing Raul's shoulder, Richard disappeared through the door without looking back. Will stared at the carved mahogany portal long after it had shut, completely oblivious to the three sets of sympathetic eyes that watched him.

RAUL moved around his bedroom, unexpectedly pleased that they had left his rooms untouched in his absence. Of course, Richard had implied that they were expecting him to return. Raul missed Alex and their house, but there was a feeling here that would always be home.

The sound of the shower stopped and he looked up to see Will walk out, water still dripping from his hair onto his bare chest, a thick towel wrapped around his waist. He walked directly to his suitcase, not making eye contact or saying anything. In fact, he'd been mostly silent since Richard had left the royal chambers more than an hour ago. Raul could feel the emotions boiling inside of him.

Sitting on the edge of his bed, Raul studied the muscle ticking in Will's jaw and the rigid set of his shoulders. "You know that she has gotten control of him again, right?"

"You didn't talk to him. I did. He was very clear about the status of our relationship."

"As he would be if she had him under another spell," Raul reminded gently. "You yourself said that you could sense a blockage."

"Maybe what I was sensing was *him* blocking me. That first time I reached out to him, it felt like he responded and then closed a door," Will said, shaking the wrinkles of out his one good shirt. It was a dark chocolate silk that he had stolen from his brother and the only thing he had appropriate for a party. He hadn't predicted a need for dressing up when he left New York.

"The Richard who left Nanna's house two days ago was more worried about your life than his own. He wouldn't have acted the way he did today unless he was under the influence of magic. Trust me on this. I've known him far longer than you have. We just have to find out what she is using to control him. Dad and Meg suspect that it is something in the food. They both said that Richard was different his first day back, before Sienna knew that he'd returned."

"And if she isn't drugging him? If this *is* what he wants? What then, Raul? You have abdicated your right to the throne. Maybe that was all he was waiting for. Maybe it was all just an act to get you to give up your birthright willingly, so they could move on," Will suggested, his eyes snapping with a golden fire. "*Together.*"

"Then it is what it is. I have never intended to rule here or even return, truth be told, but don't back out on me now. I know Richard like I know myself and this *isn't* him. If you care for him as much as I think you do, help me fight for him. Even if you don't want him for yourself, do it for me." Raul desperately wanted to add that Will was Richard's mate—that a werewolf couldn't willingly turn against his mate—but now was definitely *not* the time for that revelation, and Raul was the wrong wolf to be making it.

"I'm not going anywhere." Will shrugged, trying for a smile. "You are the one with the car and, regardless of Richard's decision, I want to see Sienna exposed and punished."

It was a small concession, but it would do for now. "Good. We have a party to attend and I seem to be without an escort. Shall we?" Raul crooked his arm, inviting Will to take it.

This time Will's smile was slightly brighter. "Goddess help me if Alex catches wind of this," he chuckled, threading his arm through Raul's.

It looked like all the pack had turned out for the impromptu welcome home party and, judging from appearances, the Cayuga pack was easily double the size of the Onondaga pack. Will told himself that he was watching Sienna, not Richard, as the two made their way from group to group around the party, but since the two were always side by side, it was hard to distinguish any real difference. Every time the slender white hand stroked Richard's arm or back, Will felt his hackles rise, making him wonder who was really the wolf in this relationship. A sharp twinge in his chest made his eyes fall—not that there *was* a relationship, according to Richard.

Reassuring himself with Raul's words in the room earlier, Will headed to the beverage table. Most of the offerings were nonalcoholic, since most of the guests were lycan, but a large metal tub of ice held a variety of beers and a bottle or two of wine. He needed to be clear-headed, but the appearance of drinking heavily might lure Sienna into a false sense of security. Picking an imported beer, he poured it into a mug, swirling the dark liquid and muttering a quick reveal charm to make sure it wasn't anything other than what it appeared. It wasn't, which didn't surprise him. Drugging an entire pack was a bit ambitious, even for Sienna.

Resting his back on a large white column, Will surveyed the festive lawn party that stretched from the patio to the trees. Tables and chairs had been set up in inviting clusters all over the manicured lawns. Kids chased between the groups of grown-ups and everyone appeared to be having a wonderful time. Even Randolf Carlisle had come down, under the watchful eye of Meg. He was sitting in a sheltered alcove with Nicolai and several elders, Raul on one side and Richard on the other. In between jaunts to the kitchen, Sienna curled at Richard's feet, always in constant physical contact.

A tall male approached the cluster, speaking respectfully to the king and princes before directing his comments to Sienna. Will was too far away to hear what was being said, but the witch got to her feet and followed the man into the house. Peering around the column, Will watched as they stepped out of sight of the royal family, stopped, and exchanged what appeared to be heated words. Sienna stalked off in one direction and her companion took the hall toward the kitchen.

Curious, Will followed, whispering a spell. It wasn't a spell of concealment—more a spell of disinterest. People would see him, but their eyes would move over him without pause. Without hesitation, he chose the direction Sienna had taken, mixing speed with stealth to catch up to her without overtaking her unexpectedly and revealing himself. A click at the end of the hall caused him to speed up.

Coming to a side exit, Will pushed the sheer curtains covering the sidelights open and watched as Sienna jogged toward a small shed attached to the greenhouse. There was no way to cross the open lawn without being easily spotted. He wasn't worried about pack members, but if Sienna was watching, she wouldn't likely be affected by the low-level concealment spell and Will didn't have the time to do anything more complex.

Heading back the way he'd come, Will went out the front door, running to the tree line and approaching the greenhouse from the back. Keeping just under the cover of the dark trees, he wished that he'd stopped long enough to tell Raul what he was doing. He smelled the strong scent of burning herbs as he stopped just out of sight of the small building. Inching forward more carefully, he spotted a large herb garden, laid out neatly to the rear of the building. This early in the spring, it was mostly evergreens and neatly trimmed-back plants waiting patiently for summer growth, but most essential herbs could be harvested and dried or grown during the winter in the greenhouse.

Will was just contemplating if it was worth the risk to try and cross the small open area from the trees to the building when Sienna came out and walked quickly back to the house, a small bundle in her hands. Waiting impatiently for her to disappear inside, Will ran to the back of the shed and tried the door. It was locked, but the old wood was warped and a firmly placed shoulder popped it open without damaging the frame.

The scent of herbs was strong to the point of overwhelming. Careful not to touch anything, Will did his best to take an inventory of the small workroom. It was obvious that Sienna used the space to prepare spell ingredients and potions. Her ritual tools were absent—they were probably stored in her home, where she'd feel connected to them—but everything else a practicing witch could need was present. The shelves were a virtual A-to-Z compendium of magical herbs, local and imported. Will's fingers itched to acquire some of the familiar herbs from Europe. He'd been making do with American substitutes, but he still wasn't used to their unique energy.

He contemplated grabbing a small handful of eyebright to cast a revealing spell on the cabinets to see if they were guarded. Sienna had been the only witch on packlands; she might not have felt it was necessary to ward her cabinets and Will was anxious to take a complete inventory of the room. Deciding not to risk it, he moved to the main worktable. Carelessly scattered ingredients in the otherwise meticulous room told him that she'd been working in a hurry. Most of the ingredients he recognized: nightshade, calamus, wormwood and catmint, but a dark, narrow leaf was unknown to him, as was a mud-colored bark. Pulling his wallet out, he used an old receipt to carefully scoop a small amount of both off the table, folding them in the paper and tucking it in his pocket.

Sienna was concocting something—something needed on an ongoing basis—and it appeared that at least one of the pack was in on it with her. Will needed to find out the identity of the tall, thin werewolf, but first he needed to get back to the party without being seen.

Chapter 13

SKIRTING the long way around the main house, Will approached the party from the opposite side. An unexpected warning shout drew his attention to the right. Quickly sidestepping, he avoided tripping over a pair of young wolves tumbling down a steep slope in a friendly tussle. He smiled, stopping to watch them wrestle, break apart, and chase each other back up the hill, barking excitedly and nipping at each other's heels. He'd never really thought about the animal side of being a werewolf, outside of the need to hunt. It made sense with the social nature of wolves that they'd play, court, and even mate in their wolf forms. Since his twin wasn't a werewolf, Will had no experience with a werewolf couple. He made a mental note to ask Raul about it later.

Rounding the grape arbor, Will caught sight of his "mystery werewolf" passing Richard a bottle of beer, using his shirt to twist off the cap before handing it to him. Every instinct Will had screamed that the liquid was drugged. It would be easy to replace the cap and hide the fact that it had been removed by taking it off before delivering it. He wanted to shout out a warning as Richard lifted the bottle to his lips, but it would draw everyone's attention and Will didn't want to let Sienna know they were on to her.

Trying to appear casual, Will quickly made his way to the royal family. Raul greeted him with a smile and a strong pat on the back. "Will! I want you to meet one of our oldest friends, Arthur Camden.

Arthur, this is Will Northland of the Onondaga Pack. Arthur is the local veterinarian and sometimes helps out our healers."

Will felt a cold chill travel up his spine. If Arthur was a vet, he'd be an ideal candidate to help Sienna create drugs that would work on lycans. He was so distracted by the nefarious possibilities that he almost missed Raul's comment referring to Will as a member of Alex's pack. Shooting his friend a quizzical look, he extended his hand to Arthur. Sometimes he could get a feel for a person's energy by touching them. Raising his own shields, he grasped the strong, callused hand. "It's nice to meet you. I had no idea the Cayuga Pack was so large, but you've all made me feel right at home."

"We are a friendly bunch, and any friend of Raul's...." Arthur left the rest of the statement to be understood.

Will noticed again how everyone deferred to Raul without seeming to grant Richard the same reverence. He wasn't a werewolf, but it raised his protective instincts and made him want to jump to Richard's defense. Didn't these people see what a wonderful...? Will stopped his rioting thoughts, taking a calming breath. He apparently had grown far more attached to Richard during their brief time together than Richard had to him. The protectiveness he felt toward the werewolf rivaled his feelings for Tristan.

Taking a seat next to Raul and as far away from Richard as possible, Will turned his attention to Arthur. He hadn't been able to read much from the man's touch, so he'd settle for a good old-fashioned grilling. "So, Arthur... what made you choose veterinary medicine?"

"Seemed like the thing to do at the time." Arthur reclined in his chair, his long legs crossed at the ankles. The beer he held rested on his thigh, leaving a dark circle on the denim from the condensation dripping off the cold bottle. He was the picture of relaxed comfort, but Will sensed an underlying unease.

Richard snorted, nudging him. "That's our Arthur. He goes with the flow."

"Never made a decision in his life," Raul chimed in.

Arthur grinned sheepishly. "Yeah, well, why bother when there are so many people around here willing to make up my mind for me? Leaves me free for important things, like thinking about Wendy." The lanky werewolf's eyes followed a gracefully curved female as she made her way out to the picnic tables with another tray of food.

Will guessed that the girl was Wendy. "Is treating a werewolf anything like treating a natural wolf?" Will asked, watching Arthur watch Wendy.

"Huh?" Arthur jumped, his attention pulled back to the group. "Oh… not as much as you'd think. Our metabolisms are very different. Honestly, werewolves are a disgustingly healthy bunch. If I had to rely on them for my income, I'd starve. Give me a bunch of neurotic lap dogs any day. So, who wants to hit the Riverfront tonight?"

"Arthur, shame on you," Sienna scolded, approaching the group with a tray of steaming ribs. "I just got my husband back and you are already trying to lure him away for a night of debauchery."

Raul elbowed Will's side, leaning close to whisper in his ear, "Arthur likes loud music and drunk women. The Riverfront is a country and western bar out on Highway 20."

Will's chuckle was cut short by the lump that rose in his throat as Sienna sat across Richard's lap, draping her arms around his neck. Raul's eyes filled with sympathy, his hand stroking Will's leg. Will tensed as Richard's hand rose to rest on the curve of Sienna's waist, his thumb caressing her side. He consciously counted three even breaths, subduing the flare of anger. They needed more information before he could let his anger loose on Sienna, and he was close to losing control and blasting something. Loud music and drunk cowboys might be a good distraction.

"Not sure if the invitation includes me, but I wouldn't mind a night on the town," Will said, forcing his eyes from Richard to Arthur.

"Great!" Arthur grinned. "We'll have a blast. If you play your cards right, there is always someone to be found at the Riverfront. You'll only leave alone if you want to."

"Never been very good at cards," Will mumbled, his gaze slipping back to Richard, watching as Sienna whispered in the werewolf's ear.

RAUL followed as Will walked through the suite into his bedroom, pulling his shirt over his head and flinging it in the general direction of a chair in the corner. "You should have seen her workroom. I need to sit down and write some things out before I forget about them," Will muttered, his head buried in his suitcase, more clothes flying in all directions as he searched.

"So you think she's using a potion to control him?" Raul asked, pulling another chair into the room and propping his feet on the bed. He'd declined the invitation to the Riverfront, so there was no reason for him to change. As soon as Will left, he was hoping to make an early night of it—after an intimate conversation with his mate, if he had anything to say about it.

"Honestly, I have no idea, but based on what you've said, it seems like the most likely idea," Will answered.

"Can't you tell based on the spell we did when we were at Nanna's?"

Will paused. "Actually, the only thing I detected then was spellwork. Of course, Richard had been away from her for over a week by that point. With a lycan's metabolism, nothing ingested would still be present after all that time. It is most likely a combination of a potion to make him susceptible and a spell to alter his behavior. She has an apothecary in that building like nothing I've ever seen—hundreds of herbs, many mind-altering and a few I've never seen. Ah, ha." Will straightened with a battered spiral bound notebook in his hands. Sitting at the desk, he began to scribble furiously, stopping to chew on the end of his pencil occasionally as he tried to remember something that he'd seen.

"Do you need to look them up? There's a library in—"

Will laughed. "I don't need a library. I've got Tristan. He's like a walking herbal encyclopedia. Even if he doesn't know the name of an herb, he can often hold it and tell you what it is likely able to do based on its energy." Will pulled the folded paper out of his jeans. "Can you send this to him by overnight mail?"

Raul took the makeshift envelope carefully. "Should I be worried?"

"I wouldn't touch them if I were you, but I doubt if government agents will show up at your door for shipping dangerous substances." Will ripped the page he'd been writing on out of the spiral journal and handed it to Raul. "I assume there is a fax machine in the offices. Can you fax this to Tristan? I don't know the number, but Benjamin has a fully equipped office on the estate so there must be a fax machine."

Raul looked down at a page filled with detailed sketches and written descriptions of several herbs. "Okay, I can handle that. What in the world made you accept Arthur's invitation? I can't see you in a honky-tonk. Your accent alone will make you stand out like a sore thumb."

Will shrugged. "Not necessarily a bad thing, mate," he drawled, exaggerating the lilt in his voice. "I've pulled more than one bloke intrigued by my voice. You Americans are so easy."

Laughing, Raul folded the page and slipped it into his back pocket. "Just remember your manners. It is one thing to have to beat off the girls, but if you come on to the wrong cowboy, you may run into a different kind of beating," Raul warned.

"Yeah, I know, but I've gotten pretty good at spotting the *right* ones and I've never had a cowboy." Will winked. "Don't worry. I'll be careful and let him make the first move."

Raul bristled at the idea of Richard's mate with another man, but held his tongue. Damn his twin for getting him into yet another untenable situation.

"Off to make myself irresistible," Will quipped, throwing a clean shirt over his shoulder and heading into the bathroom.

"Let's hope not," Raul sighed, heading downstairs to the office to find an envelope and a fax machine.

WILL tipped up the bottle in his hand, draining the last of the lukewarm beer down his throat. The heavy bass of the country-rock band pulsed in his head. Arthur was on the dance floor with yet another blonde. His hope to pump the werewolf for more information had been thwarted by an endless string of buxom airheads in skintight jeans willing to let Arthur buy them a drink and then grind against them on the dance floor. Several girls had approached Will, but after a half-dozen rejections, the word had spread and they'd left him alone.

His secondary purpose of distracting himself with a good-looking cowboy had been no more successful. The bar was full of men who fit the description, but all of them were interested in beer, girls, and beer, in that order. Raul had been right—not his crowd. Catching the bartender's eye, he signaled for another beer. Might as well get drunk, since it was obvious he wasn't getting laid. So much for Arthur's prediction that no one ever left the Riverfront alone. Of course, he couldn't blame Arthur. If Will had been interested in going home with a girl, he was sure he could have his pick.

A strong hand came down on his shoulder, snapping Will out of his pitiful musings. "I've been asking myself all night why a guy who looks like you is sitting all alone at the bar."

Will turned, finding himself facing the definition of cowboy: tall, easily six foot three, broad shoulders, narrow waist, tan Stetson and a belt buckle as large as a dinner plate. "How've you been watching me? I think I would have noticed you."

It was a flirtatious answer, but Will knew a pick-up line when he heard one. His feelings had been on a rollercoaster ride since he first spotted Richard in that jail cell and doing something just for fun held an undeniable appeal.

The man smiled, flashing straight white teeth, his blue eyes sparkling. "I've been up on stage. I'll pretend not to be hurt that you haven't noticed me. I'm Jared, the piano player." Jared stuck out his hand, grasping Will's and holding on, his thumb brushing the top with slow circles.

Will darted a glance up at the stage. Sure enough, the band was on break and a DJ had taken over the music. A spiral of attraction tightened in Will's gut—nothing compared to the reaction he had with Richard, but it didn't come with the complications either. "Ah, well that explains it. The piano hid you. You should take up the fiddle. I'm Will."

"Even before I heard the accent, I knew you weren't local. What brings you to our Podunk town, Will?"

Will made a quick decision. One night to relax and forget scheming witches, gorgeous possessed werewolf princes, and pack politics wouldn't be the end of the world. "Would you believe I heard they had incredibly sexy piano players?" Will fell easily into the banter. He might not have dated much in the last year, but he'd always been a social butterfly. Flirting was as natural as breathing… and considerably more fun.

"No," Jared answered, grinning, "but I'll let you get away with it 'cause you're cute. Can I buy you a beer?"

Will held up the cold beer that had just been delivered. "I'm good, but thanks."

Jared waved the bartender over anyway, telling him to put the rest of Will's drinks on his tab. "If I keep you in cold beer, maybe you'll hang around until I get off," Jared whispered, leaning close under the guise of being heard.

Jared's warm breath on his neck made Will shiver. "What time would that be?"

"We play until last call—two AM."

Will looked up at the tall cowboy through the thick fringe of his eyelashes. "Definitely past my bedtime. You'd better be offering incentives better than beer."

Jared leaned closer, pressing his rock-hard body against Will's briefly. "I'm offering as much as you'll accept."

"And if I'm not offering much?"

"I'd settle for just getting you to smile at me."

Someone called Jared's name and Will noticed the band was back on stage. "Go play," Will told him.

Picking up Will's hand again, Jared pulled it to his chest for a quick squeeze. "Don't disappear on me, angel."

Will spent the rest of the night watching Jared play. The piano player sang, too, usually taking the lead on the slower ballads that suited his deep, bedroom voice. Occasionally their eyes would catch, but for the most part, Jared knew his audience and played to the ladies.

Arthur finally approached Will at last call, his arm draped around a giggling redhead. "Will, buddy, Jill here would like me to see her home. Can you make it back on your own?"

"I can if you're leaving me your truck," Will said. He didn't really relish calling Raul at two in the morning to come and get him. Arthur was beginning to seriously piss him off.

Obviously flustered by a response he hadn't expected, the werewolf stammered, "I... ah, well... I can't take Jill home without a truck."

"I assume she got here somehow," Will started when a familiar warm hand gripped his shoulder again.

"I'll get you home," Jared offered.

Relieved, Arthur grinned. "There. All settled. Night, Will." Pulling Jill to his side, he hurried out of the bar before Will could object.

Will glared at the retreating couple until Jared's soft voice broke into his angry thoughts. "I'm sorry if I'm out of line. The guy's an asshole. I just thought… you weren't *with* him, were you?"

Shaking his head, Will reached down and squeezed Jared's hand. "No, just met him today. A friend of a friend. I was just pissed that he'd leave me stranded here without a second thought. Bloody wanker."

Jared smiled. "You even swear cute."

Damn, the man's easygoing attitude was contagious. Will returned the smile. "I hope you know how to get to the Carlisle place because I really don't know where I am."

Jared threw some bills on the bar to cover his tab and started toward the door. "Got it covered. I grew up around here. Went to school with the twins."

"You know Raul and Richard?"

"Well… not really. They were seniors when I was a freshman. Seniors don't socialize with freshmen." Jared laughed, pointing out his truck in the almost empty parking lot. "I'm always starving when we finish playing. You want to grab something to eat on the way?"

"Well, since you're the man with the wheels…." Will said, climbing up into the red four by four next to Jared.

Jared leaned across the seat, cupping Will's chin and turning it toward him. "You don't have to say yes. The ride home isn't dependent on anything else, but I wouldn't mind spending some more time with you."

Will sighed, releasing some of the tension in his shoulders. He'd been taking out his frustration over Richard and anger at Arthur and Sienna on Jared, who had nothing to do with any of them. "I'd like to have…." He hesitated. "What in the fuck do you call a meal in the middle of the night?"

"Dreakfast?" Jared laughed. At Will's quizzical look, he elaborated, "Brunch is halfway between breakfast and lunch. Dreakfast would be halfway between dinner and breakfast."

"Dreakfast it is. I'm assuming you know somewhere that serves it."

Jared steered out of the gravel parking lot onto the paved road with one hand; his other rested casually on Will's thigh. "The diner serves something that looks a lot like breakfast, but Nancy won't care what we call it."

WILL moved quietly up the stairs to Raul's suite. Raul had given him a set of keys so he could come in without waking anyone. He wasn't sure what time it was, but the sky had been showing a telltale glow as Jared's truck had pulled up the drive.

Will smiled, thinking about his musical cowboy—the perfect blend of handsome and humorous. If it weren't for the indefinable and undeniable feelings Will had for Richard, he'd be looking forward to spending a lot more time with Jared. Any man that could beat him at straw wrapper shooting and kiss him good night until his toes curled was worth some serious investigation. Two weeks ago, Will would have gone home with him, but even in Jared's arms, his thoughts had drifted to Richard.

Not bothering with lights, Will tiptoed across the parlor to his bedroom. Unfastening the buttons of his shirt, he sat on the side of the bed to pull off his boots. Something warm shifted behind him, warm fur brushing his back. Jumping to his feet, he screamed for Raul.

There was a wolf in his bed.

Chapter 14

HEARING the panic in Will's voice, Raul pulled himself up from a deep sleep and stumbled out of his room. "What the fuck?"

"There is a wolf in my bed, Raul," Will whispered, as if he was afraid the wolf would hear him. He'd backed away from the bed, half-undressed. He wasn't in a full-blown panic because he'd gotten used to having wolves around, but he wasn't accustomed to finding them in his bed.

Raul looked at the large amber wolf stretched over the top of Will's bed, head cocked, its yellow-green eyes locked on Will. "It's Richard." Like most werewolf twins, Richard's and Raul's wolves were identical in appearance with the exception of a curved scar on Richard's left haunch, a souvenir from a particularly dangerous adolescent prank.

"Richard? Why is he in *my bed*?" Will asked Raul.

Raul's eyebrow rose as he shot Will an incredulous look. "Not like it'd be the first time."

Will huffed. "It *is* the first time in wolf form, and he's shown absolutely no interest in me since we arrived."

Raul could hear the hurt underlying the words. The wolf rose, standing on the mattress and stretching, his considerable muscles flexing. Jumping to the floor, he shook himself, fluffing his fur, which made him appear even larger. He prowled toward Will.

"Raul?" Will called out to the other man for help as the wolf got closer.

"Calm down," Raul instructed, scenting the wafts of fear coming from the young witch. His own wolf was stirring in response to the agitation in the room. Raul had immediately smelled the stranger on Will when he'd entered the room. Richard's wolf was radiating anger and jealousy despite his calm, controlled movements. This situation could get out of control fast. "Lie down on your back."

"What?" croaked Will, looking at Raul as if he'd lost his mind.

"Just do it. You know that Richard won't hurt you."

"The Richard I knew before we got here wouldn't have hurt me, but—"

"Will, lie down!" Raul ordered. Richard's focus switched to his twin at the barked command. Eyes narrowing, he seemed to weigh the threat Raul presented. Raul continued in a more even tone, "I don't think Sienna's magic has any control over Richard's wolf, which is why he's here. He can smell another man on you and he doesn't like it."

"So what? He has no right to—" The wolf rocked his weight against the back of Will's legs. The weight of the wolf leaning into him knocked Will off balance and he dropped to his knees. Richard's wolf nudged at him with its head, rubbing his body against Will's chest like a cat brushes against its owner's ankles.

"Lie down, Will," Raul said again from the doorway. "He wants your submission."

"Submission?" Will struggled to get back to his feet. "I didn't do anything wrong. He's the one—"

"It isn't a matter of right or wrong," Raul soothed. "He cares about you, Will. His wolf doesn't give a shit that Sienna is messing with Richard's mind. He just wants you all to himself and, right now, you smell like another male. He doesn't like that. You've seen how Benjamin reacts to another's scent on Tristan."

Will looked between Raul, who was slowly backing out of the room, and Richard's wolf. He could sense that that animal was upset and felt the undeniable urge to comfort it. Sitting on the edge of the bed, he sank his fingers into the thick fur around the triangular ears. The wolf bowed his head and swayed closer. Will's arms curved around the wolf's neck, burying his face in the coarse fur. He could smell Richard and it made him ache.

All Will wanted was a chance to see what was between them. He'd never felt such an instantaneous connection with another being, and it hurt beyond belief that Sienna's conjuring could interfere with it.

The wolf's muzzle brushed against Will's neck, a low, rumbling growl rising from its chest. Nervous, Will looked toward Raul and found him gone, the door closed. He was on his own. What did he know about soothing a wolf? Following his instincts, he patted the space beside him.

The wolf jumped onto the bed. Remembering what Raul had said about smelling like another man, Will shrugged out of his shirt and shoved his jeans to the floor. Crawling under the covers, he wrapped an arm around the wolf, spooning them together. Will dug his fingers deep into the dense pelt. "You're sort of like a full-sized teddy bear," he whispered. "I guess I should be happy that one of you still wants me. Wish it was your human half. Him I knew what to do with," he whispered, petting the dense fur, each word getting softer as the approaching dawn and the steady beat of the wolf's heart put him to sleep.

WILL drifted in and out of the veil of sleep. He could feel the warmth of the sun on his face so he knew it was time to get up, but he didn't want to open his eyes. Rolling onto his back, he stretched. The spot beside him was empty and cold. Richard's wolf had left. Will wasn't really surprised. Richard ultimately had control over his wolf, and Richard didn't want to be here.

Steeling himself for another day watching Sienna and Richard together, Will got out of bed, showered, and dressed. Wandering out of his bedroom, he spotted Raul reading the paper on the balcony. He poured a cup of coffee and walked out to join him.

"Did you see Richard's wolf leave?" he asked, adjusting a chair so he could prop his feet on the railing.

"No, he must have left before I got up." Raul folded the paper and dropped it on the floor beside his chair.

"What was going on last night?"

Raul swallowed. How did he explain Richard's wolf's behavior without mentioning the mating? "Werewolves are possessive by nature. Richard's wolf sees you as his. Whatever Sienna is doing seems to control Richard but not his wolf. Last night, Richard was probably deeply asleep and his wolf took over, coming to find you."

"I can't have a relationship with a wolf, Raul."

"I know you can't, which means we need to work hard on breaking Sienna's hold on Richard. I faxed that sheet to Benjamin last night. Have you talked to Tristan?"

Will shook his head. He'd tried to connect with his brother before he came out, but his mind was too distracted to focus. "The battery on my cell phone is dead. I forgot to put it on the charger, with all the commotion of finding a wolf in my bed." He laughed. "Can I borrow yours?"

Raul handed over the phone, getting up to refill his cup and give Will some privacy. He'd been as surprised as Will to see Richard's wolf last night. Losing control over your wolf was something that happened to adolescents, not full-grown lycans.

When he returned, Will had the phone propped between his ear and shoulder and had covered his folded newspaper with notes.

"Okay, Tris...."

"When you get the package, let me know what you think of the samples I sent....

"Ah, huh... no, I think you're right....

"Yeah, I'll try and get back in....

"I'll be careful....

"Me too. Bye." Will closed the phone, handing it back to Raul. "Tristan says, 'hi'."

"Good thing I was through with that." Raul nodded at the paper. "What'd you find out?"

"The things I didn't recognize are some strong hallucinogens used in shamanic rituals, mainly from South America. Muira puama, galangal, and virola theiodora." Will laughed at the glazed look in Raul's eyes. "Guess you don't need the specifics, huh?"

"Just the highlights, please."

"Now you know why I needed your paper. I had to ask him to spell them. The interesting thing is that most of them have strong dissociative properties. If she is using them on Richard, it might account for his wolf being able to act on its own. None of them would explain Richard's behavior by themselves, but they definitely could make him susceptible to controlling spells, especially after long-term use. And if she's used them on him before, he'd be more susceptible. Sort of like an alcoholic that takes a drink after being sober for a period of time."

"So we've got the ingredients of the potion. Can you counteract it? Or can you break the spell the same way you broke the last one?" Raul asked.

Will flushed, thinking of how he'd broken the last spell. "I don't think we have *that* option and we don't really know which herbs she is using in the potion. We just know what she has in her workroom. Tristan is going to work with the herb list I gave him and see what he can come up with. We might be able to concoct an antidote of some sort that would make her spells less effective."

"In the meantime, let's go see how Richard is this morning. Maybe his wolf's nighttime jaunt has had some effect on him," Raul suggested. "Breakfast will be over and it's not quite lunchtime, so we'll have to go scrounge in the kitchen. With all the excitement, I didn't get to ask what kept you out so late last night?"

Will smiled. "I guess Arthur was right about the Riverfront. Friendly place."

The look on Raul's face vacillated between shock and horror. "You're kidding. If I had thought—damn—never mind. Did you…?"

"No, Da—ad," Will drawled, elbowing Raul in the side. "I didn't." He paused meaningfully. "The guy I met offered to drive me home because Arthur left me high and dry for some redhead. We stopped at the diner on the way and ended up talking for almost three hours. It was fun. He's a nice guy."

Raul swore silently. He had warned his brother. "I'm glad you had fun, but don't give up on Richard yet. I watched the two of you together. There is something special between you."

Will's mouth twisted ruefully. "Well then, he better come to his senses soon because I could really like this guy—and Jared doesn't come with nearly as much baggage as Richard. Not one psychotic magical wife in sight."

"Does he really make you feel the same way?" Raul argued.

"Which way, Raul? The way I felt when Richard made love to me, the way I felt when I woke up to find out he'd gone back to Sienna, or the way I've felt since he informed me that what we did was a mistake?"

"You didn't see the way he acted the morning he left," Raul said.

"No, I didn't. Because he left without saying good-bye. I don't want to see him hurt, Raul. I'll do everything in my power to help him, but I don't want to get hurt either. You got any bright ideas on how we get through to him?"

Raul shook his head. "Not really. The only thing I can come up with is to appeal to his wolf. If whatever Sienna is doing can't affect his wolf and the herbs that she is using allow the wolf more freedom to act without Richard's control… maybe we can use that."

Will eyes brightened with excitement. "Yes! I bet you are right. So what is the best way to get through to a wolf?"

Sitting back, Raul took a sip of his coffee. "Oh, that's easy—desire, jealousy, and hunger. Not necessarily in that order."

"I'm not seducing a wolf, even of the werewolf variety. Do you really think he'd get jealous over me—even under the influence of Sienna's spell?"

"Oh, yeah," Raul confirmed. "No doubt about it. Wolves are very possessive. You should have smelled the pheromones he was putting off last night to cover the other male's scent on you. I left because, in that mood, even I was a threat. And you don't have to worry about the wolf part. Sex between noncompatible species is no fun. You can't change to wolf form, so he'll switch back to human form if his desire gets strong enough."

"That reminds me—I was watching the young wolves play tag yesterday. Do you… well… do werewolves… ah, you know… do other things in wolf form… together?" Will stuttered, wishing he hadn't brought it up at all. He could have found out from Tristan or made his twin ask Benjamin.

Raul chuckled at Will's discomfiture. "Are you asking if we mate in wolf form?"

Will nodded sheepishly.

"Oh, yeah, one of the pleasures of being a werewolf. There is a primal edge to mating in wolf form that is incomparable." Raul's green eyes softened as he remembered nights spent hunting and coupling with Alex.

Will shivered, a knot of desire tugging at his groin. He wasn't a werewolf. No sense coveting what he'd never have. "So how do we get Richard alone, or do we wait for his wolf to come to us again?"

A loud grumble sounded from Raul's belly, making both men laugh. "Let's go find food and then we'll see if we can find Richard."

WENDY looked up from the vegetables she was chopping as Raul and Will entered the kitchen. "Hey boys. Hungry?" Growing up in a kitchen, she'd learned that men rarely entered the room unless they were in search of food. Gathering a handful of cut potatoes and carrots, she scattered them around a large roast sitting in a pan on the counter.

"It's okay, Wendy. We can see to ourselves," Raul said, making a beeline for the refrigerator.

Holding her knife up in front of her chest like a shield, Wendy stepped in front of the blond werewolf and guided him to the table. "Nothing personal, but I'd just as soon fix it myself than have outsiders messing with my kitchen."

"Outsiders?" Raul squawked.

"Unruffle your feathers, Raul. When was the last time you fixed something in this kitchen… if ever? That qualifies you as an official outsider. So sit!" Wendy ordered.

Will followed obediently behind, taking the chair next to Raul's. "Was she in the Marines?" he asked quietly. "She reminds me of Ken," he stated, referring to a Guardian in the Onondaga pack who was an ex-drill sergeant.

"I heard that," Wendy chimed, breaking a half-dozen eggs into a bowl and whipping them. Reaching over, she turned several patties of sizzling sausage. "If you don't want to starve while you're here, I suggest you be nice."

Werewolf ears. Will sighed. "I was being nice. I like a take-charge woman—especially one as pretty as you."

Wendy threw back her head and laughed, shaking her spatula at Will in a mock threat just as Arthur walked in the door.

"I smelled—" He stopped when he saw Raul and Will. "You scammin' my best girl?" he teased, taking the seat next to Will.

Arthur's tone was light, but Will could tell there was a serious warning behind the words. Will wanted to ask how Arthur's night with the redhead had gone, but decided to make the mature decision and let it pass. "You should probably wrap this one up and put a ring on her finger, Arthur. Pretty girls who cook like Wendy aren't likely to wait forever." Will stared steadily at the werewolf. Two could play the subtle warning game.

Raul kicked him under the table. Yeah, yeah. Play nice. "You want to share our brunch?" Will offered, the use of the word brunch making him think of Jared, and he smiled.

"Yeah. You got enough for one more, Wendy darlin'?" Arthur asked. With a playful glare, Wendy cracked four more eggs into the bowl. "So how long you plannin' on stickin' around, Raul?"

Will's senses went on alert. Arthur sounded anxious to have Raul gone.

"Not quite sure," Raul replied evenly. "Why?" he asked, putting the ball back in Arthur's court.

Arthur hedged, "Oh, no reason. It is just good to have you around again."

Wendy put three plates in front of them and conversation made way for hunger. Finished first, Arthur took his plate to the sink, rinsing it off and stacking it in the dishwasher. "I guess I'd better be headed into the office. I've got patients this afternoon." He hesitated as if he had something else to say, finally handing Wendy a note, mumbling a quick "bye" and walking out the door.

Wendy unfolded the paper, scanning it and then laying it on the counter. "The woman should learn how to cook if she's going to be so picky," she muttered, wiping her hands on her apron.

Will got up from the table, repeating Arthur's actions with his own plate and then Raul's. Leaning casually against the counter, he looked down at the note. "Who should learn how to cook?"

"Sienna. She's got a meeting tonight and left a list of what to send up for Randolf and Richard for dinner."

"Can I look at this?" Will asked, indicating the note.

Waving her hand dismissively, Wendy walked to the pantry. "Sure. Help yourself."

Will studied the note. Unless Sienna had tampered with ingredients stored in the kitchen, the food wouldn't be dosed tonight. That might work in their favor. "Who takes the king's food up when he eats in his apartment?"

"Whoever is around," Wendy answered, returning with her arms full of cans.

Will rushed forward to help. "Arthur?"

"Sometimes. Lord knows he hangs around enough."

"Wendy, can you make sure that Arthur doesn't take up the food tonight?" Will requested. "Raul and I will come get it."

The cook look puzzled. "Well… I guess. You eatin' up there too?" she asked. Will nodded. "There'll be twice as much."

"I'm sure we can handle it," Raul threw in. "I can always grab a cart."

"It'll be here waitin' on you at six. Now shoo." She waved her hands at them. "I've got work to do."

Raul draped a casual arm around Will's shoulders as they exited the kitchen. "I think opportunity just knocked," he stated smugly.

Chapter 15

RAUL held open the door as Will pushed the laden cart into the King's chambers, glass and china clattering. "Dinner is served," Will announced playfully, removing the covers from the dishes with a flourish and a bow.

He was in an exceptionally good mood this evening. For the first time since they had arrived, Will felt hopeful. He and Raul had spent the afternoon creating a plan—a plan that involved touching Richard as much as possible. With a grin, he sat down on the couch next to Raul's brother, so close that his thigh pressed against Richard's from hip to knee. Looking at the surprised werewolf with openly desirous eyes, he tilted his head and asked, "Hungry?"

"I guess so." Richard's eyes narrowed suspiciously, but Will could see the flux in his aura. The werewolf might be able to control his actions, but he was still affected by Will's touch.

Will picked a rib up off the plate, removing the tender meat from the bone in slow, deliberate bites with his teeth. Placing the stripped bone back on the plate, he proceeded to suck the sweet sauce from his fingers, glancing at Richard from the corner of his eye. The werewolf hadn't touched his food, his eyes locked on Will's mouth.

Will shot a glance at Raul, finding him deep in conversation with his father and Meg. Meg had pulled a chair up facing them, her back to Will and Richard, forming a shield that granted them a feeling of privacy. "You aren't eating," Will pointed out. "They're good." He picked up a rib from the plate and held it out to Richard.

Grabbing Will's wrist instead, Richard pulled the rib toward his mouth, taking a bite without dropping the connection between their eyes. Will shivered and watched as Richard's eyes lightened to the yellow-green of his wolf. Bingo. He placed his free hand on Richard's thigh, running his fingernails up and down the inner seam of his jeans. Every hair on his body rose at the soft rumble from Richard's chest. Boldly, he brushed the growing bulge with the tips of his fingers.

Richard released his wrist, his fingers clamping down on Will's exploring hand and moving it away. Will watched as Richard's eyes darkened back to their normal deep green. Richard was obviously fighting his wolf for control and, at least momentarily, was winning. Will picked up another rib. The night was still young.

"What are you playing at?" Richard growled under his breath.

Will shrugged. "I can't forget how it felt to have your hands on my body," he whispered seductively. "The feeling of you moving inside me. I want to feel it again."

Richard's eyes flickered again. "I told you—"

"I know what you told me," Will interrupted, "but I know what we experienced was real. More real than what I see between you and Sienna."

Richard stood abruptly at the mention of Sienna. *Damn*, Will swore silently. He shouldn't have mentioned her name.

"That isn't true," Richard declared. Turning to his father, Richard mumbled an abrupt good night and left the apartment.

Will moved over beside Raul, unsure of what he should say in front of Randolf and Meg. "I didn't mean to run him off."

Randolf smiled, his eyes full of warmth as he looked at Will. "That's okay, Will. My son is stubborn, but he'll come around."

Will's eyes opened in surprise. Had Raul told his father about their plan?

Raul's arm wrapped around his shoulders, squeezing him close and then releasing him. "It's a start, and the fact that he didn't eat before he left will work in our favor. Hunger is pretty much an undeniable need for us. If he doesn't eat dinner, his wolf will be more demanding."

Will nodded, collapsing back into the corner of the couch and drawing his knees up in front of him. Richard had taken Will's appetite with him when he left.

RICHARD twisted in his bed, restless and frustrated. He could feel Will's touch on his thigh and moaned as his cock jumped and swelled harder. Rolling onto his stomach, he moved his hips, allowing the sheets to fill the need for friction that he wouldn't allow himself to indulge with his hand.

"Fuck," he swore, arching his back and pushing himself into the mattress until the pressure was almost painful. He tried thinking about Sienna, but the calming sensation he normally felt was elusive. Thoughts of Will filled his mind... his smell... the feel of his skin... the sound of his cries when he came.

His doubts about Sienna's treachery were even returning. Where did she go when she disappeared like she had tonight? She had done this ever since he'd known her. Why was he just now wondering where she went?

His eyes focused on the crisp white pillowcase. The image of Will's dark curls tangled on the pillow at his grandmother's rose in his mind. Swearing again, he sat up, swinging his feet to the cool floor. Feelings from the time he'd spent at the farmhouse flooded him. His wolf strained impatiently to go to Will, craving his mate's touch.

His mate. How could he be feeling that again when he'd been so certain that it had all been an illusion? Werewolves weren't supposed to be fickle. The mating instinct was supposed to be certain. When he was with Will, he doubted Sienna, but when he was with Sienna, he doubted Will. There was one difference—he had never felt mated to Sienna. His head hurt and his wolf's need was making it hard to think. Something important was just out of reach. If he could just focus, he knew he could find the answer.

He was halfway to the door before he realized that he'd moved. His need for Will overwhelmed him; he'd been about to walk out of his house without a stitch of clothing. Hastily grabbing a pair of sweatpants and a T-shirt, he jogged barefoot up to the main house, choosing to climb the tree to his brother's balcony, as they had when teenagers, instead of having to knock on the door to the hallway.

He immediately caught Will's scent drifting through the open French doors, guiding him toward the sleeping witch. This close, the need eased slightly, the restless urge to move evaporated, allowing him to stand and stare down at the man who held his heart. Looking at Will, his sleepy-scent soothing and arousing him at the same time, Richard had no doubts that this man was his mate.

He needed to figure out what was going on with Sienna, but that could wait. His desire to join with his mate—to reaffirm their bond—could not. Reaching out, he touched the soft curls splayed across the pillow, just as they had been in his memory.

Will stirred, opening sleepy, unfocused eyes. His breath caught in his chest as he looked up at Richard. He watched desire flood his lover's eyes as they switched between the yellow-green of his wolf eyes and emerald green of his human eyes. He felt a surge of emotion. They were both there. This wasn't just Richard's wolf taking over. That indescribable feeling in his chest was back, making it impossible to turn Richard away. Without a word, he reached up and pulled him down to the bed.

Richard skimmed his lips over his lover's cheek. Will sighed, leaning into the werewolf's strength. His breath hitched as Richard's mouth glided down his neck. Turning Will's head, Richard kissed him, licking at the seam of his lips, pushing his tongue inside as he cradled the back of his head in his hand. Pulling back just a breath, he said, "I want to take this slow, but I have to have you, Will. I need you."

Will's breath left his lungs in a shaky rush. The plan had been to seduce Richard's wolf, but he hadn't expected to get this far this fast. They wanted to shake Sienna's hold on Richard, but it appeared that they had cracked it completely. He felt like he should push Richard away, wake Raul and talk this out between them, but the feeling of Richard's arousal pressed hard against his thigh eroded his best intentions. They could talk after they made love.

Slanting his mouth across Will's, Richard locked his mate against him, one hand fisted in his hair, the other wrapped firmly around his waist. He buried his nose against Will's neck. Memories of another man's scent on Will's skin taunted him. Now. He would reclaim what was his, right now. Re-mark Will with his scent.

Will's heart swelled in his chest as Richard murmured endearments, his voice rough and primal. Desire spiraled in his gut, robbing him of his breath and all logic. His chest rubbed against Richard's as the werewolf crushed them together. Even the thin cotton of Richard's shirt was too much of a barrier. Impatiently, he lifted at the bottom, demanding that his lover remove it without being willing to separate their mouths to voice the plea.

Separating for the briefest moment, Richard pulled the shirt over his head and pushed his pants down his legs, kicking them to the floor. Will's nipples tightened into aching points as the wet velvet of Richard's mouth closed over one of them, his tongue a rough contrast to his lips as he suckled lightly. Hot little darts of agonized pleasure shot directly to his cock, now trapped between their bodies. Arching against his lover, he buried his fingers in the thick silk of Richard's hair.

Richard shifted him, aligning their bodies while his mouth feasted avidly on Will's chest. He moved from one nipple to the other, leaving the wet gleaming tips to throb hungrily for more. One big hand guided Will's leg around his waist and the witch eagerly lifted the other, hooking his ankles at the base of Richard's spine, reveling in the intimate contact. He shuddered as Richard started to rock against him, dragging the hard length of his shaft against the sensitive skin between his thighs. Richard's hands cupped his ass, the fingers of one hand pushing into the crevice between the smooth cheeks. Slowly, Richard kissed a path across Will's collarbone, scraping his sharp teeth along the tendons in the witch's neck until Will sobbed out his name.

Will whimpered. He had never felt anything this intense. His head fell back, begging Richard for more.

Richard's eyes opened, the emerald eyes burning into him. Against Will's mouth, he growled, "You are mine. I will never get enough of you." Then the werewolf kissed him, his tongue parting Will's lips and diving deep, stroking in and out in a way that stole Will's breath.

Will's hips jerked as Richard's hands raced over naked flesh, caressing, teasing. The werewolf lifted his fingers to Will's mouth. "Suck them," he rasped. Will wet them thoroughly, realizing he had nothing better to aid their joining. Richard's mouth returned to his lips, swallowing Will's moans as two fingers pushed inside the tight channel of his body.

Richard pulled away slightly, staring at his mate through slitted eyes as he pumped his fingers in and out in a maddeningly slow rhythm.

Will felt a teasing pressure as Richard's fingers swept around his prostate and he sobbed out his lover's name, pushing into the touch with erratic thrusts.

"You're so hot, so tight. Made for me," Richard whispered, his entire body quivering as he attempted to tame his wolf. He wanted this experience for himself.

When he opened his eyes again, Will trembled at the blind hunger he saw in Richard's gaze.

The needy quiver combined with the intense scent of arousal pouring off his mate was pushing Richard's control to its limits. "Damn it, Will, I just can't control myself around you."

"Then you'll just have to make love to me again… and again until it gets to be old hat," Will moaned as the world spun. He clung to Richard's shoulders, dizzy.

Richard moved down the length of Will's body with studied determination. The rough rasp of his unshaven face teased the smooth skin. Lifting Will's hips in his hands, he leaned down, drawing his tongue from the entrance to his mate's body, over the tight sacs and up the length of his shaft before closing his mouth over the swollen head. This would never get old.

Will screamed, his hips rising to meet Richard's mouth, his fingers tunneling into the thick silk of his golden hair. "Richard," Will gasped, his hips circling against his lover's mouth.

Richard continued to tease the tight muscle, pumping his fingers in and out as he worked his tongue against the sensitive head, until Will was screaming and digging his heels into his back. Another long finger steadily pressed against the tight pucker of his ass, slipping inside his body.

The extra pressure crossed directly over Will's prostate and he exploded, his eyes wide with shock, bright pinwheels of color exploding as he came in one hard convulsion after another.

Richard's mouth nuzzled against his mate tenderly, his tongue stroking soothingly along his length as the climax tore through him, his wolf happily savoring the taste of his lover's release and the intensely erotic smell of sex. Now Will smelled like he should—like him.

Will's eyes closed as he collapsed limply, his body still racked with harsh shudders. The warmth of his lover was suddenly gone, replaced with a breeze of cool air that made him shiver. His lashes opened and, through the dark fringe, he saw the gleaming gold of his lover's body rising above him.

Will shivered at the look in his werewolf's eyes, blatant hunger as tangible as a caress. Seconds later, Richard covered his body, hands spreading his thighs wide. Will felt the slow drag of the steely hard length of Richard's cock. His lashes fluttered closed as he felt the blunt head probing against his entrance.

"No. Don't close your eyes," Richard commanded, the tone of his voice driving through the satiated fog that clouded Will's brain. Dragging open his eyelids, the witch stared up at Richard as his lover pushed into his body, his sheath pulsing around the hard shaft as it breached the first tight inches.

"Oh, Goddess, yes," Richard growled. "That's it. Look at me while I take you...." His voice trailed off as Will arched against him with a hungry whimper, his hands digging into the muscles of his back, trying to draw him deeper. "Ah, hell, so perfect," he rasped, pulling out slightly and working his length back inside. "Tight. Made to fit me."

Will cried out as Richard plunged deeper, withdrawing and driving back inside him, a tense, strained look on his face. Draping Will's thighs over his own, Richard cupped the slender hips, hitching his lover closer. His entire body ached from the tension of holding his wolf back. He started to rock, not thrusting, just circling his hips in the cradle of Will's thighs, rubbing against the sensitive bundle of nerves, one hand cupping the curve of his ass, the other hand stroking the satiny skin of his back as he watched his lover's cock start to harden again.

Will lifted up, bracing his weight on his arms to be able to push back into Richard's gentle thrusts. "Take me," he rasped, wanting to see Richard lose control like he had at the farmhouse.

Richard's eyes widened, lightening to peridot as he lost his internal battle for dominance and his wolf took over. The scent of his hunger was heavy in the air—that crisp scent that was purely Will's surrounding him as he started to thrust harder.

Will's muscles clenched around Richard's cock, and the werewolf growled hungrily, shifting to cup his beloved's head in his hands. Taking his mouth greedily, Richard drove his tongue inside, drinking down the sweet taste of his lover as Will shuddered and groaned into his mouth. Sweat gleamed along their bodies as Richard gave in to the wolf inside him that whispered, "Harder, harder.... Now, now...." He sank his teeth into the curve of Will's sleek shoulder, marking his mate as he took him higher and higher. "Again," he whispered against the fragrant flesh. "I want to feel you come around me."

Will's damp hair clung to his face and neck. Gasping for air, his heart thundered in his chest, but he could feel the tingle of another orgasm twisting low in his body.

"Come for me," Richard growled, catching Will's knee and bringing it up over his shoulder, sliding his fingers down the sweat-slickened skin of his thigh and squeezing the supple curve of his ass before stroking his fingers down the crease between Will's body and thigh. He cupped the tender sacs, rolling them in his hand until Will's body trembled and clenched around him, a startled wail falling from his lover's lips.

Will flinched and then moaned as Richard's fingers slipped between his legs, massaging the tender spot beneath his balls. Abandoning all decorum, he rocked his hips hungrily to press into those feather-light strokes. Nails raking across Richard's broad back, Will threw back his head and screamed as Richard's fingers brought him to orgasm, his lover's thick length buried deep in his body.

A fiery sensation built in Richard's groin when Will contracted around him. The sensuous tremor of his mate's channel gripped his cock, leaving him swearing and sucking air into his lungs. Richard howled out his mate's name and flooded his body. The moment seemed to last forever as his body peaked, plateaued, and peaked again. Holding Will in a viselike grip, he emptied himself inside the willing body. Slowly, he came down on top of his lover with a weary, replete sigh.

Will stroked his fingers up Richard's arms, wrapping his legs around his hips and hugging him close. His lids drooped and he sighed blissfully. His entire body felt warmed from the inside out, and he sprawled boneless on the damp and wrinkled sheets.

Richard rolled them so Will was cuddled against his side. His heart clenched in his chest as Will rasped out his name in a hoarse, awe-filled voice.

"Richard...."

"Rest," he whispered, already succumbing to sleep himself.

WILL woke suddenly, immediately missing the feel of Richard spooned behind him. The bed dipped as Richard sat up. Damn. He was getting extremely tired of being left after every time they made love.

An unexpected ripple of magic skittered along Will's skin. Every sense on alert, he held completely still instead of turning to confront his lover. He felt Richard flip the sheet back and sit on the edge of the bed. Something was wrong. Richard wasn't just sneaking out in the middle of the night—the energy in the room was different. Slowly turning over, Will reached out to touch Richard's back. "Richard?" he called softly.

The werewolf got to his feet, pulling on his clothes.

Will sat up, an eerie feeling of déjà vu swamping him. "Richard."

Still no reaction. Richard walked toward the door that led into the suite. Will rose to follow, meeting a sleep-rumpled Raul in the living room. Raul made a move to intercept his twin, but Will motioned him away. "Can't you feel it?"

Raul shook his head, puzzled. "Feel what? What's wrong with him?"

"He's being compelled. I can feel the magic. It is a strong spell." Will whispered a few words and twisting bands of light appeared, drawing Richard to the door.

Raul stepped toward Richard again, and Will grasped his shoulder. "No. It might hurt him to interfere."

Richard walked into the hall, leaving the door standing open behind him. Will moved to the balcony to watch as Richard appeared from the side door, walking down the path to his house. Wide awake, Will made his way back into the living room, plugging in the kettle for tea.

Raul shadowed his steps. "What in the hell is going on?" he asked, his fingers raking through his hair.

"That is what we are going to find out."

Chapter 16

RAUL paced, trying to ease his agitation. "He was like a zombie. He didn't seem to even see us."

"I don't think he could," Will stated, calming his own nerves with the familiar ritual of making tea. His rational mind might understand that Richard's actions were being controlled by Sienna, but his heart felt battered and bruised. "Whatever she was using on him tonight is not what she usually uses. We speculated that she's using a potion to make him more receptive. He hadn't had any today. She probably tried calling him back with her regular spell and he fought against it. She had to up the power of the spell to get him back under her control."

Sitting on the arm of the sofa, Raul's eyes lit up with excitement. "If he can fight against the spell she's using, we might be winning. She can't keep him walking around like a zombie all the time."

"No, but once he is home, the first thing she will do is have him drink more of the potion. Most likely, we'll see the same Richard tomorrow that we've seen since we arrived." Will stared into space, his mind exploring the implications of what they knew. "There is more to this than just the potion. She had been gone several hours by dinnertime, and Richard was still under her control. Something changed between then and when he came to me."

"His wolf came to you once before and she wasn't even gone."

"Yes, but this wasn't just his wolf. Richard came to me in human form and I didn't see his wolf take over until I begged—" Will stopped, flushing. Raul might not want that much information about his twin's love life.

"So something changed while she was gone. Maybe the spell just wore off?" Raul suggested.

Will shook his head. "Spells don't wear off. It can be a matter of proximity. She might have traveled out of the range where she can control him, but I'd think, especially with us here, that she would be careful *not* to do that."

Raul yawned, the adrenaline from the middle-of-the-night excitement wearing off. "So we're right back where we started. Tomorrow she'll have reestablished control over Richard and we still don't know what spell she is using."

"No, we've learned quite a bit tonight." Will stood up, walking to the sink and rinsing his mug. "Our plan to engage Richard's wolf works. There is definitely a potion involved and without it Richard can resist, if not completely fight off, her spells; and we have a window of opportunity when she isn't around. I'll have to think more on that."

Will wandered into his bedroom, obviously lost in thought. Raul got up, shaking his head. "See you in the morning," he called after the retreating witch.

PROPPING his head up with his hand, Will tried to keep his eyes open. Between Richard's lovemaking and Sienna's magical machinations, he hadn't gotten much sleep last night. Tristan had found some interesting information on compulsion spells and sent it to him via e-mail. Will was convinced the answer was in the pages before him, he just had to keep his eyes open long enough to find it.

When he and Raul had gone down for breakfast that morning, they found Richard exactly as Will had predicted—clueless and safely ensconced at Sienna's side. Catching Richard alone in the kitchen for a brief moment, Will had tried playing to his wolf, but failed miserably. Clearly exasperated, Richard had repeated that Will was a mistake, adding several unflattering adjectives that didn't bear contemplation.

The ringing of his cell phone provided a welcome distraction. Digging it out of his pocket, Will got up from the desk, walking out onto the balcony. "Hello."

"Hey," Jared's soft voice drawled, "how's my favorite dreakfast companion this morning?"

Will laughed. "It's almost two in the afternoon."

"Yeah, well for a barfly like me, that's morning."

"I guess that makes sense." Will leaned back against the railing, unable to keep himself from smiling. It felt good to have a conversation where he wasn't constantly examining everyone's motives. "So what do you do during the daylight hours?"

"Actually, that was why I was calling. I've got the night off and thought you might want to come for a ride with me. I'll feed you lunch," Jared suggested.

Raul entered the suite, a serious look on his face. Spotting Will on the balcony, he walked through the open doors.

Will laughed again. "Two o'clock in the afternoon, remember?" He mouthed at Raul, "It's Jared from the other night."

"Fine. Linner? Or maybe Lupper?" Jared suggested.

"It doesn't have quite the same ring," Will teased back, hesitating. "I'm not sure I can get away...." Will's voice trailed off as Raul started motioning at him.

"Hold on a sec," he said into the phone, covering the receiver with his hand. "What?"

"You should go," Raul urged.

"Huh?" Will asked, confused.

"You saw how Richard responded to the scent of another man. Basic drives, remember. And jealousy is one of the deepest."

Will felt like banging his head against the nearest wall. Why couldn't he fall for an uncomplicated man? Richard might do explosive things to his equilibrium, but he was married and next in line to lead his pack. Even if they got rid of Sienna, Richard would have the same issues with Will—he wasn't a werewolf and the pack wouldn't want to change him because he was a witch. It wasn't like there was anything official between them, other than some words whispered in the heat of passion. The only comment Richard had ever made about their relationship outside of bed was that it was a mistake. It all made his head hurt.

Shrugging, Will gave up trying to decide what was best. "I'd like to come," he told Jared. "I don't have a car, though."

"What kind of gentleman would I be if I didn't come pick you up?" Jared sounded playfully indignant that Will would even suggest such a thing.

Will chuckled. "What time?"

"Since you've informed me that lunch is over, we'll aim for dinner. Can you be ready by six?"

"No problem."

"Jeans and boots. I don't do fancy and you look good in jeans...." Jared's voice trailed off seductively.

Tristan's voice sounded in Will's head, *I'm not sure this is a good idea....* But he purposefully ignored it. Surely Raul knew Richard better than anybody else. "I'll see you in front of the house at six," Will confirmed, closing the phone.

RAUL watched Will out the window. He really hoped that things went well when Jared arrived to pick up Will. His worries for Will's friend's safety kept him glued to the spot. When Jared arrived, Raul wanted to be there to run interference. No one knew better than he how dangerous a werewolf jealous over its mate could be.

Ever since Richard had chosen to mate with Will, Raul had been worried about the ramifications of his twin's rash behavior. If Richard had been in a position to woo Will properly, it might have worked, but instead he was doing everything he could to push him away and he wasn't even doing that consistently. Raul knew that the hot and cold mood swings were hurting Will more than the young witch was revealing. Raul wasn't sure which of them he was worried about more.

It was nearing twilight when Jared's truck arrived in the circular drive in front of the house. Sailing down the stairs, Raul pushed through the front doors just in time to see the black pickup pull up and Richard step out of the shadows.

Richard had been in a state ever since Will had announced he was going out for the evening. Despite whatever spell she'd cast on him, if Sienna hadn't stepped forward and taken Richard's arm, Raul was convinced his brother would have followed Will and started an argument. Proximity was definitely a component of Sienna's power. Just her touch on his arm and Richard had visibly relaxed.

In keeping with the plan, Raul had done everything he could to keep Sienna out of contact with Richard all day, enlisting the help of the kitchen and household staff to summon her for a variety of problems only *she* could solve. While she was absent, he had needled his twin, bringing up Will repeatedly and speculating on what might happen on his date.

"Where are you going?" His brother's voice was low and dangerous. Raul couldn't see his eyes in the fading light, but he'd be surprised if his twin was operating from his human side.

"Not really your business, is it, mate?" Will shot back flippantly.

Jared started to get out of the truck, but Will leaned through the passenger window and said something Raul couldn't hear.

Raul stepped into Richard's field of vision, trying to distract him from Will. "Richard, I think Sienna is looking for you."

Will shot him an incredulous look for bringing up Sienna's name. Walking toward Richard, he stopped directly in front of the blond werewolf. "You made your choice and it wasn't me." Even though he was playing a role according to their plan, he couldn't keep the subtle break out of his voice.

Raul stepped up behind Will. He could smell Jared through the open windows and knew Richard would recognize the scent. He could feel the waves of jealousy radiating off his twin and the sharp spike of emotion when Will's voice broke. Possibly the only thing worse than a werewolf's possessiveness was their insane desire to protect their mate. Will was obviously hurting and Richard instinctively would be driven to fix it—only in this case he was the cause of it. What a mess.

Richard looked over Will's shoulder and growled at Raul, warning his brother to back off. Raul knew he was treading dangerously. Their twin bond would mean very little if Richard really perceived him as a threat to his mate. "I'm only trying to keep him safe, Richard," Raul soothed.

"From me? I wouldn't hurt him!" Richard exploded.

"Wouldn't you?" Will whispered softly, looking up at the man right in front of him. "You already have." He let all of his confusion show in his eyes.

Raul took a step back as Richard swept Will into his arms, moving him against the stone wall, shielding him with his body. "Never. I—"

"Richard!" Sienna's voice broke through the quiet night air.

Raul watched as every muscle in Richard's back tensed. Richard took a faltering step back from Will like a drunk trying to make his way out of a bar.

Sienna came around the corner, scowling at Raul. The blood drained from her face as she spotted Will still partially hidden behind Richard. Quickly composing her expression, she pasted on a false smile. "Richard, honey, I've been looking all over for you. You told me to come find you as soon as I was done, remember?"

Richard squinted at her, his eyes darting back and forth between his wife and Will. Sienna closed the distance between them, wrapping her hand possessively around Richard's arm. The tension in his shoulders eased and he smiled at her. "I'm sorry. I don't know what—"

"It doesn't matter, sweetheart. Let's go home," she inserted quickly, already pulling Richard away. Turning her head, she smiled at Raul. "Have a good night, Raul." The smile only faltered slightly as she added, "Will."

Raul put a comforting arm around Will's shoulders. It seemed like every time they took a step forward, Sienna would appear and push them two steps back.

"Well, that sort of worked. Think she knows about me and Richard?" Will asked, watching them disappear down the walk.

"If she didn't before, I think she does now. Now, what are you going to do about Jared?" Raul noticed for the first time that the young man had gotten out of the truck and was clearly debating whether or not to intervene.

"I called him earlier, after we talked. He knows I'm in the middle of a breakup and is only here as friendly distraction. I'm gonna go ahead and have dinner with him. Honestly, I could use a friend who isn't a wolf right now. No offense."

Raul squeezed Will's shoulder. "None taken. I think you are doing amazingly well considering."

"I won't be late." Will smiled at Jared as they climbed into the truck. He waved out the open window as they pulled away.

Chapter 17

"So, should I take a shower before bed or not?" Will asked from his position on the couch. He'd been rereading Tristan's e-mails about compulsion spells before bed, but still hadn't spotted the key piece of information he sensed they possessed.

"What?" Raul asked, looking up from his own stack of papers.

"I asked if you think I should take a shower."

Raul's forehead furrowed. "I heard you the first time. I just don't understand the question. You've never consulted me about your personal hygiene before."

"I may not be a werewolf, but I know I smell like Jared after having dinner with him. I think odds are good that Richard's wolf will show up here tonight, so do I wash the scent off me or not?" Will elaborated.

Raul hesitated, obviously weighing the options. "I'm not sure. I don't want to see you get hurt."

"You said that outside earlier. Do you really think Richard would hurt me?"

"No, Richard would never *intend* to hurt you, but you aren't a lycan and he isn't in control of his wolf. When a werewolf gets really jealous, it can be a volatile situation... the sex can get... well, feral."

Will couldn't suppress his smile. "I'm not averse to *feral*."

Raul chuckled. "Me either, but I'm worried about Richard's control. Trust me, Richard's wolf wants you enough as it is. You don't need to incite him into more."

"All right." Will shrugged, standing and stretching the kinks out of his back. "It has been a long day and I didn't get much sleep last night. I think I'll take a shower and go to bed. I'll see you in the morning, okay?"

"Yeah, I'd tell you to sleep well, but I'm hoping you don't sleep at all because it'll mean we are making progress."

Laughing, Will disappeared into his room, closing the door behind him, but making sure the French doors were open in case he had a nighttime visitor. Stripping off his shirt, he pressed the warm cotton to his face and inhaled. Even he could smell Jared's light, citrusy scent. Tossing the shirt on a pile of clothes to be washed, he removed his jeans, kicking them in the same direction. Standing naked in the moonlight, he stared out into the night.

Was all this worth it? How *did* he feel about Richard? There was no doubt he desired him—more than anyone he'd ever been with. When Richard touched him, he melted, every nerve vibrating. But if he was honest with himself, it went deeper than that. In Richard's arms, he felt safe, protected, loved. That was the real draw to the handsome werewolf. When Richard held him, Will felt complete in a way not even Tristan made him feel. Logically, it made no sense, but magic had taught him that not everything was exactly as it appeared.

Magic had also taught him that intent was everything. He was afraid to commit to Richard because there was a slim chance of success and a great chance of total heartbreak, but unless he really committed himself to freeing Richard, was there any chance that he would succeed?

Not likely.

Will glanced down at the discarded clothes and then at the door, deciding that it was time to take a chance. Foregoing the shower, he slid between the sheets of his bed and prayed to the Goddess that Richard's wolf would find a way to come to him.

WILL woke with an awareness that he wasn't alone. His heart thumped and the hair on the back of his neck rose as he let his eyes adjust to the low light in the bedroom. A menacing growl filled the room. Moving only his eyes, Will watched as Richard's wolf paced around the bed, stopping to sniff at the pile of discarded clothes. The amber wolf snarled, grasping Will's shirt with his teeth and shaking his head violently. Anchoring it to the floor with his paw, he arched his neck, methodically tearing the fabric to shreds. Turning toward the bed with the remainder of the shirt still hanging from his mouth, the wolf's eyes narrowed.

Will had a split second to register the bunching of the muscles in the wolf's powerful haunches before it was in flight. In one easy leap, the wolf landed on the bed, the mattress giving with his weight and rolling Will toward him. Will tried to lift himself up to a sitting position, but Richard's wolf knocked him flat.

Last time, Richard's wolf had come seeking reassurance. Tonight, things were different: he had come to reclaim what was his. Without his human side to filter it, Richard's wolf was acting on the anger and jealousy that Will had seen in Richard earlier. He was demanding Will's submission and would accept nothing less. Will shuddered, the untamed strength of the wolf that straddled him arousing and scaring him at the same time. His body responded to the wild energy, his cock hardening against his stomach, his blood pounding through his veins.

The wolf tasted his chest with a long, slow drag of its tongue; its teeth scraped lightly against his throat, causing a wave of goose bumps. Turning his head, Will offered more of the tender flesh, having no fear of the powerful animal above him despite Raul's warning. Richard's teeth settled into his neck, not breaking skin, but controlling his movement, making sure that Will was aware of exactly who was in charge. Will gasped, holding his breath, his body arching, begging to be claimed.

A growl issued from deep in the wolf's chest—pleased now, not angry. Will's arms reached up to circle the wolf's chest, his fingers sinking into the thick pelt. He could feel the vibrations and pulled the wolf down, rubbing himself against the soft, downy hair of its underbelly. Hoping Raul was right about Richard changing form if he wanted Will enough, he begged, "More. Take me."

In a split-second shimmer of form, the amber wolf shook and a gloriously naked Richard loomed over him. Grasping both of Will's wrists, he pinned them to the mattress above his head in one large hand. The other hand stroked Will's cheek in a surprisingly tender gesture. His eyes were still unwaveringly yellow-green.

Richard's wolf was in charge and needed no more encouragement to claim what he wanted. He pressed in close, pinning Will's hips with his own, pelvis to pelvis, his spine curved to hold Will down. His arousal was growing, pressing hard into Will's stomach. Will felt the blond man shiver and could see the hunger in his eyes, reflecting what he was sure showed in his own, the hammering of his heart now fueled more by arousal than fear. He could see the gleam of desire in his aura as it radiated off his body.

Richard slid one knee up between Will's thighs, tight to his undulating body. Will pushed back against him, encouraging Richard to ride him. The werewolf's cock stroked against the smooth skin of Will's abdomen, sliding alongside Will's matching erection. Will's legs fell open, his body crying out for Richard's touch. He desperately wanted the big, solid shaft—rhythmically running over the muscles of his stomach—inside him.

The fluid they were producing wet his stomach, lubricating the track Richard's cock rode over his flesh. His own erection throbbed painfully, aching for more stimulation. Richard seemed oblivious to his pleas and blatant squirming as Will attempted to align their bodies in a way to encourage penetration. Burying his face against Will's throat and lapping at the thundering pulse, Richard pushed a second knee between his thighs, spreading his legs, making him completely vulnerable.

Will's sigh of relief changed into a moan of pleasure as Richard pushed his knees up farther, resting long and demanding against Will's entrance. Will gasped, moaning his approval as the head of Richard's cock, slick with fluid, pressed into his welcoming body. Eyes locked on the fierce, beautiful face above him, Will struggled to free his hands so he could touch… stroke… hold Richard as they made love. His body trembled from head to foot. Bowing off the bed, he locked his legs around Richard's hips, allowing the werewolf's thrusts to move them as one.

Richard's eyes raked over Will's body, just the heat of his gaze pulling Will's nipples into sharp points. Will's erection rose, flushed and hard, between their bodies. A satisfied snarl flowed from the werewolf's throat. Changing the angle of their bodies, Richard snapped his hips forward. Will cried out, his eyes rolling up in his head as the edges of his vision fluxed. "Oh Goddess, fuck me! Hard! Now!"

Richard's length throbbed inside his mate. He bared his teeth as he moved faster, grinding into Will as he writhed and squirmed.

Reduced to gasps and begging moans, Will tried to encourage more speed with his hands, clutching and grasping at sweat-slippery skin. He could feel his release growing, a tingling rush moving up from his feet, down from his shoulders, and washing over him until he shot his pleasure between them.

Richard stopped then, still hard and heavy inside Will's body, his yellow-green eyes searching Will's face. A quick pulse of his hips made Will cry out, his body hypersensitive. Bending his arms, Richard lowered his body, rubbing himself in the released seed on Will's belly and chest. Now that Will had come, he seemed in no hurry to find his own release. Slow, almost lazy, strokes kept Will on the knife's edge of pleasure, every sensation causing a renewed ripple of aftershocks. He whimpered as Richard slid deeper and deeper, picking up speed as he neared his own climax.

Still pressed chest to chest, Richard's hips were the only part of his body that moved. Capturing Will's face between his hands, he claimed his mouth for the first time. Like a circuit completing, the connection of their lips triggered Richard's climax. Arching his spine and throwing back his head, he cried out in a human howl as he filled Will's body. The sound spiraled in a tight knot in Will's gut, starting the cycle of arousal again.

Reaching up, Will curved a hand around the back of Richard's neck, pulling him down to his chest. A panting mess, they held each other close as their heartbeats slowed. "Stay with me. Be mine tonight," Will whispered into Richard's ear.

THEY made love twice more during the night. Each time slower, more lingering and deliberate. Richard left just before dawn, pinning Will to the door and kissing him until his knees wobbled before shimmering into his wolf and disappearing down the hall.

Standing at the door long after the wolf had disappeared, Will felt Raul walk up behind him.

"I told you he'd be human for you."

"He never said one word." Will turned, shutting the door quietly and walking toward the teakettle. He scratched distractedly at the skin just above the elastic of his boxers while he waited for the water to boil, thinking that *now* he definitely needed that shower, but was reluctant to wash Richard from his skin.

"Wolves tend to speak more with actions than words. Richard is safely locked up by Sienna's spell. They share a body, so Richard's wolf can force a change of form, but I doubt it would even occur to it to speak."

Will glared at the slow kettle and then curled up in the corner of the couch, pulling his legs up and wrapping his arms around his knees. "At least, he didn't disappear while I was sleeping this time. I feel like we're making progress." Will laughed. "It is easier to watch him go than to wake with him gone. I asked him to come back tonight."

"That's brilliant. Some of this has got to be slipping through to Richard. The more we can court his wolf, the more progress we'll make." Raul poured the hot water into Will's mug and handed it to him. "You should try and get some more sleep."

Will shrugged, blowing the steam off the top of the hot liquid before taking a tiny sip. Setting the mug on the table, he picked up the stack of papers from Tristan. "Maybe in a little bit."

"Okay," Raul agreed, reluctantly. "We don't need you run-down."

Will looked up at Raul and smiled. "You either."

Raul laughed. "You don't have to convince me. I'm going back to bed. I'll see you at a decent hour."

Shuffling the papers to find a particular article, Will sat back, papers propped against his thighs.

The sky brightened from gray to pink to blue as Will read. Sometime after eight, he heard Raul rustling around in his bedroom and the sound of the shower starting. Finally, his eyes landed on the paragraph he'd been looking for. Swinging his feet to the floor, he bolted upright. He must have read this paragraph six times, but this time an idea formed that seemed so simple he berated himself for not thinking of it sooner. He stood quickly, the papers dropping from his lap and scattering in a messy pile on the floor. Running to the bathroom, he burst through the open the door without knocking.

"I've got it, Raul!" he screamed over the running water.

"Got what?" Raul peered out from behind the shower curtain.

"I've got an idea about how we can break Richard free!" Will was so excited he was bouncing on the balls of his feet.

"That's great," Raul answered, genuinely pleased, but uneasy about the transparent shower curtain between them. It wasn't an issue of nudity. Will had seen Raul unclothed at several ceremonial gatherings, but Will was Richard's mate and just the thought of what

Alex would do if he could see them.... Raul shivered. "Can I finish my shower first?"

"Oh. Oh, of course," Will stammered, backing out of the bathroom. One day he'd learn to think before he acted. He stood for several minutes outside the bathroom door, vibrating with excitement. When the water didn't immediately shut off, he forced himself to calm down. Ten minutes or twenty wouldn't make any difference.

He needed to share his breakthrough with somebody, however, or he was going to explode. Walking out onto the balcony, he stood in the warm morning sun and started to go through his morning yoga poses. When he reached the still point deep in the center of the exercises, he crossed his legs and reached out to Tristan.

His twin was sound asleep, in the middle of an erotic dream about Benjamin. Will shook his shoulder. "Wake up before you embarrass us both," he ordered gruffly.

Tristan turned away from his twin, pulling the covers up over his head and mumbling something indistinguishable.

"Come on, Tris," Will wheedled. "It's important."

Throwing back the covers with an exasperated flop, Tristan pulled himself up to a sitting position, his back against the headboard. "This better be good," he warned.

"It is. It is. I was reading the papers you sent and I got an idea. The author had used it for a completely different purpose, but I think it will work. Based on his behavior when Sienna is away—"

Tristan held up a hand and stopped the rapid flood of words. "What's the idea?"

"Oh... yeah... we find a place that I can magically shield and then lure Richard inside it. All connections with Sienna should be severed. I started adding up the pieces of what we know. She obviously uses touch to control him, so the closer she is to him the better. The one time she left packlands, he seemed to come back to himself, which means she is using a spell that has geographical limits. His wolf wants me and doesn't seem to be affected by Sienna's spells, so if we can get him to a place where she has no magical control over him, maybe we can talk some sense to him."

"Sounds reasonable. It'd work best in a natural formation... rock, preferably. Are there any caves in the area?" Tristan asked, leaning forward, elbows on his knees. He loved a good puzzle.

Will stretched out on the bed next to his brother. "I'm not sure, but Raul'll know. He and Richard grew up here. I'm sure they explored every inch of this place."

"Probably, and if not, a good topographic map'll tell you. Does the spell shield an area from magic by creating a perimeter that magic can't cross, or does it create an area where magic doesn't work at all?"

"I'm hoping for the first. I'll be in that cave with Richard and I'd rather not lose my access to magic while I'm there. If I can't raise a perimeter that will hold, I'll have to do the other."

Tristan reached out and entwined his fingers with Will's. "You should be powerful enough to pull it off. It isn't like you have to make it hold indefinitely."

"No," Will agreed, "but once Richard goes off her radar, Sienna will be actively searching for him, so the barrier will be tested."

"If you do get a perimeter to work, you should try working a little bonding magic of your own, if Richard is agreeable. If the two of you form a consensual bond, it should help protect him from her magic even once he leaves the area," Tristan suggested. He grinned, shrugging. "Plus, it is a hell of a lot of fun bonding with a werewolf."

"Well, I don't know about the bonding part. I think Richard's wolf may be more interested in me than Richard is," Will explained.

"Boy, does that sound familiar—the wolf desiring you before the man catches up. All I can say is wolves make good partners. Between the two of you, you'll wear his human side down and then... look out."

Will raised an eyebrow, looking up at his brother. "I don't want to have to 'wear him down'. I'd prefer a lover who actually wants to be with me."

"Richard wants to be with you," Tristan soothed, his fingers combing through Will's curls. "I don't think it is possible for a werewolf and his wolf to be in complete disagreement about something as important as love and mating. The human half just is capable of intellectually fighting the more instinctual impulses. Doesn't make them right," he ended with a laugh.

"Well, I guess we'll see. It wouldn't hurt to have a potion of some sort to counteract any drugs she might have given him. The shield will break magical bonds, but it won't affect organic things in his system. Can you work on something based on the list of herbs I found?" Will asked, sitting up.

"I've already been working on it. I should have something ready for you by tomorrow. I want to test a couple of combinations and I had to order some of the herbs. When you get the spell done for the shield, send it to me. I'd like to see how you put it together," Tristan requested, getting to his feet and pulling his twin into a tight embrace. "You've been gone too long. I miss you."

"I miss you too," Will agreed. "I can't imagine what Raul is going through."

Tristan shuddered just thinking about being separated from Benjamin for more than a few days. His mate was only downstairs in his office and he felt his absence. "So figure this out so you can bring him home."

"I'm working on it." Pressing a kiss on Tristan's cheek, Will closed his eyes, relaxing back into his still point with several deep breaths. Opening his eyes on the sunny balcony of Raul's ancestral home, he planted his hands on the warm stone and pushed up into the next motion to finish his morning yoga cycle and ground the energy he'd raised traveling to talk with Will.

TRISTAN pulled on a pair of sleep pants that had been carelessly thrown to the floor the night before. Padding through the house barefoot, he attempted to sneak up on his lover, who was working at his desk, apparently engrossed in the constant stream of figures on his computer screen.

Just before Tristan's arms wrapped around his chest, Benjamin swung his chair around, pulling his lover across his lap. "'Bout time you got up."

"Ha! I'll have you know I've been up for hours. I was talking with Will."

Tristan's words were playful, but Benjamin could see the unspoken worry in his mate's eyes. "Do you want to go to him?" he asked gently.

Tristan threw his arms around his lover's neck and kissed his cheek. "You know me so well. Are you sure you're okay with it? You sort of orchestrated Will going because you didn't want me to."

"Yeah… well… I won't be worried about you going if I go with you," Benjamin said, hugging Tristan to his chest. "And something tells me we won't be heading south alone."

Chapter 18

RAUL stepped from the top of a jagged rock to a narrow ledge several feet away. Reaching behind him, he held out his hand for Will, to steady him as he crossed. They'd been scouting possible locations for several days. Every day they spent the daylight hours looking for the ideal spot to set Will's shield spell and every night Will worked on composing the elements of the spell. He had snuck into Sienna's herb shed twice, sneaking out small amounts of the herbs he thought he might need and whispering spells to reduce the potency of the herbs he left behind. He wasn't sure if the spells would make much difference. Most of an herb's power is intrinsic, but he figured it couldn't hurt.

He hadn't seen much of Sienna, Richard, or Arthur, which worried him some, but Richard's wolf was coming to him regularly, every night now, if only for a few hours. He could feel the bond between them growing and had even sensed the wolf approaching before it entered the room on the last two nights.

Will glanced at his watch. It was nearly dusk and they'd need to head home soon. The last thing he wanted to do was miss one of Richard's visits. "How close are we?" he called to the blond several yards in front of him.

"Just around here," Raul answered, his fingers searching for a handhold to steady himself as he rounded a sharp corner. "I was considerably smaller last time I was up here," he muttered as he overbalanced, swayed backwards and then clung to the rock for a moment, letting his heart rate slow.

Will watched each step Raul took, recreating the placement of his hands and feet exactly as he rounded the corner. The ledge broadened immediately into the opening of a good-sized cave. If it was deep enough, it would be perfect. Raul was already inside and Will could see the beam of his flashlight illuminating the space. Pushing aside a curtain of vines, he followed.

The cave was tall enough to be able to stand without stooping once he was past the first six feet. The main chamber was approximately the size of a bedroom with smaller passages leading off in two directions. Neither would be easily navigated. A man would have to crawl on his hands and knees.

"How far back do these lead?" Will asked, pointing into one of the smaller tunnels. He presumed correctly that two young boys wouldn't have been able to resist exploring them.

"Not far. During the spring when we get a lot of rain there is a spring that runs out of this one. There are no other entrances." Not knowing exactly what Will was looking for, Raul leaned back against the wall and watched as the witch ran his hands over the stone and explored every nook and cranny of the cave.

Finally appearing satisfied, Will sat in the middle of the space, crossed his legs and closed his eyes. He took several deep breaths and Raul held very still, not wanting to interrupt what he didn't understand. It was like Will had explored the physical layout of the cave and now was exploring it using senses Raul didn't possess.

With each breath, Will expanded his energy into the space around him, feeling it rebound when it reached the walls of the cave. There was ironstone in the ground here, mixed with dolomite, calcite, and quartz, and it served as a natural barrier that would work to his advantage. He could feel the water under the rock, but it wasn't flowing into the cave at the moment, so it wouldn't be a problem. He could isolate this area. Placing his hands flat on the ground on either side of him, he softly chanted a string of words and pushed the power they raised into the rock, feeling how it flowed. He sensed Raul fidget and step away from the rock as the power ran up the wall behind him.

Yes, this was the place. Now he just needed a strong spell, a potion from his twin and his recalcitrant lover.

"Well?" Raul queried as Will opened his eyes.

Will smiled. "It's perfect."

"I love it when a plan comes together," Raul exclaimed, rubbing his hands together. At Will's puzzled look, he added, "It's a line from a TV show. Oh, never mind… So what do we need to do next?"

"I call Tristan and tell him I need his potion *now*. It would be best if we could dose Richard with it for a day or two before we try this. I'll work on the spell up here, practicing taking it up and down. The rock will absorb the energy of the spell. It should get easier to raise it each time I cast it. The first few times, I'll have to guide the energy through the rock to make sure it closes off the cave completely, but after that it'll be like a river flowing back into a dry riverbed. It should follow the path already carved out." Will shuffled his feet, reluctant to make his next suggestion. "If you'll agree, I can put some harmless spells on you and we can see how they are affected by the shield."

Surprisingly Raul agreed, not even stopping to think about it. "Makes sense to me. Just no warts or anything," he teased. Will lunged forward, catching Raul in a sudden hug. "What was that for?"

"Just for being you and trusting me. You have no idea how much that means to me," Will said.

"Well, you're practically family—" Raul started, breaking off before he revealed too much.

Will nodded, stooping to open the backpack he had dropped to the ground just inside the entrance and pulling out his sketchpad and pencil. "I forget how the pack defines family."

Raul let Will think that he was referring to his connection through Tristan and Ben. "What are you drawing?"

"Just the general shape of the cave." Will reached back into his backpack and pulled out a small electronic device about the size of a cell phone. "GPS," he said. "I want to look up this area on the county maps and see what else is around. I need to collect samples from some of the plants and trees around here."

"Maybe you can collect and I can write what you tell me," Raul offered.

"That'll save time." Will turned to a clean page, handing Raul the pad and pencil. Zipping his backpack, he turned to the cave entrance. "We can do some on our way back, but we'll have to come back tomorrow to finish up. We aren't far from dark and I don't want to have to go back down that uneven trail when I can't see my feet."

"Plus you have a date with a wolf," Raul drawled.

Eyes twinkling, Will agreed. "Plus I have a date with a wolf."

ONCE they had a location, everything else seemed to fall into place. The spell, as Will had written it, worked beautifully. Starting the following afternoon, Will and Raul worked together; Will casting different spells on Raul. If a spell was cast outside the perimeter and either Will or Raul entered the cave, it was severed, but a spell cast with both of them inside the cave functioned normally.

Will was tempted to go ahead without Tristan's potion, but they only had one shot at this. If it didn't work and Richard reported their attempt to Sienna, they wouldn't get a second chance. They needed everything working in their favor, which meant waiting on his brother. Unable to connect with his twin, Will had resorted to using his cell phone to reach him. Tristan had promised to get the potion to him by this afternoon. While he waited, Will studied star charts and times of day, searching for alignments that would benefit them.

"What are you researching now?" Raul asked, walking into the suite and spotting the papers strewn all over the table, the seat of every chair but the one Will was sitting on, and down onto the floor.

"Alignments. Moon phases, times of day, planetary locations all have an influence on magic," Will answered.

Raul peered over his shoulder. "I had no idea that magic involved so much research. I thought it was something you were born with." He shifted some of the papers around. "Some of these charts seem to contradict one another."

Will grimaced. "Well, yeah, sometimes they do. You just have to go with what feels right. Magic is more of an art, not a science."

"I'm learning that."

"What have you been up to?" Will asked. "I haven't seen you since lunch."

"I've been with my father. He needed to know our plans."

Will put down his pencil, sitting back in his chair and staring at Raul. "Is he okay with all of this?"

"He wants Richard back. Meg has managed to keep his food and drink clear since Richard first returned home and he is getting stronger each day, but he isn't getting any younger and I'm no longer heir to the throne. He needs Richard free of Sienna's control so he can lead our pack. If we can accomplish that, Father's behind whatever we come up with." Raul poured himself a cup of coffee and leaned against the back of the couch. "Besides... he likes you."

Will's eyes widened in surprise. "Me? He hardly knows me."

He knows you are Richard's mate. "Werewolves rely on their instincts more than humans. He formed an opinion of you from your scent the first time he hugged you."

"The world might be a better place if we all relied a little more on our instincts," Will mused, picking his pencil back up. "We need to stock the cave with food and other camping supplies."

"Why?"

"Well, we are hoping that Sienna's spell will be broken like the spells I cast on you, but we know that she has been using some form of organic control as well. We don't know if Tristan's potion will work. We might have to keep Richard in the cave until Sienna's potion is metabolized out of his system," Will explained. "That could be several days."

"I hadn't thought of that." Raul paused. "Why don't you let me do that part? I can handle getting the cave stocked and let you worry about the magical elements that I don't understand. I'll also arrange for a couple of trusted Guardians to watch the area outside the cave."

"They might also be helpful if Richard doesn't wish to stay voluntarily," Will added. He was hoping that everything would play out exactly as planned, but he would be a fool not to consider the variables.

"How are we going to get Richard up to the cave in the first place?" Raul asked. "Do I ask him to take a walk and get lost?"

Will smirked. "Actually, I was planning on taking the wolf up with me at night."

"Ahh… now the truth comes out," Raul crowed. "Why didn't you just tell me to stock the cave with furs and lube?"

Blushing, Will crumpled a piece of paper and pitched it at Raul's head. "Fuck you."

"Well, I see your vocabulary hasn't improved," drawled a familiar voice from the doorway.

"Tristan!" Will shrieked, jumping to his feet and rushing to hug his twin. "What are you doing here?"

"You ordered a potion. What was I supposed to do—send it Fed Ex?"

"Yeah, that was kind of what I had in mind."

Tristan held his brother close, whispering directly against his ear. "You came across an ocean to stand by me when I needed you most. The least I could do was cross a couple of states."

Will swallowed to clear the tightness in his throat.

Tristan pulled back just far enough to lock eyes with Will. "We are stronger together and I could feel how important this is to you. It's no longer just about helping Raul."

Will felt his eyes well with tears. "No. No, it isn't." He buried his face against his twin's neck. "I've fallen in love with Richard."

Tristan rubbed Will's back. "I know, and if you hadn't said it, I'd have made you admit it. And for the record, I'm happy for you. I wholeheartedly endorse taking a werewolf as a mate," he teased, lightening the exchange and letting his twin get a hold of his emotions.

Will straightened, brushing the wet trails off his cheeks with the back of his hand. "I guess I've been bottling up my emotions a little." Tristan rolled his eyes at the understatement. Will asked, "Speaking of mates… how did you convince Benjamin to let you come?"

"By agreeing to bring me with him," Benjamin interjected, coming through the door. "Nice little cottage you've got here, Raul," he said, dropping a suitcase on the floor and embracing his friend.

Raul's hug lifted Benjamin completely off the floor. "Goddess, I've missed you."

"Bet I brought someone with me that you missed more…" Benjamin taunted.

Raul's arms dropped to his sides, limp. "You mean … ? But how … ? He'd have had to …." Without waiting for answers to any of his half-questions, Raul bolted out the door.

"Alex came too?" Will guessed.

"Not yet, but it's just a matter of time," both Tristan and Benjamin replied in unison, all three men breaking into laughter.

Chapter 19

RAUL ran down the hall to the balcony overlooking the foyer. Grasping the rail, he looked down. His mate was standing in the middle of a large circle of dignitaries and guards, talking with the king. Alex's clear hazel eyes immediately lifted, his look so charged with energy that everyone in the room reacted to it. All eyes followed Alex's look, settling on Raul. The king took a step back, making room for his son to join them, a knowing smile on his face.

Ten minutes ago, when Raul had thought it would be days if not weeks before he could be with his mate, the loneliness had been bearable; but having Alex here, only steps away, was intolerable. He felt like he was about to crawl out of his skin. Oblivious to everyone but his mate, Raul flew down the stairs and into Alex's arms.

Alex's control had reached its limits. He knew how important protocol was—especially in this first meeting with the alpha of another pack (not to mention his mate's sire), but the feel of Raul in his arms overshadowed everything. Tearing his face away from Raul's neck, he looked up and directly into the amused green eyes of King Randolf. A barely perceptible nod was all the permission he needed. With a powerful swoop, he bent, lifting Raul over his shoulder and heading for the stairs. The crowd parted, the scents of Alex's desire and possessiveness clearing the way. Twice when someone got too close, a warning growl sent them scuttling. No one was stupid enough to mess with an alpha in Alex's current state.

Following his mate's scent, Alex unerringly stalked toward Raul's suite, kicking open the door with his foot. Peripherally, he registered Tristan and Will's startled jumps and Benjamin's pleased expression, but nothing was going to deter him from reclaiming his mate.

The instant the door closed behind them, Alex dropped Raul to his feet, counting on his mate's werewolf reflexes to keep him from falling. Grabbing Raul's wrist, he slammed him up against the wall, hands caught over his head and hips pinned by the weight of Alex's body. "Mine," he snarled, baring his teeth as he leaned in close, smelling the desire and need rolling off Raul's skin. He was more than familiar with every little nuance of Raul's scent, but he had never smelled a need this strong.

Raul stared back at him, relaxed, exhibiting complete submission. Alex's wolf surged forward, impatient with the human interaction slowing the physical reclaiming of their mate. Alex growled, fighting himself and his wolf as he tried to regain some control. He tightened his grip on Raul's wrists, chest flattened against chest, his hips driving Raul back into the unforgiving wall. He thrilled at the sharp exhale against his mouth, the desire in Raul's eyes, and the unmistakable erection pressing against his thigh.

"Claim me," Raul whispered. He knew Alex was fighting his wolf. He could feel the slight tremble of Alex's muscles, the hitch of breath against his chest, the way his cock got even harder between them. "It's been too long. I need you to let go."

Alex searched Raul's eyes. He'd been able to think of little else but making love to Raul since he'd left New York. He wanted their first time to be slow and intense, but as usual, he had underestimated his need when it came to his mate. He wanted to lick, suck, bite, scratch, thrust and fuck Raul until he was *screaming*.

"Mine," Alex snarled, dropping his voice to a low rumble. "Mine." He seemed unable to produce any other thought. He transferred Raul's wrists to one hand, keeping them pinned over his head, feeling Raul arch against him. His other hand wove into the soft blond hair, grasping the strands, and jerking his head to the side, prompting a strangled moan. Enflamed, he dove forward, sealing his mouth over the pulsing vein of Raul's throat, teeth sinking into the flesh so hard he thought he was going to break skin, sucking at that spot, wanting, *needing* to leave a mark so everyone would know that Raul was *his* and that they had better keep their hands off if they valued their lives. He felt more than heard Raul groan, wrists twisting in his grasp, hips bucking forward, head slamming back against the wall and tugging against the fingers twined in his hair, but all Alex could think was *mine, mine, mine.* He growled again, dropping both the hands just long enough to tear Raul's shirt open, careless of the buttons ripping from their holes and flying through the air, needing only to touch, claim and mark. Grabbing Raul's wrists again, he pinned his hands next to his head, tearing his mouth from Raul's throat, pulling back to stare into his beloved's flushed, wide-eyed face with a feral grin.

"Mine," he rasped again, eyes flicking over the livid bruise on Raul's throat. His cock throbbed hard as Raul let out a low, rough moan, head falling back against the wall.

"Alex," he gasped, shuddering, and Alex took that as his cue, dragging his mouth down over Raul's neck and chest, biting down hard on a nipple and groaning as he felt Raul jerk against him. Skimming his teeth back up over trembling flesh, he dropped one of Raul's wrists and reached between them, tearing open the fastenings of Raul's trousers and shoving them down past his hips before reaching for his own, opening the flies and dragging his aching cock out, his need too urgent to bother with undressing.

"You are *mine,*" Alex snarled, every repetition making it feel more true. He slammed his hips forward so that their cocks slid against each other and gasped as Raul arched against him, wantonly seeking more. Alex wanted more, too, needed more, and then Raul was kicking his shoes off and fumbling out of his trousers and Alex groaned, sliding his hands down to Raul's armpits and lifting him bodily off the ground until their faces were even, until the head of his cock was pressed against Raul's eager, grasping hole.

Raul shuddered, wrapping bare legs around Alex's clothed hips, fingernails clawing at Alex's arms and head lolling off to the side as he hissed, "Please, Alex... please, fuck me!"

Alex barely had the presence of mind to spit in his hand and provide a minimum of lubrication before he was slamming forward, burying himself in his mate's body in one smooth, forceful, possessive thrust.

Raul *howled*, clutching at Alex's arms for dear life, heels digging into the small of Alex's back. His head tilted back, skin already slippery with sweat where it slid against Alex's clothed chest. His nails scratched at the cloth stretched over Alex's shoulders.

Alex sucked in a sharp breath, driving Raul back as he began to move, slowly at first, gaining speed with each thrust, hips pistoning forward and up as he fucked Raul mercilessly into the wall, lapping up every grunt and moan and gasp and desperate flex of toes against his back, dig of fingernails into his arms, and twist of forehead against his shoulder. The muscles in his legs screamed as he drove forward again and again, tongue flickering out to drag along the curve of Raul's neck, tasting salt and sweat and sex clinging to the flushed, salty skin. He could feel Raul tensing against him, his thighs clamping around his waist, the violent hitch of breath and strangled moans as Raul tried desperately to hold back, but Alex didn't want him to hold back. He wanted to feel Raul fall apart in his arms. He wanted confirmation that he was the only one who could make him feel this way. Raul belonged to him.

Shoving Raul's head to the side with his cheek, he bit down on the already-purpled bruise on his throat. That did it; with a hoarse, strangled shout, Raul seized, fingernails sinking into Alex's arms hard enough to draw blood, heels digging desperately into the curve of Alex's ass, head thrown back and spine arched so hard Alex thought it might snap as he shook and clenched and *came* in long, hard, sticky pulses over his stomach and Alex's shirt. The feel of that tight hole squeezing around his cock was too much and Alex followed with a gasped, choked cry, "Raul! Mine... mine... my love."

Alex's legs gave way, sending them both tumbling to the carpeted floor in a tangle of limbs and a sprawl of shaking, sweaty bodies. He panted against Raul's throat as he struggled to blink the haze of his orgasm out of his eyes, hyperaware of Raul clinging to him, body trembling with aftershocks. Tired, sated, and almost unbearably happy, Alex flicked out his tongue, swiping it over the possessive mark on Raul's throat.

Raul shuddered hard, dropping his forehead to Alex's shoulder. "Mother Goddess, Alex!"

Alex nodded, letting out a sharp bark of laughter as he wound his arms around Raul's back, lying flat and pulling his mate on top of him. Holding him close, he relaxed as Raul touched him, feeling all of his tension from their time apart dissipating with every wet kiss Raul pressed to his throat, every stroke of smooth hands over his back. Raul buried his face in Alex's neck, breathing softly against the skin.

After a long silence, during which he couldn't clutch Raul close enough, Alex finally moved, propping himself up on one elbow and looking at the other half of his soul, silently vowing that they would never be separated again. "I didn't hurt you, did I?" he murmured. Werewolves could take more than humans and healed fast, but the thought of causing Raul pain, no matter how fleeting, was intolerable.

Raul stared at him blankly, and then burst into laughter. "Hardly! I don't think I've ever felt better," he snorted, shaking his head.

"Good," Alex said, raising a hand to smooth his palm over Raul's cheek, then resting two fingers atop the bruise and pressing lightly, a frisson of pleasure twisting his spine at Raul's hiss and flutter of eyelids.

"Our friends may have a few colorful comments to make about our entrance," Raul said, catching his hand and lifting it to his mouth to kiss the rough fingertips.

Alex shook his head. "Don't care." Twisting his fingers around Raul's, he pulled their clasped hands to his chest and shut him up rather effectively with a forceful, possessive kiss. A trill of desire shot down his spine as Raul arched into him with a soft, pleased moan, swollen lips parting beneath his.

"So do we go out there?" Alex murmured when he finally let Raul up for air.

"Hardly," Raul barked. "I'm not done with you yet."

Alex grinned. Gathering Raul into his arms, he stood and walked toward the bed.

RAUL smelled dawn. Without opening his eyes, he curled closer to Alex, burying his nose his lover's warm fur. They'd changed to wolf form around three a.m., heading off into the woods to hunt and frolic. Completely exhausted, they'd returned, curled up in the center of the bed—making a mess of the sheets—and fallen asleep.

Raul didn't want to wake up now. The steady beat of his mate's heart and the familiar musk of his fur were lulling his wolf back to sleep, but his mind kicked in, making him feel guilty. He had wasted an entire day satisfying his desires. He'd been supposed to stock the cave, help Will get ready for the full moon in two days' time. He readjusted his position, his wolf still campaigning for more sleep.

Alex's head came up, curving over his back and nudging him back down to his side. Raul relaxed for a few more minutes until he heard Will and Tristan talking in the outer room. Standing, he extended his paws on the bed and stretched. Between the sex and the run, his muscles were sure to be sore and stiff today. Alex's teeth nipped at his haunch and he yelped, bounding to the floor, shimmering into his human form and pouncing on his lover.

Before Raul's body impacted, Alex changed to his human form, leaving them naked and pressed chest to knee. Raul reacted immediately, his cock hardening and his hips thrusting forward instinctively. Bracing his arms, he lifted himself away from temptation. "Fuck, we can't do this," he groaned, backing off the bed.

Alex's arms circled his waist, pulling him close. "Seems like we can," he snickered, glancing down at the matching erections nestled between them.

Swatting Alex's shoulder, Raul attempted to roll to the side. "I don't mean we can't. I mean we shouldn't. We are very close to breaking the spell on Richard and Will needs my help. I forgot all about him last night, and I need to make it up to him."

Alex bristled even though he understood what Raul was trying to say. Threading his fingers into the soft blond hair, he pulled his mate close for a deep, hungry kiss that he ended reluctantly with a series of slow, sweet tugs on Raul's bottom lip. "If you insist," he groaned, allowing Raul to slide out of his arms. "Will you at least feed me first?"

Raul headed for the bathroom. "You're hungry again? We just ate three hours ago."

"We've burned a lot of calories since then," Alex reminded him, standing and starting to follow Raul.

Blocking his entrance with the door, Raul shook a finger at him. "Ohhh... no. If you come in here, it'll be lunchtime before we get dressed. Go find us coffee."

The door shut and Alex heard the click of the lock just as he was reaching for the knob. *Damn, Raul knew him too well.* With a resigned shrug, he pulled a pair of boxers from the floor and headed toward the sound of voices.

WILL looked up as Alex walked through the door. Pausing just inside the room, the werewolf king looked around, really seeing the room for the first time. "Good morning," he greeted. Scratching at his bare chest, he walked out onto the balcony.

"Raul'll want coffee," Will said, getting up from the couch and walking over to the bar.

Tristan's eyes followed Alex and then darted back to the closed bedroom door. "You two have gotten to know each other inside and out, haven't you?"

Will's mouth pulled up into a grin. "Yeah, I guess we have. He didn't trust me at all when we first started, but he let me put spell after spell on him over the last few days and didn't even blink."

"Wow! That's some change." Tristan watched his twin fix Raul's coffee with sugar and cream. "You need to be careful. Even I can sense the easy intimacy between the two of you. Alex won't like it."

"What?" Will looked up, startled. He couldn't believe his twin would even say such a thing. "He's mated and I'm in love with his twin. I'd never—"

Tristan laid a hand on Will's shoulder to calm him. "I know that and Alex does, too, but it won't stop him from reacting like you're a threat. It's his job to care for his mate, not yours." He motioned to the steaming cup in Will's hand.

"Should I pour it out?" Will asked. "I hate coffee." It was obvious that things were going to change now that Alex had joined them. He hoped he could stay one step ahead and prevent a serious social gaffe. Even living among werewolves for the last few months, he still didn't think like one.

His twin circled his neck, pulling him close in an affectionate squeeze. "No, just make one for Alex too. It is only special attention to his mate that will bother him. Speaking of mates, I should go find mine."

Quickly pouring a second cup, Will walked out onto the balcony where Alex was scanning the countryside. "Coffee?" he offered, handing over the mug. "I didn't know how you liked it."

"Black is fine. Where's Ben?"

"I think he's still in bed. Tristan just went to go find him."

"I may as well go back to bed then. They'll be hours." Alex chuckled, leaning back against the railing and crossing his feet as he sipped his coffee. Shrewd hazel eyes studied Will. "Do you think you'll be able to help Richard?"

"A week ago I wouldn't have been so sure, but I think we've got it figured out. Some of it will depend on Richard. We can free him from the spell, but he has to decide what he wants. If he goes back to Sienna voluntarily, there is nothing I can do."

"I don't think you have to worry about that." Will shifted under Alex's intent stare. "Werewolves mate for life and they have no tolerance for anyone who interferes with that bond."

Will bit his lip, wishing he drank coffee so he'd have a mug in his hand—a place to focus his gaze. He couldn't look at Alex. The Rajan's eyes were too knowing. "I'm the one messing with bonds."

"Are you?" Alex asked, breaking off as Raul walked out of the bedroom. Covering the distance between them in a handful of long strides, the werewolf king enveloped his consort.

Will watched, his chest aching. He wanted the kind of easy intimacy the couples around him shared.

Chapter 20

"READY?" Tristan asked, drawing Will's gaze away from the moon hanging low and full in the sky.

"No, but it's now or never," Will muttered, walking through the open French doors into the living room. He was worried about tonight—about Richard's reaction. He hadn't voiced his fears to anyone but he could see that Tristan knew something was on his mind. "What if it isn't the spell? What if he really wants to be with her?"

Tristan cuffed his twin's shoulder, attempting to lighten the moment. "Who in their right mind would choose her over you?"

Will's eyes narrowed, staring at his twin. "Oh, I don't know… any heterosexual man?"

"I think we've established that Richard is not strictly heterosexual. He couldn't keep his hands off you from the moment you met and he's been coming to you every night in spite of a strong spell. You're overthinking this. Your power comes from your emotions—your heart, not your head. We've prepared everything we can think of. It's time to quit worrying and act. Sienna is already suspicious over our arrival. We don't want to give her the time to figure out what we're up to."

Will nodded, swallowing the last of his tea before putting the mug on the bar. "I guess I need to go to bed then and pray for a nighttime visitor."

"You've been slipping him our potion, right?" Tristan asked, waiting for his brother's affirmative answer before continuing. "And he's been coming every night?"

Unable to resist, Will grinned and winked. "Sometimes more than once."

"Fucker." Tristan slapped at his brother's head as his twin dodged the blow.

"Children!" Raul called, walking into the room with Alex and Benjamin following him.

"He started it!" both brothers accused, pointing at each other before collapsing into a giggle heap on the couch.

"Do I even want to know?" Alex whispered, leaning close to Benjamin's ear.

"Probably not," Benjamin answered. "I've noticed before that they sometimes respond to stress with silliness."

"Everybody knows the plan, right?" Raul asked, completely ignoring the twins wrestling on the couch.

"And Raul responds with stoicism," Alex supplied, sharing a look with Benjamin. "Shall we intervene?"

Benjamin shrugged. "I guess we are going to have to." Reaching down, he wrapped a strong arm around his lover's waist, lifting him off Will. "Behave or I won't—"

He didn't even have to finish his threat. Tristan immediately calmed at his lover's touch, standing placidly at Benjamin's side as soon as the werewolf lowered his feet to the floor.

"Right," Raul continued, "Will gets Richard up to the cave. Tristan helps with the spell while Benjamin patrols the perimeter."

"And you and I make sure Sienna stays here," Alex finished the duty list.

"I've been thinking," Will added, "someone should have eyes on Arthur. I'm still not sure what his role is in all this, but he definitely isn't as innocent as he appears."

"Hell, subtle won't matter if this works… and if it doesn't, Arthur will be the least of our worries. I'll just have Dad order the Guardians to sit on him," Raul suggested.

Will shrugged. "Why not? Keep him away from phones so he can't warn Sienna."

"Done," Raul pronounced, picking up the phone.

Tristan pulled his brother into a hug. "We're gonna head up to the cave. I've not been up there after dark. The moonlight will help—it's bright as day out there—but I'd rather not have to rush on that trail."

"I'll be right behind you," Will whispered into Tristan's curls.

"I've got your back. Sienna's going to learn tonight that you don't mess with the Northland twins."

"Damn straight."

"Ahh… guys," Raul said.

Will turned to find Richard's wolf prowling in through the balcony doors. Its gaze instantly locked on Alex. Richard had been introduced to Alex in human form, but his wolf was clearly not happy to have any alpha this close to his mate. His lips drew back in a snarl, baring his teeth, the fur on his back rising.

Will took a step forward, but Raul's hand on his arm stopped him. "If this is going to blow up, you don't want to be in the middle of it."

"I can't… That's your mate and your twin. Don't you care if they kill each other?" Will argued.

"Alex is better than that," Raul whispered, his tone showing his complete confidence and trust in his mate.

Alex's eyes met Raul's and he held out his hand. Raul immediately went to his side, pressing close, Alex's arm moved around his shoulders. The couple held completely still, eyes lowered, not wanting any sudden move to be perceived as a threat. Alex was the alpha of his pack, but Richard was heir here and his wolf deserved respect and deference, if not submission.

"What are they doing?" Will asked Benjamin in a hushed voice.

"They are giving Richard's wolf time to process their scent as a couple. A mated alpha isn't a threat—at least to you, which seems to be all Richard is worried about. The fact that the alpha is mated to his twin doesn't hurt either." Benjamin nodded to the door. "We should leave the room."

Will shook his head, still worried. Richard had quit growling, but his hackles were still up. "No, he won't hurt me. Take Tristan and go up to the cave. We still have work to do tonight, if things don't blow up in the next ten minutes."

Raul had told Will to stay out of it, but every instinct the witch had was pushing him forward. He took a hesitant step. Raul's eyes shot up, silently warning him not to come any closer, but Alex's hand tightened on his mate's side, countermanding the admonition. Will's eyes darted from Raul to Alex and then down to the amber wolf as he made his decision.

This was about him, and Richard needed to know that Alex was no threat. Taking another step, Will dropped to his knees at the wolf's side. Sinking his fingers in the dense fur, he buried his face against the wolf's neck. The wolf rocked its weight against him, knocking him to the floor and lying down across his chest. Turning his eyes away in submission, Will relaxed, his hand rising to burrow into the soft fur of the wolf's underbelly. He didn't use words, but every touch screamed, "I belong to you."

Will could feel the wolf's heartbeat slow. The muscles under his fingers were still tense, but the fur was no longer bristling. The wolf nudged at Will's chin with its muzzle and the witch looked up, catching Alex and Raul disappearing through the door in his peripheral vision. The wolf stared down at him with a steady yellow-green gaze. Reaching up, Will smoothed the fur back from his face, pausing to rub the thick ears. He always looked forward to Richard changing to his human form, but he had to admit that he was developing a serious attachment to his wolf. Rising up on his elbows, he wrapped his arms around the wolf's neck, whispering soothing sounds into the coarse fur.

Richard's wolf rolled to the side and Will sat up, an idea forming in his mind. He'd been struggling with how to get Richard to the cave. They didn't communicate verbally during these nighttime encounters so he couldn't just ask, and he didn't see himself putting a leash on Richard's wolf, but maybe he could use another one of the wolf's natural behaviors....

Will pounced forward unexpectedly, toppling the wolf onto its side and burying his face in the soft white fur of its belly and blowing. Laughing, he turned and crawled away, throwing a look over his shoulder that clearly challenged, "Come and get me."

Richard's wolf was on its feet barreling into him before he reached the couch. The heavy weight pinned him to the floor, but then eased just enough for Will to wriggle free. Getting to his feet, he sprinted for the balcony, the wolf literally snapping at his heels. Will laughed again as adrenaline surged through his system.

The chase was on.

Bracing his hand on the railing, Will propelled himself over, landing gracefully on the grass and running for the trees. Before he could gain any speed, the wolf tackled him, sending them both rolling. This time the wolf was the first to his feet, leaving Will to be the pursuer. Their game of tag continued, until Will was out of breath and more than a little sore. He'd managed to guide their game to the base of the path that climbed to the cave but didn't relish being tackled on the narrow, rocky path. Surging forward, he grabbed at the wolf and they both hit the ground in a tight embrace.

Following the rhythm of their game, Will should have gotten to his feet and bolted, but instead he held tight, resting his head on the furry chest while he tried to catch his breath. Will could feel the blood pounding in his ears, matching the beat of the heart under his cheek. He stroked the rough fur and called to his lover, "Richard," his desire evident in his tone.

In the span of a heartbeat, Richard changed, his arms pulling Will close and his mouth claiming a heated kiss. All of the energy raised during their chase flowed into their kiss, leaving both men aroused and panting. Richard yanked at Will's clothes, intent on removing the last of the barriers between them, but Will firmly stilled his hands.

"This way," Will rasped, keeping Richard's hand in his and leading him up the path to the cave. Richard was as surefooted in human form as he was as a wolf, steadying Will as he slipped on loose rocks, the uneven ground not seeming to bother his bare feet.

By the time they reached the cave, Richard seemed to know where they were going, rounding the corner and entering the opening with no hesitation. Had his human half been in charge, the prepared setting might have made him pause, but Richard's wolf was focused on claiming Will, and the pile of soft furs was the only thing in the well-stocked cave that caught his attention. Sweeping his lover off his feet, he dropped him into the soft bed.

Will kicked off his shoes and reached for the buttons on his shirt, as anxious as Richard to release the energy of their chase, but his lover wasn't waiting. The shirt was easily ripped open, buttons flying in every direction. Will managed to get the buttons on his jeans open before Richard stripped them off with a single strong tug from the bottom that lifted Will almost completely off the makeshift bed. The light from the lantern disappeared as his lover loomed over him, magnificent and aroused. Will shivered, all doubts about Richard's desire for him evaporating.

This was right. This was real. All that was left was to break the bonds of evil that Will could feel, like oil scum on the surface of the ocean, and he knew just how to do that. Letting all his love show on his face, he opened his arms. He'd been wanting to apply his magic to breaking through Sienna's spell for days, anxious for Tristan's potion to reach full strength.

Richard crouched immediately, stretching his body on top of Will's and pressing the slender witch deep into the luxurious furs. Distantly Will remembered Tristan sharing that Benjamin had formally claimed him as his mate in a very similar setting. The second Richard's mouth touched his, all thoughts of anything but the feel of the man above him vanished. His hands clutched at the rolling hips as Richard moved against him.

Since Richard's wolf had begun breaking free for nocturnal visits, the first time between them was always explosive—raw and hungry. Tonight was no different. If anything their game of chase had heightened their need. Spreading his legs, Will wrapped them around his lover, pulling him into an intimate embrace. His hand searched the furs for the lube Raul had teased him about stocking. Fingers closing around the smooth plastic, he worked a hand between them, circling his lover's hot, hard shaft.

Richard pushed up, supporting his weight on his arms to allow Will more freedom to touch him, a low rumble of approval building as the slippery hand moved up and down his erection. Slipping his hand between his own legs, Will quickly spread the excess lube. His patience gone, he lifted his legs to Richard's shoulders. The werewolf didn't need more of an invitation, penetrating the tight hole with a steady thrust, retreating and then slamming deep.

Will cried out, his body arching. Richard pushed up onto his knees, lifting Will's hips off the furs and allowing him to plunge deeper into the welcoming channel. Will's head tossed from side to side, his hands scrabbling for purchase in the silky furs. A steady stream of curses and praise fell from his lips, forming a worshipful chant. Every thrust pushed him higher in the soft pile.

Reaching above his head, Will's hands connected with the cold stone wall. He pressed them flat, bracing himself. Focusing on his building orgasm, Will opened himself to the energy flowing up from the earth. He could feel his body flushing with heat, Richard's movements speeding up as the energy flowed through their connected bodies into him. Will held back as long as he could, his heels pressing into Richard's back as he encouraged him to drive faster and deeper. At the first twitch of the werewolf's climax, Will let go, his own orgasm washing through his body. He opened himself completely, becoming a conduit for the energy flowing from Richard and the earth and pushing it into the spell that would shield them from the world. As the burning heat of the energy spread through the rock, he felt the familiar presence of Tristan's magic joining with his, making the barrier stronger and thicker, guiding the raw power flowing from his twin. The circle of magic closed on itself, the force physically jarring Will's body as it locked them inside.

Chapter 21

RICHARD collapsed forward into Will's arms, his body shaking. Will didn't know if it was from the force of his orgasm or a response to the shield being put in place. Worried, he lifted his lover's head to be able to see his face. Steady emerald eyes stared back at him, blank at first and then growing unfocused before settling into confusion.

"It's okay. You're safe," Will reassured, his hands running in soothing strokes up and down Richard's back and arms.

"Will?" Richard's brow furrowed as he attempted to piece his disjointed thoughts together.

"Yeah," Will whispered. "How do you feel?"

"Like I was hit by a bus and left on the side of the road." Richard looked around the cave. "Where are we?"

"A cave northeast of the house. Raul helped me find it so we could be alone," Will explained. Once he determined Richard's state of mind, he'd complete the explanation.

"I… shit…." Richard scrubbed his fingers through his hair, pushing himself off Will and sitting up next to him. "I can't…." The agitation rolled off of him in waves.

Will turned to his side, propping his head up with his elbow. "It's okay. Take it slow."

"It feels like someone has made a jigsaw puzzle of my memories. I have all these disjointed thoughts—just flashes of moments or feelings. How long have I been home?"

"Several weeks. What do you remember?" Will coaxed.

"I remember being at the farmhouse with you and Raul." A soft glow warmed his eyes as he looked down at Will. "I remember being so angry... up in my father's suite... and then nauseous... and a terrible pain in my head."

Will sat up and pulled the werewolf into his arms, holding him close to his chest. "Does it hurt now?" he asked cautiously, smoothing Richard's hair with his hand in much the same way he'd pet his wolf.

"No, nothing hurts now. Everything feels right again."

Will relaxed, releasing the tension he'd been holding for days. "I've missed you." He felt a prickling as his eyes filled with tears, but he blinked them away. He would not give in to tears of relief when he'd managed to refrain from tears of frustration and pain.

"She did it again," Richard stated matter-of-factly. "And I let her. I've been a real asshole to you." Pulling back just slightly, he cupped Will's cheek with his hand. Will turned into the touch, placing a kiss in the smooth palm.

"Why are you still here?" Richard asked. "Why didn't you leave me here to straighten out my own mess?"

Will leaned forward and placed a gentle kiss on Richard's lips. "Because I care what happens to you," he admitted softly. "And I wasn't alone. Your wolf was around to keep me company. I wasn't about to leave him at her mercy."

The confusion flooded back into Richard's eyes. "My wolf?"

Will wondered exactly how much Richard would remember of the time when his wolf was in charge. As the herbs worked their way out of his system, he would probably remember more. "He's been sneaking away from Sienna and coming to me at night."

Richard chuckled, his head falling forward to rest on Will's shoulder. "He always was smarter than me."

"Oh, yeah?"

Lifting both hands to cradle Will's face, Richard looked straight into Will's dark eyes. "Yeah... he knew right away what we had found in you. What you meant to us."

Will swallowed the tightness rising in his throat. "What do I mean to you?"

Richard looked away with a nervous shift that made Will tense again.

"Richard?" he prodded gently. "There's a lot of shit going on out there and we have a limited amount of time. We're only going to beat Sienna for good if we're completely honest with each other. I need to know how you feel about me. *You*. Not your wolf."

The werewolf took a deep breath and faced Will again. "There isn't a difference, you know. I can try and ignore my wolf, but there isn't one feeling that we don't share. I should have been honest with you back at Nanna's house."

Will shivered, wishing suddenly for his clothes as if they would protect him from whatever it was Richard was about to say.

"That morning we first made love... the morning I got my memory back...." Richard paused, reaching for Will's hand, pulling it to his lap and fiddling with the long fingers.

Will turned his hand over, threading their fingers together and squeezing. Richard's eyes rose from their joined hands to make contact again. "You can tell me anything," Will said. "If I'm still here, fighting for us, with the way you've been treating me the last few days...."

Richard nodded. In a voice just above a whisper, he said, "I bonded with you that morning. I know I didn't ask or even tell you what I was feeling."

Will had felt the power of their joining that morning; he had used it to help break through the spell that bound Richard's mind, but he didn't really understand.

"I claimed you as my mate," Richard blurted, stopping Will's racing thoughts.

The witch froze, focused completely on the word "mate." He knew what mating meant to a wolf. "But I—"

"I know," Richard continued, preventing Will from saying something he didn't want to hear. "I was wrong and I may pay for it the rest of my life."

Will's forehead wrinkled. "How were you wrong? I didn't think there was any doubt when a werewolf found his mate."

"There isn't," Richard confirmed. "But that doesn't mean you have to feel the same way. I chose you as my mate, but you aren't a werewolf. You don't have to stay with me. Based on the way I've treated you since we've met, logically, you shouldn't."

Silence filled the cave until Richard could hear Will's heartbeat and the hiss of the lantern became almost overwhelming. He held his breath, waiting for Will to answer… to say something… anything.

Will finally spoke. "Good thing I'm not all that logical then, huh?"

Richard watched as Will's mouth turned up in a slow smile and then moved toward his mate. Catching him en route, Richard pulled him the rest of the way, tilting his head so their mouths fit together perfectly.

Breathless and aroused, Will forced himself to pull away from Richard's intoxicating kiss. "We've got to talk first. We always end up making love and not saying the things that need to be said. I need to tell you why we're here," he started, unable to stop himself from stealing another quick kiss. "Sienna has been controlling you with potions and spells. I don't know exactly which ones, but her control seems to correlate with her proximity. I've spelled this cave. It has a shield around it, blocking all magic. As long as you are in here and she is out there, her spells can't affect you."

"So we're just living in here for the rest of our lives?" Richard joked. At Will's scowl, he quit teasing. "Well, your shield is obviously working. My only desire is to see her gone. So what do we do now?"

"Well... I have an idea, but...." Will's eyes shifted everywhere but Richard's face.

"You're not sure I'll go for it. You are my mate. I'll deny you nothing within my power," Richard vowed.

Will felt the truth of Richard's words and met the steady green gaze. "If we can raise enough energy and channel it into a bonding spell between us, it should be strong enough to protect you from any spell she could cast."

"For how long?"

"Theoretically—forever. But...." Will's voice trailed off. "That means the bonding would be permanent as well."

Richard took Will into his arms and held him close. "I've claimed you as my mate," he whispered, stroking the dark curls back from his lover's face. "I've already committed my life to you."

"This would be intentional."

"My choice to claim you as my mate was intentional. I had my memory back by the time I made my choice," Richard confessed.

Will looked flabbergasted. "You risked your feelings not being reciprocated after a couple days of hot sex?"

Richard shrugged. "I risked nothing. You were mine... or, I guess more correctly, I was yours from the moment our hands touched at the jail. Claiming you was just the formality. My heart and my wolf would have been yours anyway. It just made sense to enjoy being able to claim you physically when you already owned me emotionally, but what about you? Binding yourself to me seems rather extreme to help a werewolf you hardly know."

Richard was fishing and Will knew it. He could sense no tension in the werewolf and Richard wouldn't be nearly this relaxed if he wasn't certain that his feelings were returned. It wasn't taking much effort to support the shield with Tristan's energy augmenting his power, but it couldn't be maintained indefinitely, so there was not much to be gained by playing coy.

"I may not have a werewolf's instincts to help me identify my perfect mate, but I know my heart… and it belongs to you. If the mating instinct is never wrong, then this choice is as right for me as it is for you," Will reasoned. "This spell will be the equivalent of my mating ritual."

Will's hand stroked up Richard's chest, his eyes dancing with mischief. "I know it will be a hardship, but the best way to raise the energy we need will be an extended period of passionate sex."

A possessive growl rose from Richard's throat as he lunged forward and sealed his lips to Will's. Falling back onto the cushion of furs, he pulled Will on top of him without breaking the kiss. Mouths open, lips, teeth, and tongues explored at a leisurely pace. Richard surrendered to the scent and taste of his mate. His cock hardened, trapped in the tantalizing friction between their bodies, but he felt no urgency to do anything except hold Will close and learn every spot that made his mate squirm and sigh. His hands ran freely over every inch of exposed skin.

Cupping Will's perfect ass, Richard lifted him higher so his mouth could reach the tempting dark nipples, each nub receiving the same focused attention until Will's hands were fisted in his hair and his pleading had been reduced to a continuous babble of moans and curses. The tips of Richard's fingers slid into the damp crease defining his lover's ass, spreading it open to graze over the recently fucked hole.

Will gasped, twisting in his embrace. "Fuck, Richard! Please!"

"Too soon," the werewolf reminded. "You said extended and I haven't had the pleasure of indulging in the appetizing scent you give off when you are turned on. My wolf is acting entirely too smug from lying with you without my participation."

Richard's hands skimmed up Will's sides, hooking him under the arms and lifting the witch even higher. Scooting down between Will's legs, Richard's mouth had complete access to his cock and balls as the witch knelt over his face. Whimpering, Will fell forward, bracing himself on the stone wall to keep from collapsing altogether as Richard's mouth sucked at the sensitive skin, pulling first one and then both orbs into his mouth. His tongue flicked and jabbed, pushing up between the clenching cheeks. He could taste his release on Will's skin and the mixture made him reach for his own dick, stroking it leisurely, all of his attention still fixed on pleasuring the man above him.

Will shamelessly rode Richard's face, his thighs moving him up and down as he fucked himself on his lover's tongue. Wanting… no, needing… to come, his muscles quivered. His hand closed around his cock, shuttling rapidly up and down the hard shaft.

Richard's fingers circled his wrist like steel. "No, don't touch yourself," he commanded, moving Will's hand away from his erection.

"But…." Will pleaded. "I…." His balls ached and his cock slapped wetly against his belly with each bounce.

"I know what you need," Richard rasped, his lips teasing the inside of Will's thigh, his nails grazing the ticklish skin along the bottom curve of his ass.

Will cried out, his thighs trembling and threatening to give out completely. "So give it to me!"

A satisfied chuckle rumbled up from Richard's chest. He'd clamped down hard on his wolf. It was struggling to be freed, but Richard wanted a little more time to enjoy Will exclusively with his human side. The desperation in their mate's voice was making his wolf restless. The wolf's nocturnal visits had forged a deep bond with Will, and he wasn't happy being held back. *Just a little longer,* Richard thought, his hand reaching up and circling Will's cock, pulling him firmly down and sucking at the pink opening. Sliding his free hand up Will's thigh, he slipped a finger in next to his tongue.

"Oh, fuck... Richard!" Will screamed, his body rocking helplessly between the dual stimulation of his cock and ass. Falling forward, he caught himself on shaky arms. The new angle allowed Richard to guide Will's leaking cock to his mouth, leaving his fingers to fuck the tender hole.

"You're gonna kill me," Will panted, his hips thrusting erratically. "I can't think. I need to concentrate to be able to—"

Richard sucked harder, taking more of Will's length into his mouth, his mate's taste coating his tongue.

"Fuck. We need to use this energy." Will struggled to get away from the overwhelming stimulation. "We'll lose the—" A strong shudder seized his body.

Richard pulled his mouth away long enough to rasp, "Send it to me. Send me the energy." He hadn't given many blowjobs in his life, his wolf resisting the submissive position, but pleasing his mate this way felt completely different. His wolf's agitation had nothing to do with fighting against submission. It was pure need to take and claim his mate in every way possible. There was nothing he wouldn't give or do for Will.

Will threw his head back, keening until the sound filled the room, echoing off the rock. Clamping down on Richard's fingers to hold them in his body, he came down his lover's throat, one hand falling from the stone to thread into the soft blond hair, opening a conduit for the energy exploding out of him. Massaging Richard's head, Will rode out the violent aftershocks. He gasped as Richard guided him to lie down in the furs without withdrawing his fingers.

Pulling his mate into the protective circle of his arm, Richard rode the dual feelings of his own arousal and his mate's sated completion, his body humming with the excess energy. Shifting Will closer and fitting their bodies together, he brushed soft kisses over the damp curls, his fingers moving in slow, lazy thrusts that kept Will half-hard and unable to collapse into the post-orgasmic stupor he craved.

Summoning the last of his power, Will tried to pull Richard on top of him. "We need to continue to build the energy or we'll lose it."

Richard twisted his fingers, grinding his erection against Will's hip. "There is one more thing I have to tell you before you bind yourself to me."

"Now you bring it up. I think you may be stacking the deck in your favor," Will moaned as Richard's fingers brushed his prostate, keeping him on the brink of a second orgasm.

"I hope so." Richard's cock surged and threatened to spill as Will's eyes closed, a wave of sensual pleasure washing over his face. "If you stay to be my mate and consort, you will have to be changed."

Will's eyes flew open. *Changed?*

Chapter 22

Doubt etched a furrow between Richard's eyes as he waited for Will's reaction. He could feel the energy that had been pulsing within him start to diminish. "I wish I hadn't goaded Raul into giving up his birthright, but I'm committed to ruling our pack, and the king's consort must be a werewolf." He started to pull his fingers from Will's body. It wasn't fair to try and influence Will's decision by distracting him with passion.

"Wait! I knew that; I just hadn't thought it through." Will's fingers locked around Richard's wrist, holding his hand in place. "Don't stop."

"But—"

"We'll do what we have to do." Will tossed a leg over Richard's hip, using the leverage to rock them together, Richard's fingers sliding easily in and out of him.

"Don't you want—?"

"Is it that hard to believe that I want to spend the rest of my life with you no matter what? I may not have your innate instinct to mate, but I felt the same connection between us that you did."

"I don't know what it will do to your powers," Richard said. Intellectually, he doubted that anyone would surrender themselves so selflessly, even though his heart, body, and wolf were in complete agreement: Will was theirs and needed to be claimed.

Will pulled up to his knees, straddling Richard's thighs and dragging his fingertips down the furry chest to brush over the full shaft rising from the tangle of dark blond curls. "Do you want me for my powers?"

Richard's breath caught, his eyes squeezing shut. "No-o."

Will smiled, power surging through him at the raw desire exposed by the tremble in his lover's voice. He let the energy trail out his fingers and dance over the surface of Richard's skin as he stroked. "Then let's finish this. We'll talk details later. Open your eyes. I want you to look at me while you claim me."

Richard's wolf swelled with satisfaction at their mate's willingness, but Richard kept him controlled. He wouldn't let this moment be lost to mindless desire. Grabbing Will's hips, he rolled his lover beneath him. "You'll always be mine."

When Richard finally opened his eyes and looked down at Will, he murmured, "Just looking at you under me this way is enough to make me come: do you know that?"

Will's breath caught in the back of his throat, and he felt hot color suffuse his cheeks.

"If you wouldn't stay, I'd find a way to leave," Richard added quietly.

Will's eyes widened in surprise. He watched Richard's gaze dart between his eyes and his mouth. Wrapping a hand around Richard's neck, he pulled himself up for a kiss. Their lips brushed together, and then Richard buried his face in Will's neck, sucking in mouthfuls of taut skin and placing wet kisses along his jaw to his ear.

Will shuddered under the assault, almost desperate for Richard to let go and ravish him. "More."

"Soon. You said to make you mine." Richard lifted Will's hand, kissing the tip of each finger, the rough pad of his thumb teasing his palm. Will felt the soft press of Richard's fingertips as they drew on the tender skin of his wrist, circling his pulse point and traveling up the inside of his arm, continuing steadily over the silky skin to his chest. Will sighed and twisted his body instinctively into the touch. The hand moved lower, the fingers joined by the press of a palm as Richard's hand mapped Will's body. Teasing his side, Richard's thumb strayed onto Will's chest to circle his hard nipple before moving again. He followed the shape of Will's waist to the ridge of his hipbone, letting the fingers stray down to caress the slight swell of Will's buttock. The hand continued along Will's thigh, which was bent upwards and wrapped around Will's hip. It finally stopped at Will's knee and began a slow return journey.

It was such an intimate, possessive touch that Will felt ready to explode. This tender exploration felt a thousand times more personal than the dozens of times they'd had hot and passionate sex. He could feel the power he'd released earlier pulsing between them, growing with each touch. Richard's face held an expression of satisfied possession. It was a look so intense, it felt as if Richard could see inside him: his deepest secrets, his greatest desires. But even that exposed, he felt safe, cherished... loved.

"Mark me," Will challenged, offering his neck. When Richard hesitated, he raised a knee, pressing his thigh firmly between Richard's legs and prompting a hair-raising groan.

Richard's mouth dropped to the tender flesh, his tongue rasping up the smooth skin and his teeth nipping at the tempting earlobe. Will's body undulated under him, his hands grasping Richard's hips to pull him closer. "Shhh...." Richard soothed, allowing the frottage until Will's chest flushed and the pulse in his neck pounded. Lowering his mouth to the pounding vein, he sucked, lifting the taste of his mate's desire from the skin. Will's hands delved deep into his hair, urging him on. He increased the suction, pulling the skin between his teeth and biting.

"Ah, fuck!" Will screamed, his hips bucking off the fur pallet. "Fill me. Please!"

A satisfied chuckle rose in Richard's throat. This is how Will should always be: naked and begging. "Soon," he purred, his hands sliding underneath Will's hips to lift him tighter to his body. Sliding down, he raised matching bruises to the left of Will's nipple and in the hollow of his hipbone. His head turning to nuzzle the musky curls, he rubbed his lips and cheeks over Will's cock and balls, painting himself with the arousing scent. He could feel his own power mixing with the energy Will had channeled into him and knew he couldn't hold it much longer.

Richard braced himself over Will's trembling body. "Damn, I have no control when it comes to you."

Will's face glowed. "And I love that." Reaching between their bodies, he wrapped his hand around Richard's cock, lifting his knees and guiding it into his body. "Now make me scream."

Swooping down to steal a hard kiss, Richard thrust forward. "Mine," he growled, letting his feelings show in his eyes. Sensing it was important for him to hold nothing back from this moment, he released his wolf.

Will watched as Richard's eyes warmed to the deepest green he had ever seen and then shifted to the more familiar yellow-green of his wolf. Will's body responded immediately, his cock twitching in anticipation. He'd experienced extreme pleasure under that luminous stare over the last few nights, and that reminder on top of the extended foreplay almost sent him over the edge.

Richard reached across the makeshift bed to recover the discarded bottle of lubricant, painting his erection liberally from top to bottom. Will reached out, his hand joining Richard's in slow, leisurely strokes. With a warning growl, he pushed Will's hand away, his fingers moving to the entrance to his body. Will spread his legs as wide as they would go, offering himself. Richard groaned as he knelt between the open legs, staring down with a look of undiluted lust.

Will rolled his hips, begging Richard silently to get on with it and take him. It was strange how easily he slipped into nonverbal communication at the appearance of Richard's wolf's eyes. He lifted his legs and circled Richard's hips, coaxing his body forward into position. Angling his hips up sharply, he hooked his heels together in the small of Richard's back and pulled him in. As he tightened his legs, Richard's cock breached him, rubbing him in all the right places.

Will didn't know it was possible to want anything as much as he wanted this. Every part of his body screamed for Richard's touch. He wasn't used to Richard's wolf having this much control. Focusing on his lover's face, he was surprised to find the deep emerald gaze staring down at him. Goddess, he had both of them. His heart rate jumped and he gasped raggedly, "Make me yours."

Richard covered Will's body with his own, balancing his weight on his forearms and bringing their faces close together. Will's vision was full of Richard's eyes, and a small tilt of his chin brushed their lips together. Reluctantly, he released the tempting mouth, caressing Richard's muscular back and running his fingers through the curtain of hair that fell around them.

"Sore?" Richard whispered as he slid carefully into Will's body, gazing intently down at him as he joined their bodies.

Will shook his head, never once looking away from Richard's face as he replied, "No. Give me all of you. Don't hold back." He watched Richard's eyelids slide halfway down and then close altogether in reaction to Will's words. For a minute or two, Will stared up into Richard's face, watching the flicker of emotions. He loved that he could affect Richard so deeply.

Richard bit his bottom lip and Will knew he was attempting to maintain control. His eyelashes were dark and longer than his blond hair would suggest they should be. Will watched his eyelids flutter but stay closed, his tongue darting out to lick his lips.

"Open," Will rasped, his hips lifting to meet every thrust. "I want to see your eyes, remember?"

Richard shook his head, eyes still pressed tightly shut. "Can't."

"Why not?"

"If I look at you, I'll lose it. We need the energy."

"The energy comes from our connection. It isn't how long we fuck, it's how powerfully we connect," Will explained. "Look at me."

Richard acquiesced. With an evil grin, Will tightened all his muscles around Richard's cock, making his withdrawal difficult and extremely pleasurable. Richard gasped, the muscles in his torso and arms trembling, and he plunged back in with a quick snap of his hips. When he was completely buried, Will arched up so that their sweat-slicked bodies pressed together.

Will gave up on begging. Richard was obviously going to claim him in his own way. There was something he desperately needed, however. "Kiss me," he whispered. Richard didn't need to be asked twice. He lowered his head and pressed his mouth to Will's, flicking his tongue out and lapping carefully at Will's lips. They both groaned as they fell into the kiss. Richard thrust into him, adding a slow twist of his hips each time and drawing increasingly intense ripples of pleasure from Will's body.

Will wrapped his arms around Richard, letting his hands wander over every piece of accessible skin, stroking and tickling and teasing, returning the pleasure of Richard's sensual exploration. Threading his fingers in Richard's long hair, he cupped the back of his head, gently at first but with growing force as the kisses became more desperate, more passionate.

The kisses destroyed all control. Will lost any composure and whimpered into Richard's mouth, scoring red tracks into his back. He registered in the back of his mind that he needed to keep enough focus to be able to complete the spell, but he was losing the ability for coherent thought fast.

Between kisses, Richard murmured, "Scream for me. I want you to tell me how you want it."

The plea ignited something inside Will. He choked out, "*Harder, fuck me harder... I want you!*"

Richard's kisses became so all-consuming that neither of them could draw a proper breath. His hips doubled their pace and he slammed into Will's body as hard as he dared, reveling in the loud slap of flesh on flesh at the moment of impact. Will screamed. On every inward thrust, he cried out, the needy noises eating away at Richard's composure.

"I have to come," Richard gasped out in warning between his own grunts and groans. "I'm sorry… I have to."

Their eyes met briefly before their mouths crashed together again, both consumed with their need for each other. Richard ground his hips into Will's body, all semblance of gentleness shattered under the demand of his wolf.

Will wrapped his arms tightly around Richard, whispering the words of the spell, lips pressed to skin. Splaying his hands flat on Richard's back, he opened every level of himself—physically, emotionally, spiritually, and magically—allowing the power to cycle through them both with no barrier, pulling more energy from the earth beneath them. The feel of the magical charge triggered Richard's orgasm. It flooded out of him, filling Will and sending a second stream of power flowing through their bond. A look of pleasure so intense that it bordered on painful crossed Richard's face, tipping Will over the edge into his own climax and a third surge of power that expanded the aura around them to a pulsing ball of gold light.

Richard collapsed on Will, muscles shaking, strength depleted, his wolf sated and sleepy. They lay in that panting, gasping pile for many minutes, their bodies a sticky palette of sweat and sperm. Eventually, Richard managed, "Holy Mother Goddess."

Will just laughed quietly, too tired to manage anything more expressive. He could feel the energy binding them and was in no hurry to be any farther from Richard than he was now.

It took a little while longer for Richard to gather the energy to roll off Will, and once they were parted, the air cooled them quickly. They lay side by side, touching at the arm and leg, fingers wound together tightly.

Will felt sleep pull at him and groaned quietly. He knew they needed to get up and leave the cave. They need to test the bond, find the others, and finally confront Sienna. He just couldn't seem to convince himself to open his eyes, let alone move away from the incredible warmth of Richard's body. *Just a few more minutes*, he convinced himself. *I can't face Sienna completely drained of energy.*

Chapter 23

WILL stirred in the warm furs. Richard's arm came over his side, pulling him back into the cradle of his body and nipping his shoulder, his breathing returning immediately to a slow, steady cadence that signaled to Will he hadn't really been awake. His own eyes were just closing as he felt a second twinge like the one that had woke him up. Focusing, he reached out, exploring the cave and the shield still thrumming through the rock around them. A small whirlpool in the protective shield developed, pulling the energy outward and causing a corresponding twinge in Will's stomach.

Now Will was completely awake. Carefully shifting away from his sleeping lover, he sat cross-legged on the bare rock, dropping into a light trance. He didn't want to lower the shield or have Richard venture out of the cave until they knew for sure it was safe. Following the stream of the protective energy, Will flowed with it down into the whirlpool the next time it tugged. The ribbon of light led directly to his twin.

Tristan was sitting just outside the cave in an almost identical position, deep in the trance that was maintaining the shield. Will reached out with his mind to connect with Tristan but was brushed away. Since they connected through magic, the shield was preventing Will from reaching him. The energy tugged again, and Will felt pulled toward his twin with no outward sign that Tristan could even sense he was there. Will concluded that Tristan needed him and was using the energy to cross the barrier and call to him.

Bringing himself up out of his trance, Will used a towel and bucket of water warming by the fire to clean up and pulled on his clothes. Kneeling next to Richard, he pushed a lock of hair back from his face and kissed his cheek. "I'll be right back," he whispered to the sleeping werewolf. "Sleep." He added a small bit of suggestive magic to the last word, not wanting Richard to wake and find him missing.

The shield was designed to prevent magic from crossing, not humans, so Will had no problem leaving the cave. He could sense the Guardians watching the entrance but couldn't see them. Tristan was maintaining the shield so it wouldn't fail. Stepping out into the dark night, his eyes followed the trail of silver light up to the full moon in the inky black sky. He whispered a prayer of thanks to the Goddess for her help in protecting Richard and bringing them together. Following the twisting path twenty yards down the mountain, he found Tristan in a niche hidden by a thick stand of brush. He could feel the shield and knew that the cave must be straight through the rock Tristan leaned against as he concentrated.

Will didn't want to break Tristan's trance, so he sat next to him and descended into a trance of his own, reaching out to Tristan on the spiritual plane.

Tristan's sarcastic voice greeted him. "'Bout time you showed up."

"You rang?"

"I've been 'ringing' for more than an hour."

"Sorry, I guess we were a little out of it," Will apologized. It had been thoughtless of him to allow Tristan to maintain the shield alone for this long.

Tristan swayed toward him, bumping their shoulders together. "It's okay. I know how it is, but Alex sent a Guardian up to speak with Benjamin. He and Raul saw Sienna enter the house after dinner, but now they have the feeling she isn't there. They didn't want to go in and check without knowing what was going on up here, and Ben didn't know what to tell them. Plus I was a little curious...." Tristan grinned.

"I don't like the idea of Sienna being in the wind. She has to have felt Richard's absence by now."

"I thought she'd come looking for him the second the shield severed their connection."

"So did I. I figured it would take her several hours to make it clear out here if she was searching blindly. We would have been shielded from any tracking spell." Will frowned. "I don't like this at all. Something is wrong. I'm going back to Richard. I don't want him alone."

"Not so fast. Did the potion work?" Tristan asked as Will started to move away.

Will couldn't restrain his satisfied grin. "Oh yeah. He was himself the second the shield fell in place, and the bonding spell was stronger than anything I've ever cast. She'll never mess with him again. The bond lit up the cave."

Tristan mirrored the grin. "I suspect it wasn't the spell that was so powerful, but the feelings behind it. I'll want details later."

"Definitely. I have some serious questions to ask you and Ben, but let's get through the rest of this night first." Will stood up, stretching his legs, and jogged back to the mouth of the cave. Richard was still sleeping peacefully. Reaching into the stream of magic, he pulled it to him, placing his hands flat on the rock and releasing the energy back to the earth with a prayer of thanks. He'd come out tomorrow and leave an offering.

Lying down beside Richard, Will ran his hands up his back, the warm skin making his palms tingle. He wished he was waking his lover for another round of lovemaking, but there was work to be done. Switching the polarity of his previous suggestion, he whispered, "Wake up."

Richard mumbled groggily, turning over and attempting to pull Will into his arms. Will felt Tristan and Benjamin arrive just outside the cave. They wouldn't come in until Will invited them, but all of them needed to head back to the house and confront Sienna. Will pushed gently out of Richard's arms and stood.

Completely awake, Richard stared up at his mate, frowning. "Why are you so far away… and dressed?"

Will chuckled at his petulant expression. "I've dropped the shield. How do you feel?"

"Lonely." Richard yanked on Will's hand, tumbling him into the furs and claiming his mouth.

Will struggled for about fifteen seconds before surrendering to the kiss with a moan. Richard affected him in a way that had to be fate. Summoning every ounce of willpower he possessed, he broke away from the kiss with a gasp. "We need to go help Raul and Alex," he got out before Richard managed to align their mouths again.

The effect of the words was delayed, but Richard eventually pulled away. "Where are Raul and Alex?"

"Watching your house. Sienna was there earlier, but they think she might have left. Is there a way out that can't be seen from the outside?"

Richard shook his head, sitting up. "Not that I know of, but if she escapes, I'll spend the rest of my life looking over my shoulder and fearing for you." He got to his feet, making a face at the dried mess on his stomach.

Will laughed, reaching for the pot of water. "Here, let me help."

Richard caught his hand with a rueful smile. "I'd better do that or we'll never get out of here." He looked around for his clothes. "How did I get up here?"

"Your wolf followed me." Will grinned, handing him a clean stack of clothes.

"Figures."

Still amused, Will poked, "If I didn't know better, I'd think you were jealous."

"I guess I am... a little." Tossing the cloth to the floor beside the fire, Richard reached for his jeans, a pair of tan silk boxers falling from the folded denim. "You planned for everything, didn't you?"

"I wasn't sure how long we'd be up here." Will pulled a bottle of water out of a cooler of ice, taking a big swallow. "How can you be jealous of your wolf? Isn't that kind of like being jealous of your arm?"

"Normally," Richard answered as he finished dressing, "but usually we share experiences. I was shut out of his time with you."

Will pressed himself to Richard's back, laying his cheek against the warm muscle and hugging him tight. "We'll make more memories so you don't feel left out."

Richard turned in his arms, his hands running down Will's sides to grasp his ass and pull him close. "I doubt we can beat tonight. I've never felt that close to someone before, not even when I was claiming you at Nanna's."

Will shivered at the tone in Richard's voice as he said the word "claimed." He liked the idea of belonging to this strong werewolf. "We were both focused on the same goal."

"Mind-shattering orgasms?"

Will stepped away, cuffing the side of Richard's head. "Wanker."

Richard shrugged, an unapologetic smirk tugging at the corners of his mouth. Reaching for Will's hand, he drew him close, his head bending to capture his lips in a kiss. "You are mine... forever."

Tristan's voice shattered the moment. "Should we make ourselves comfortable out here?"

Will buried his face into Richard's neck. "Let's go finish this so we can send them home."

"Is it bad that I just want her gone without having to do anything about it? I don't want to waste even one more minute on her," Richard murmured into his hair.

"No. It's perfectly understandable—not realistic, but perfectly understandable. Come on." Will took Richard's hand and pulled him toward the mouth of the cave. He didn't want to invite Benjamin and Tristan inside. The cave had become a sacred place for him—a place that belonged just to him and Richard. "The sooner we start, the sooner we can come back."

"You'll come back here with me?"

"Definitely. We aren't done here yet."

Stepping out into the moonlit night, Will noted that the Guardians had come forward. Richard signaled one of them to stay and one to follow. "No one goes in the cave but me or my mate," he instructed.

The Guardian nodded. "Yes, sir."

As they walked down the path, Will whispered, "You called me your mate."

"You are."

"I know that, but how will he know?"

"You wear my scent. They've known since you arrived. I'm sure my behavior earlier confused them, but they wouldn't question me or my choices."

"Ohh...." Will thought about the time he'd spent with Jared. Members of the pack had seen him greet Jared with a hug and leave in his truck. *I wonder what they thought about that?*

RICHARD would have changed into wolf form and run back to the house, but Will and Tristan couldn't have kept up. He had no idea what would happen when they confronted Sienna, but he wanted—needed— Will at his side. The morning he had left Nanna's to face Sienna, he'd been sure he could handle her alone and had been proved wrong—spectacularly wrong. He wasn't making that mistake again. Will, Raul... hell, even Alex, Benjamin, and Tristan, he'd take all the help he could get to remove Sienna permanently from his life and get her away from his pack.

Will filled him in on the rest of the plan as they moved down the mountain. Crossing the yard, Richard led them straight to Raul, easily locating his twin's scent. "Is she in the house?" he asked without preamble.

"Sienna came back here after dinner. We saw her walking between the bedroom and the kitchen and reading in the living room," Alex answered.

"Maybe she just went to bed," Richard suggested. "It *is* the middle of the night."

Will shook his head. "No, she would have felt the severing of her bond with you."

"Don't call it a bond. Control. Spell. But not bond." Richard's hands cupped Will's face, turning it up so he could stare down into Will's eyes. "A bond is what I share with you, and I've never shared that with her."

Will covered Richard's hands with his own, rising to his toes to press a quick kiss to his lover's lips. "Got it. When her spell was severed, I'm certain she reached out with her magic to find you. Depending on how she did it, she either got nothing back or felt her magic being deflected by the shield. Even if she felt the deflection, she wouldn't have been able to locate us. I built that into the spell. She would have been worried, maybe even panicked."

Richard looked at the house he'd shared with Sienna and silently vowed to burn it to the ground at daybreak. "We won't know if she's in there unless we go in or she comes out. I'm not much interested in waiting."

"The best defense is a good offense," Benjamin quoted.

"Let's go," Raul and Alex said together.

Richard led the way, all fear of Sienna fading. With Will at his side, he could face anything. He could feel the magic thrumming through him, glowing like a shield around his body. Opening the door cautiously, he debated calling out a casual greeting to put her at ease, but Will had said she would know that her control had ended. She was either entrenched to fight or gone.

Silently the group split up, heading into different rooms. They methodically searched each room, meeting back in the living room when they were done. "Anything?" Richard asked.

One by one each man shook his head. "We need to actually lay hands on every inch of wall, ceiling and floor. Each bookcase, picture and piece of furniture needs to be examined," Will explained. "Sienna is a master of illusion; she makes things appear as they are not."

Reenergized, the team searched again, running hands over walls and baseboards, fingertips checking the rim of every shelf and lampshade. "What exactly are we looking for?" Richard asked, setting a large portrait on the floor.

Tristan paused, looking up from his place behind the couch. "Anything that reveals a means of escape. Raul and Alex watched her enter this house and she's never left—at least by conventional means. There has to be something we are overlooking."

Benjamin found it.

The wall above the tub in the master bathroom appeared to be solid tile, but when he reached toward it, his hand disappeared up to the elbow. Calling to the group, he climbed into the tub.

Richard reached the room first to find Benjamin only visible from the waist down. "What the fuck?"

Benjamin withdrew, grinning. "It's a tunnel."

Chapter 24

"A TUNNEL?" Will climbed into the tub next to Benjamin. Leading with his hands, he passed through the image of a solid wall to find that the room had been shortened by several feet, creating a narrow passage. Crawling into the space, he stared down through an open trap door into a tunnel approximately sixty inches in diameter. A ladder led down into the hole, with the tunnel heading north. He couldn't see more than a few feet with the beam of light from the bathroom. "We need a torch."

Something solid tapped him on the shoulder. Reaching up, Will's fingers circled the cylindrical barrel of a heavy flashlight. He switched it on, illuminating another few feet of the tunnel, but still not seeing a turn or end. Sienna was nowhere in sight.

Richard crawled through to kneel beside him. "Damn. It is the perfect hiding place. I haven't taken a bath since I was eight."

Will winked at him, his hand slipping into the back pocket of Richard's jeans and squeezing. "We'll have to remedy that. I like the idea of having you warm and wet and soapy in my arms." Richard growled, his eyes flashing yellow in the low light.

"Cut that shit out!" Tristan ordered, leaning through the opening and slapping Will's hand away from Richard's ass.

Will rolled his eyes, pushed Tristan back into the bathroom, and stepped out of the passage. "It doesn't look like it was used much, which means she isn't familiar with it. It would be slow going. Even with her head start, she won't be far. Any idea where it might come out?"

"It appears to head due north, but there's no telling how far. Nothing but woods north of here. It could come out anywhere." Richard rubbed his neck to ease the growing tension. "How in the hell did she get that dug without me noticing?"

"Probably a combination of magic and labor. She may have hired someone to tunnel in from the opposite end. She could do a small amount from here and then guide the way with magic to have the tunnels meet." Will frowned, picturing the layout of the property. "Isn't her gardening shed north of here?"

Tristan almost bounced with excitement. "Yeah, it is. If this tunnel connects the two, she could have made a run for the trees from behind the shed."

Will shook his head. "I don't think so. She needed a completely safe way out. Even if the tunnel stops at the shed, I'm betting it continues. That way it would provide a secret escape from both places and allow her to get in and out of her shed without being seen. Tris, I'm going to take the tunnel. You go to the shed and see if you can find a hidden entrance like this one. I'll meet you there."

"Ohh… no." Richard's hand closed like a steel band around Will's arm. "You can go with Tristan. I'll go into the tunnel."

"I don't have time to argue with you—" Will started.

Raul interrupted him. "Alex and I will go with Richard."

Fists on his hips, Will faced the three large werewolves. "And how do you plan to stop her? Not one of you knows a lick of magic and that's what she'll be using."

"You said that your magic would protect me from her," Richard reminded him gently.

"Yeah, it'll keep her from controlling your mind, but it won't stop her from killing your body," Will argued.

"As long as she can't turn my mind, we'll be safe." Richard brushed a dark curl off Will's face. "We can travel much faster as wolves. I won't be able to focus if I'm worried about you. Please stay."

"Fuck," Will swore softly. If Richard had yelled at him, bossed him around, he might have stood a chance, but his mate's soft, heartfelt appeal went straight to his core, melting his resistance. "Fine. Tris and I will look for a hidden door in the shed."

Richard turned to Benjamin. "While they examine the shed, can you go fill my father in?"

"I'd be happy to," Benjamin agreed. "When I'm done, I'll join them in the shed. Can't hurt to have an extra set of eyes."

Richard gripped Benjamin's arm. "Keep him safe for me."

RICHARD stole a hard kiss from Will before climbing down into the tunnel. It wasn't tall enough to allow him to stand straight, and he was glad that his wolf was better designed for both the space and almost complete darkness. The feeling of rock and earth around him reminded him of the cave and Will's enthusiastic surrender to their bonding. The memory spread warmth through his body, chasing away the chill of the bare earth around him better than any fire. He felt Raul step into the tunnel behind him and Alex after that. *The gang's all here.*

Alex reached forward, laying a possessive hand on Raul's back. "It's good to have you here," Raul whispered, leaning into his lover.

"I was wrong to let you come alone."

Richard felt the strength of the bond between his twin and the king of the Onondaga. He was glad that Raul had found someone so special. Raul had been born to lead and Richard had no doubt that Alex and Raul made a formidable royal couple. His mind drifted to images of Will beside him on the dais of the Cayuga council room, the power of his feelings for his mate making his wolf bristle. *He's ours,* he whispered to his wolf, easing his agitation, *and no one will ever take him from us.* Now he just had to stop Sienna so he could keep that promise.

"We should have a plan for when we find her."

Richard was pleased that Raul had said "when" and not "if." He needed to confront Sienna—to know that she would never hurt him or Will again—and the soon-to-be king in him wanted assurance that she wouldn't try her trickery on another unsuspecting pack. He was certain that her ambition would never allow her to stop. Since she'd failed here, she would attempt to insinuate herself into another pack somewhere else. The thing that really scared him was not knowing her final goal. She obviously wished to be turned. Had she chosen him just because he was susceptible, or was ruling over a pack also in her plan?

"I think you should let Alex and me handle her," Raul continued.

The unexpected comment startled Richard. "What? Why?"

"I watched her. Whenever she needed to control you, she touched you. If you touch her, I'm afraid she could regain power over you. Will taught me that magic can be trained. If you do something repeatedly, it becomes easier. She has conditioned you to react to her magic. I don't want to lose you again."

Richard shivered. The air was damp and cool, but it was the desperation in Raul's voice that caused the chill. "You won't lose me. The bond between Will and me is complete and stronger than anything she could conjure. It will protect me from her magic. You, on the other hand, might be vulnerable."

Alex growled. "She wouldn't take another breath if she dared to touch Raul's body or mind."

"Not that I'd be upset to have her eviscerated, but I want to see her tried and condemned for what she's done. Her magic obviously works best in close proximity. I'm immune so I'll stay in the lead." Richard shimmered into wolf form and ran off in an easy lope, Raul and Alex on his heels.

WILL and Tristan sprinted for the shed. Several yards from the door, Will held out a hand, catching Tristan in the chest and stopping him. "I didn't find any external wards last time I was here. Do you think she'd put the tunnel entrance inside or outside?"

"I'm sure it's inside. The whole purpose was concealment and escape. She wouldn't want to be exposed." Tristan cast a revealing spell on the outside of the garden shed and the ground around it. "I don't see anything. Do we search out here or just start inside?"

Will nodded toward the door. "I vote for inside."

Moving slowly, Will scanned for something that appeared out of place. Reaching for the door latch, his hand hovered over the metal while he whispered a low chant. The iron heated, glowing orange. A series of sigils appeared, glowed brightly, and were extinguished with a quick hiss. The twins waited until the metal returned to its normal gunmetal gray before touching it. Thumbing the lock, Will pushed the heavy door open and looked around.

The room was a mess. Drawers had been pulled free and dropped to the floor, their contents scattered. Bottles and jars lay on their sides, herbs and other spell ingredients strewn over every surface. Cabinet doors stood open, revealing bare shelves.

"Well she's obviously been here, which means we're right about an entrance." Will pointed to the opposite side of the large room. "You take that half and I'll start here. Be careful what you touch; some of this stuff is caustic."

Tristan nodded, methodically working over surfaces with his hands as they had in the house. Less than five minutes into their search, Benjamin arrived. "The king has sent a group of Guardians down the tunnel to help Richard and Raul." Standing in the middle of the room, he looked around, stunned. "I take it she didn't always keep it in this condition."

Will shook his head. "No, it was meticulously organized. She was trying to find something, and in a big hurry."

"I think it might be more that she was trying to keep *us* from finding something," Tristan suggested, straightening from a crouch. "Nothing over here."

"Yeah, that makes sense. It's hard to tell in all this chaos, but I have a pretty complete list of what was here. We can compare it to what's here now and determine what she took with her." Will's hands skimmed the surface of the heavy worktable before running down the stout legs to the floor. When his hands moved to the tile beneath the table, it shimmered like the still surface of a lake when a leaf lands. "I think I've got it."

Will reached down, his hand appearing to sink into the solid tile. Tristan stooped, reciting three quick lines and pushing his hand through the illusion. The tile floor disappeared, revealing a hole in the ground identical to the one they had found in the bathroom. A similar wooden ladder was propped against the rim. They couldn't see the bottom. Will rose to his feet, pulling open one of the few closed drawers. "Did we bring the flashlight with us?"

"I don't think you'll need one," Benjamin said, peering down into the hole. "I can smell Raul and the others and it's getting stronger."

"They should have been past here by now." Unable to wait, Will climbed down the ladder. He was tempted to call to Richard, but knew his voice would carry and didn't want to alert Sienna if she was still within hearing distance. Taking a deep breath, he flattened his hands against the walls, reading the energy flowing through the earth. He could feel Richard moving closer, the power of their bond stretching between them through the rock and soil. Ignoring the magnetic pull of his bonded, Will pushed out farther, searching for Sienna's magical signature.

There. He concentrated harder, using the earth to amplify his spell. A faint wash of scattered magic. It was diffuse, like static electricity, indicating that the witch was rushing, scared, or panicked and unable to focus. He was about to call to Tristan to come down so they could join their powers when he heard a familiar growl from the tunnel to the south.

All his attention immediately switched to Richard. Walking toward the sound of Richard's wolf, Will followed the wall of the tunnel around a slight curve until he met the trio of wolves. Richard changed—one step a wolf and the next a man—pulling Will into his arms. His smile made Will's pulse pound. Wrapping an arm around his lover's waist, he molded his body to Richard's side. "How did we get ahead of you?"

"There was a cave-in and we lost time digging through."

Will frowned. "Do you think she did it on purpose?"

"I think it was natural. There were signs that she had to dig through it as well, but she might have collapsed it again once she was through." Richard shrugged. "It would make sense to try and keep others from following her. What did you find?"

"Ben is back, so the king knows what is going on. He sent some Guardians in after you. Maybe you should wait until they catch up," Will suggested.

Richard frowned. "We don't have time. We need to keep moving. Was there anything upstairs?"

"Sienna ransacked the shed, but it'll take time to figure out what she took. It wasn't a small amount of stuff, however, so it would have taken her time to get it together and it is probably heavy and bulky enough to really slow her down. If you hurry, you might be able to catch her before she gets out of the tunnel."

Raul's wolf butted against Richard's leg, obviously eager to get moving. Richard's fingers delved into the dense fur. "We'll catch her. Even if she's out in the woods, it's miles to get off packlands. We can track her."

Will squeezed Richard's hand. "I'm coming with you."

Wrapping his hand around the back of Will's neck, Richard massaged the tension out of his muscles. "No—"

Before Richard could finish his refusal and Will could object, Raul shifted into human form. "Maybe you could scry for her, like you did when we were searching for Richard. If you can find her location, you might be able to find the end of the tunnel before she comes through it."

"Tristan can do it," Will objected.

"I don't want to be separated from you," Richard interjected calmly, "but we travel faster and see better as wolves. We both need to use our strengths. Go do what you do best and help us catch her."

Will stepped back, his hand lingering on Richard's arm before finally falling to his side. "Go! You're wasting time."

The brothers shimmered into wolf form and bolted down the tunnel with Alex. Will watched them until the darkness swallowed them. "Be safe."

Reluctantly, Will climbed the ladder. "They're tracking Sienna."

Tristan hugged Will to his side. "He'll be okay. Raul and Alex will keep him safe."

Will rested his head on Tristan's shoulder. "I know. We need a map and a crystal. Raul wants me to scry for her."

"Brilliant idea! Why didn't we think of that?" Tristan asked, moving efficiently around the room. "I poked around while you were down in the tunnel just to see what was here. These should work."

Tristan laid a pad of graph paper and a teardrop shaped crystal on the table. The top page of the pad had a sketch of the grounds and gardens on it. It wasn't exactly a map, but it would indicate location… as long as she hadn't left packlands. Will picked up a length of twine and knotted it around the crystal. He cleared the table with a sweep of his arm. Benjamin jumped back from the falling cascade, eyebrows raised.

Will shrugged. "Well, it's not like it could get any worse in here." He oriented the drawing to the proper directions, closed his eyes, and took several deep breaths. The scent of mugwort filled the room. He smiled; Tristan was helping. Mugwort helped to still the mind and awaken higher consciousness. His twin had obviously found some of the herb among the ingredients left behind and was rubbing it between his hands to release the fragrance. Taking a deep breath of the herb-laden air, he concentrated on Sienna, released his conscious will, and let the energy from the earth flow through him into his hand, down the string, and out through the crystal. The makeshift pendulum began to swing, the pattern changing from a line to an ever-widening circle. Finally drawn to the surface, it stuck, the point piercing the paper.

Will opened his eyes. Tristan's finger was already marking the spot as he bent over, examining the drawing with Benjamin. "She's too far east for the tunnel to run due north."

Benjamin followed the path from the shed north with his finger. "They might have hit rock or water when they were digging it and had to deviate. It looks like she's headed to this road. We might be able to cut her off with the car."

"Bring the drawing," Will ordered, heading for Benjamin's car at a run. He was tempted to slide in behind the wheel, knowing that the keys were usually left in the ignition, but his lack of experience might hinder their speed. Yanking open the back door, he slid across the leather seat, letting Tristan in beside him. Benjamin took the wheel. The tires sprayed rocks as they took off, racing over narrow, deserted roads at more than twice the posted speed limit.

It took only minutes to reach the spot where the road intersected the projected line from the shed to the location the pendulum had marked. Will climbed out before the car stopped. He wasn't sure how much ground the running wolves could cover, but they had to be close, unless they had been blocked by another cave-in. Outside, he paced back and forth until he could feel the difference in the density of the earth under his feet. "This way," he cried, breaking into a run as he followed the incongruity back toward the south. The eastern sky was just beginning to glow. In an hour the sun would be completely up.

Chapter 25

A DOZEN yards off the road, he stopped, Tristan crashing into his back and almost knocking him off his feet. He turned to find a large black wolf standing next to his twin. Will's eyes connected with the wolf's. "There's a fluctuation in the energy here. I think she's close. Can you help?"

The black wolf's eyes deepened in color, much like Richard's would when he was controlling his wolf. With a firm bob of his head, the wolf put its nose to the ground and darted around the immediate area until he let out an excited yip and started digging.

Will pushed the wolf out of the way, falling to his knees and placing both hands open on the disturbed dirt. He felt Tristan's hands spread across his back and their powers joined. He could feel Sienna beneath them and the growing sphere of power she was gathering. Fear and anger radiated from her, tainting the magic. This was magic intended to destroy, and Will could only think of one thing she would want to destroy in that tunnel.

The men who were pursuing her.

Will cried out in frustration, slamming his fists into the earth. She was directly beneath him, taking aim at his lover and he couldn't reach her to block the spell.

"Why can't you?"

Tristan's voice startled Will. They had combined their powers, but Will had been so focused on Richard that he hadn't felt his brother in his mind. The air crackled around them with the magic Sienna was raising.

Ben's wolf paced, circled, and whined, uneasy with the energy coming from the earth. With a pained yip, he shifted back into human form, jumping up onto a fallen log as if the ground was burning his feet. "They're coming. I could hear them running toward us."

There was no time to find the exit to the tunnel. There was no time to plan or even think. Will took four big steps south and dropped to his knees. He took a deep breath, focusing his own energy and pulling power from Tristan, kneeling behind him. Clenching his hands into fists, he struck down into the earth in much the same way he had in frustration moments earlier. This time he struck with intent, pushing a wall of energy into the earth like a giant guillotine. Keeping the flow open, he channeled power into the wall of energy—making it thicker and stronger.

Simultaneously, Sienna released her spell. The shield reverberated as her spell ricocheted back. With a loud rumble, the ground shook beneath their feet. The sound of wood cracking was the final warning and a crater opened, dirt falling into the collapsed tunnel below.

Will and Tristan fell backwards, carried by the tide of dirt. Sliding with the shifting surface, they came to rest at the bottom of the hole. "That was some spell, little brother," Tristan rasped, his throat dry with exertion and dust.

Will sat up, brushing dirt and leaves out of his hair and coughing. "Not exactly what I intended." He could no longer sense Sienna. Wherever she was, she was no immediate threat. The magic was dissipating, seeping back into the earth.

Benjamin jumped down into the hole, his hands carefully examining Tristan for serious injuries. Gazing at Ben's bare, muscular body, Will realized that he had become inured to the werewolves' blasé attitude toward nudity. His knees shook and threatened to give out when he tried to stand. Benjamin reached out to steady him. "Are you hurt?"

Will shook his head, the movement causing him to sway. Gripping Benjamin's shoulder to regain his balance, he searched the area for signs of life. "We need to find Richard and the others. They could be trapped by the cave-in."

"Richard is your mate." Benjamin put his hands on Will's shoulders, making him meet his eyes. "You should be able to sense him. Focus your mind on him."

Will closed his eyes, calming his thoughts by controlling his breath. He reached out for Richard, something he hadn't tried since he had left the farmhouse. Subconsciously, he'd been afraid of what he'd find. All it took was picturing his lover as he'd looked braced over him in the cave and opening his mind, and he was flooded by a rush of love so intense it made his knees weak again. Will projected his feelings of love and relief in return. Sending a final image of himself secure in Richard's arms, he withdrew from the connection and opened his eyes.

"They're just through there." Will pointed at a corner of the crater. "The way back is still clear, but I don't think I can wait that long. Help me dig through." He started throwing broken branches to the side, clearing off the top layer of rubble.

Tristan stooped to help and Benjamin changed back to his wolf, digging faster than either of them could with their scooped hands. The clamor of pack members arriving to investigate the strange noises grew as they worked. As people arrived, Will put them to work. One group was helping clear the way to Richard, Raul and Alex and one group was attempting to unearth Sienna.

"What happened?" All activity ceased as the king approached. The man commanded attention even dressed in blue jeans and a T-shirt. The sun was up now and it was easier to see the extent of the damage: piles of loose rubble, toppled trees, and exposed roots.

Will knew that Benjamin had given Richard's father the basics, so he cut to the finale. "Richard, Raul, and Alex were tracking Sienna through her escape tunnel. She attempted to cast a spell to stop them and I was able to block it. The collision of the spells caused the tunnel to collapse. Richard and the others are fine; I can feel them. They should be just through here. I have no idea what happened to Sienna."

The king called a Guardian over and ordered him to round up the families that hadn't arrived and have them bring shovels and a first aid kit. Every Guardian was on duty until they had his sons out. He walked over to the spot where a smaller group was working to uncover Sienna and scuffed the charred dirt with his boot. Will hovered near him, not knowing if he'd been dismissed or was still needed. "Do you think she's dead?" Randolf asked, turning back to Will.

"That would be my guess. She was casting a powerful spell that rebounded. If that didn't kill her, the collapsing tunnel would have. I can't sense anything but residual energy from her spell."

"Can't say as I'm sorry. The penalty for her actions would have been death anyway. She violated our most sacred laws."

"Her own as well," Will added. *"Eight words the Wiccan Rede fulfill, An' it harm none, do what ye will.* She used her gift to harm and manipulate others and it came back on her threefold."

"Wise words," King Randolf agreed, watching as Will's eyes continually darted to the workers digging out their prince. "They *will* get him out." The king's voice was steady and sure. Years of practice had polished it to the perfect pitch to instill confidence and serenity.

This situation had stretched Will's nerves beyond soothing. A nervous laugh escaped Will's throat and he shoved his hands in his pockets to keep from twisting them. "Yeah. I know they will, but I can't seem to stand having a barrier between us." Will realized for the first time exactly how tall the king was as a strong arm wrapped around his shoulders. Sick and wrapped up on the couch, he had seemed almost frail.

"Don't worry, son. That obsessive need to be with each other will lessen in time."

Will thought about Tristan and Benjamin and Raul and Alex. "It must take a lot of time," he mused more to himself than in response to the king.

Randolf laughed and squeezed him tight. "I guess it does, but it's not such a bad thing to be so in love that you can't bear to be separated. You bring a great strength to our pack. My son is lucky to have you."

A lump rose in Will's throat. The tightness probably would have led to tears if someone hadn't called out that they'd broken through. Pulling away from the king, Will ran toward the workers. Richard emerged first, still in wolf form. Shaking the dirt from his fur, he scanned the group for his mate. Spotting Will running at him, he shifted, standing just in time to catch Will in his arms.

Will clung to Richard's broad shoulders, burying his face against his neck. Richard's hands cupped his ass and lifted him even closer. "Don't ever... ever... do that to me again!" Will ordered, covering Richard's shoulders and neck with kisses.

Richard laughed, spinning Will off the ground. Unfazed, Will wrapped his legs around Richard's hips and held tight. "Got it. No being possessed by evil witches."

Will bit into Richard's shoulder. "Fucker."

"I needed you safe," Richard added in a more serious tone.

"Well, I needed... need to be with you," Will retorted.

Giving the couple a moment to be alone, the king stood to the side, talking with Raul and Alex. Most of the wolves went about their tasks, flowing around the embracing couple with averted eyes as the pair expressed their love and relief with kisses.

Richard reluctantly raised his head, catching Raul's amused gaze over Will's shoulder. Nuzzling the soft skin of Will's neck, he whispered, "Think we can leave them to this and go hide in our cave?"

Will sighed, pressing closer to Richard's chest. "We need to find Sienna. If she isn't down there, we need to start a search immediately."

"Damn. Why does this woman keep fucking with my life?"

"Richard...." Will rolled his eyes. "I think we can survive a few more minutes to make sure she's out of our lives for good."

"Can we?" Richard's voice dropped, low and husky, and Will trembled in his arms. His wolf pulsed with energy over the obvious effect they had on their mate. At the moment, all he cared about was binding them closer by making love until neither of them could breathe.

An unexpected hand on his shoulder surprised him and Richard spun, shifting Will behind him in one smooth motion. "Just me," Raul said quickly, feeling his twin's edginess.

Richard forced a neutral expression. He didn't like all these people around his mate, sharing in his delicious scent: aroused and still wearing the mark of their lovemaking.

Raul smiled, easily seeing beyond Richard's carefully schooled features. "We've found her."

Richard stepped away from Will. Threading their fingers together, he walked to his father, surrounded by a small group of Guardians with Alex at his side. They were all looking down. The gathering parted at their approach.

Sienna lay half-buried, dirt clinging to her skin and hair. She looked asleep—small and innocent. Even like this she was beautiful. *Not a glamour then....* Richard looked up at his father.

Randolf nodded his head, resting his hand on Richard's shoulder. The warm grip and slight squeeze strengthened him. "She's dead," the king confirmed.

Will shivered, his hand still firmly clasping Richard's. "I didn't—"

Tristan immediately interrupted, stepping forward to hug his twin. "You *didn't*. She did it to herself."

Richard bristled at anyone touching Will—even family—but remained silent, knowing he was being irrational. Benjamin stepped forward, gently pulling Tristan to a more comfortable distance. Richard sent Benjamin a silent thank you with his eyes.

"You knew where she was," Tristan continued. "You could have cast to kill her and you didn't. You chose a spell to protect those you love. *Her* spell was designed to kill and it did."

"Divine retribution," Alex added solemnly.

The group stood silently for several minutes, Richard finally taking an audible breath and turning away. "Son?" the king queried, ceding authority over how they would proceed to Richard.

Everything seemed so clear to him that Richard was surprised by the question. There was no doubt—no grief—in his mind. "Take her off packlands and bury her."

"I should go," Will said.

Richard tensed, scowling at Will. "Why?"

Will laid his hand open on Richard's chest over his heart. "She was working in dark magic for years. Her body should be cleansed of the energy it still contains and her grave warded."

Richard held his tongue. He wanted to scream, *no*! They were done with Sienna. He didn't want Will anywhere near her body, but he knew nothing of magic. He trusted his mate. If Will said it needed to be done, it would be done. All of this ran through his head as the others waited patiently for his response.

Lifting Will's hand to his lips, he kissed the underside of his wrist. "Thank you, my love, but I have lost enough of your time to Sienna." Turning to Tristan, he bowed slightly. "Tristan, would you do my pack the supreme service of supervising a proper burial for Sienna?"

Tristan smiled, returning the gesture of respect. "I'd be honored."

"You'll need—" Will started.

Tristan assured, "I think I can find everything I need in the garden shed. Go. Enjoy your mate. After the last few weeks, you two deserve an uninterrupted honeymoon."

"This won't be it, however," Randolf interjected. "That will come after Will has been accepted into the pack and officially becomes Richard's consort." His tone brooked no argument.

Richard's mouth whispered directly against Will's ear. "That doesn't mean we can't spend the rest of the day and night practicing."

"I heard that," the king growled, his indulgent smile making a mockery of the tone in his words. "But before you disappear, there is another member of this pack who needs our attention. The Guardians are still detaining Arthur."

Chapter 26

RICHARD strode into the room, his eyes locking immediately on Arthur. He looked bone-weary and miserable; Richard felt his anger melt into a wave of sympathy. He nodded toward the door and the Guardians stood, exiting the room. Richard watched them assume a post on either side of the door before swinging his gaze back to the man he'd called friend for most of his life. Arthur sat on the couch, his lanky frame curled inward, his eyes fixed on the floor.

Randolf and Raul had agreed that Richard should be the one to handle the interrogation, as both the wronged party and the future ruler of the pack. He knew that everyone was watching him, gauging his skill and power as alpha. Will would be joining him, but his mate had detoured to Raul's apartment to collect what remained of Tristan's potion. This, like all important decisions in the future, they would be handling as a couple.

Richard paced. With every pass, Arthur crumbled into a smaller ball. He finally snapped, "Why don't you just kill me?"

"Because first we need to know what you did and why," Will interjected from the doorway. His eyes immediately sought Richard, seeking permission to continue.

Giving a curt nod, Richard stepped back, ceding the space in front of Arthur. Will pulled a vial out of his pocket, holding it up to the light to measure the remaining contents. He held it out to Arthur. "Drink this."

Arthur looked up and started to say something, but a stern look from Richard shut his mouth. He lifted his hand and took the vial, tossing the contents back on one swallow.

"Don't you want to know what was in that?" Will asked.

"I have no right to question our heir or his mate. It is by your good will only that I still breathe."

Will shook his head. Under stress, werewolves always reverted to formality and custom. "True, but the contents will cause you no harm. It is a potion created by my brother to counter the effects of Sienna's brews."

Arthur's forehead furrowed, his eyes darting up again before fixing on the point between his feet. "They told me that she tried to kill you and Raul. I didn't know. I thought she loved you... that she was your mate and then when Will showed up... I guess I felt sorry for her."

"You felt *sorry* for her," Richard growled.

The miserable look on Arthur's face intensified. "You were her mate and you bonded with another."

"I think maybe we'd better start at the beginning," Will suggested, pulling a chair over from the small table in the guest room and sitting down directly in front of Arthur. "Tell us what Sienna was doing for you and what she asked you to do in return?"

Arthur glanced at Richard for permission before speaking. Receiving another quick nod, he took a deep breath and began. "I'm in love with Wendy. I've known for years that she's my mate, but she won't give me the time of day."

"I thought the mating instinct was always mutual?" Will looked up at Richard.

"It is. I've never heard of an instance between two werewolves when it was not." Richard rested his hand on the back of Will's chair. "Are you sure she's your mate?" he asked Arthur.

"Completely. That was why I agreed to let Sienna help me. She said that she could brew a potion that would make me irresistible to Wendy."

"And what did she ask in return?"

"Errands mostly. Most of them involved spending time in the kitchen, delivering groceries, taking meals up to your dad. She said it was important to spend as much time around Wendy as possible so that the potion would work."

"You aren't really that stupid, are you?" Richard asked, incredulous.

Arthur's shoulders fell another few inches. "No. I began to suspect that Sienna wasn't just trying to help me when your father started to get sick. I just wanted Wendy so badly and she wouldn't...." His voice fell off and he buried his face in his hands, breaking down into shuddering sobs.

Richard took Will's arm and pulled him out of the room and away from the door. The Guardians could still hear them, but he had complete trust in their discretion. "If what he's saying is true, she could have easily controlled him. A werewolf will do anything for their mate, and they are incredibly vulnerable if they are in an unrequited relationship."

"I thought you said that there were no unrequited relationships."

"It happens. Infrequently. Usually when a werewolf falls in love with someone outside the pack who isn't lycan."

"That's what you risked with me?"

Richard cupped Will's cheek, his fingers stroking the sensitive hollow behind his ear. "Being with you is worth all risks."

Will's eyes lit up. "Is it possible that Sienna was dosing Wendy as well? She was able to keep you from acting on your bonding instinct with me. Maybe she was doing the same thing to Wendy to keep Arthur helping her? She played on his need for Wendy and then his empathy by convincing him that she was going through the same thing with you."

Richard shrugged. "I guess anything is possible, but how in the hell did she keep it all straight?"

"It would have been a juggling act, which might account for the times her control slipped and you were able to react to me. When she was focusing on you, her control was complete, but she had to keep her other balls in the air. When she had to focus her power on someone else, you were able to break free—if only a little bit."

Richard nodded, turning quickly to look down the hall. The Guardians also tensed, alert and ready.

"What?" Will asked.

Just then Wendy appeared, dragging two Guardians with her as she stormed toward them. "Where is he?" she shouted the second she saw Richard. "Where is Arthur?"

Richard motioned for the Guardians to release her. She stopped at the door, scenting Arthur, obviously torn between her loyalty to Richard as the pack's heir and her desire to get to Arthur.

"I guess that answers that question," Richard whispered to Will.

Will nodded. "He's fine, Wendy. Let us talk with you for just a minute and we'll let you—"

Overlapping Will's words, Richard said, "Go to him. I'd like you both to stay here tonight and we'll talk in the morning."

Not needing to be told twice, Wendy was through the door. Will turned to Richard, who had a small smile on his face as he looked at the closed door.

"Tomorrow?" Will asked, cocking his head.

Richard pulled him close, burying his face in the dark curls and inhaling deeply. "They are mates that have been denied consummation and kept apart far too long. Neither of them will be any use to us until their wolves have been satisfied." He paused. "It might be the day after tomorrow."

Will chuckled. "You're a giant softy."

"Hardly," Richard snorted. "I am to be the king of this pack. The successful mating of its members is my job. I let them down and endangered them by bringing Sienna into the pack and letting her manipulate us." He took Will's hand. "Come on."

Passing the Guardians, he slowed. "They don't leave the room, but see to it that they get food and anything else they need. Send someone to their rooms to bring them fresh clothes." To Will he added, "There is a bathroom and bedroom. I doubt they will need much else."

Both Guardians nodded their understanding. If they had an opinion on the way Richard was handling the situation, they kept it to themselves.

IN THE end, they didn't return to the cave as Richard had wished but to Will's room in Raul's suite. There was still too much up in the air to justify cloistering himself so far from the estate. Raul and the others were still out dealing with the aftermath of the confrontation. Richard's house held too much of Sienna's energy and was filled with workers. Tristan would collect most of her belongings to be buried with her or burned over the grave. Will would be happy to burn the house and the garden shed to the ground as well... and he just might do it if Richard agreed. They had tumbled into Will's bed, intending to make love and take a quick nap, but it appeared that they had slept through the rest of the day and into the next.

Will could see the sky lightening along the horizon. Stretching his hands above his head, he groaned as muscles sore from tension and hours of lovemaking complained. Turning to his side, he pulled a pillow under his head. Richard's solid warmth curled close to his back, and a large hand pressed flat to his abdomen, pulling him backward to fit them together.

"Mmm..." Richard hummed, lips grazing Will's neck. "Too early to get up. Sleep."

"We were supposed to get up for dinner," Will teased, "*last night*."

Richard mumbled, "Already missed it. Not time for breakfast yet. We're good."

Will's eyes closed, but his brain refused to surrender to his weariness. *I'm going to be changed. I'm going to be a werewolf. I wonder if it will hurt. It couldn't hurt any more than the idea of losing Richard. I might lose my magic.*

"Goddess, you think loud," Richard complained, rolling onto his back and stretching, the sheets pulling low and exposing his chest and stomach.

Will turned toward him and rested his head on the warm chest, his fingers swirling in the soft hair. "Sorry. When will they do the changing ceremony?"

"Probably tonight."

Will sat up. "Tonight! That soon?"

Richard tugged him back down to his chest. "It has to be done during the three days when the moon is the fullest. Our night in the cave was the first night of the full moon and we just slept through the second night. It doesn't leave us many options unless we want to wait until the next full moon and I don't want to wait that long to make you mine. Are you having doubts?"

Will shook his head, his cheek brushing Richard's nipple and causing it to harden. He snickered and placed a kiss on the pink nub. "You're insatiable."

"Only for you." Richard rolled Will beneath his body, kissing him soundly. "What do you know of ceremonial changing?"

"I was present for Benjamin's, but I don't think it was normal and I was assisting Tristan, so I missed large portions of what Alex and Ian, his shaman, were doing."

Richard's fingers stroked through Will's hair, smoothing it down his bare back. "Our pack doesn't have a shaman. Apa will conduct the ritual. Raul and I will be present, but Apa has to actually change you since you are to be my consort. Raul has agreed to present you to the pack for membership. It will ensure that they accept you."

"You mean there's a chance that they won't accept me?" Will sounded slightly panicked.

"Shh…." Richard soothed. "All will be well. They have a choice to accept you just as they will have a choice to accept me as their ruler."

"What happens if they don't?"

"Don't accept you or don't accept me?"

"Either. Both!"

Richard laughed, squeezing him tight. "I guess we go live with Alex's pack."

"But this is your home. I don't want—"

"It would be no home without you. With all that has happened with Sienna, I can't assume that the pack will accept my rule. When Apa presents me to the pack, they have the right to present another alpha to challenge me. According to pack law, another alpha has the right to challenge the leader of the pack at any time, but it is most likely to occur when leadership is changing."

Will shivered. "I don't like the sound of that." He remembered Tristan's description of the fight between Alex and Benjamin's wolf. "I don't want you hurt."

Richard shrugged. "It will be what it will be. I will ask forgiveness from the pack when I ask them to allow me to bond with you officially. If they accept that, there will likely be no challenge to me taking the throne. They wouldn't change you, knowing that you are my mate, and then separate us by exiling me from the pack."

"Exiling you? I thought we were talking about fighting for the throne."

"We are, but if I were to lose, the new alpha and king would never tolerate having me around. A defeated alpha is dangerous."

"And I thought my brain was whirling a few minutes ago when all we faced was my changing."

Richard sat up, swinging his legs to the floor. "You think too much. I hear Raul. Let's get up and see what plans were made while we slept."

"I need a shower." Will looked over his shoulder as he walked to the bathroom. "Want to join me?"

Richard's chest rumbled, his eyes shifting as he charged Will, pushing him into the bathroom, pinning him to the tile wall and ensuring they got sticky and sweaty enough to really need the shower.

Chapter 27

MOONLIGHT shimmered off the water. The Cayuga pack ceremonial meeting place was along the river and surrounded by a circle of willows. An inner ring of stones set aside the sacred space with the royal dais located at the northern curve. Several hundred had gathered inside the circle of trees to bear witness to the night's happenings.

Will knelt between Tristan and Wendy to the right of the royal dais, just outside the ring of stones. Randolf was seated in the center of the dais, his throne the highest of the seats. Raul and Richard flanked him, with Alex in a place of honor at Raul's side. Several inches lower and slightly back from the royalty, the pack council sat in six chairs: three to the right and three to the left. Arthur knelt next to the dais, head bowed. His sentence was the first thing to be dealt with tonight. Richard had explained that it was important to bring closure to the past before moving into the future.

Richard stood and motioned for Arthur to rise. Clothing was never worn during rituals. Richard was adorned only with the copper torque, armbands, and circlet of his position. Arthur stood calmly facing Richard, adorned only with a leather thong tied around his right bicep, his eyes respectfully lowered. Will could feel Wendy tense beside him and wanted to comfort her in some way.

Richard began, his voice deep and clear, traveling easily through the still night air. "Arthur Braun Camden, son of Frank and Amelia, you stand before this council charged with betrayal of your pack. Your actions aided the witch Sienna in her efforts to harm the royal family and, through deception and perverted use of magic, to gain control over this pack."

"Yes, my lord. All I've been charged with is true and was done by conscious decision," Arthur answered, his voice equally clear, although the volume was reduced as his eyes were still directed at the ground.

Wendy gasped. Will reached over and caught her hand, squeezing. There was nothing he could say to ease her distress. Things didn't look good for Arthur, and Will was beginning to suspect that Richard had given them the previous night knowing that they would have nothing more.

Richard stood perfectly still, staring at the man in front of him. Arthur shuddered as the silence grew to the point that it felt like the air would shatter if someone whispered. "Face your pack," Richard finally ordered.

Arthur turned, his eyes rising to face the people he was accused of betraying. Wendy's hand clutched Will's so hard he was losing feeling in his fingers, but he wasn't about to deny her that small amount of comfort. He had his own fears about how the rest of this night would go for his mate and was glad Tristan was at his side.

"Arthur Camden, you have confessed to endangering our pack... our family... all we hold dear." Richard's eyes shifted from Arthur to the crowd circling the field. "The punishment for this offense is death or exile. Do you understand?"

"Yes."

"Were you aware of these consequences when you made your decisions?"

"Yes."

"Did you initiate any of the actions that led to members of the royal family being harmed?"

For the first time, Arthur hesitated before answering. "No, my lord."

"In each action, you were following the direction of another?"

No hesitation this time. "Yes, my lord."

"Did you make any of these decisions under duress?"

"It is not an excuse for my behavior, but I was separated from my true mate, my lord."

"How long did you go before you were able to bond with your mate?"

"Twelve months." Arthur's voice trembled. A joint gasp went up from around the circle. A sob broke from Wendy and Will tore his eyes away from Richard to look at her. Tears were streaming unchecked down her cheeks, her eyes locked on her mate.

Richard looked down at Arthur. "Turn and face me. In all things, do you accept my authority to pass judgment on you?"

"Yes, my lord."

Raising his eyes to the assembly, Richard asked again, "Do you, as my pack, accept my authority to decide his punishment?"

"We do," the crowd chorused, their voices solemn but resolute.

Will noticed that Randolf smiled behind his son as the pack showed its unwavering support. Apparently Will wasn't the only one who had been worried about the pack's acceptance of Richard as leader.

"Arthur Camden, it is our decision that you were unduly influenced and manipulated with the use of potions and spells by the witch Sienna. Your actions were forced by the denial of our most primitive and instinctual need—mating. You are not blameless in these events, but neither are you responsible for them. Your intent was not to harm your pack. You will leave the Cayuga pack—"

"No!" Wendy cried, jumping to her feet and lunging for Arthur. A Guardian stepped forward, preventing her from running to her mate. Neither Richard nor Arthur looked toward the disturbance.

"Do you accept this?"

"Yes, my lord." Arthur's voice was softer, subdued, but no less clear.

"An exiled werewolf must exist alone or convince another pack of his worthiness. If he succeeds in finding a new pack to accept him," Richard continued, "his new alpha can request that his mate and any family be allowed to move to be with him."

Richard paused, and it was obvious that Arthur didn't know if he was supposed to respond to this statement that held no question. A new voice filled the void and Will immediately understood what his mate had orchestrated.

"I, Alex Hanover, Rajan of the Onondaga Pack, accept Arthur Camden as a member of my pack." He stepped forward, facing Richard formally. "I request the honor of accepting his mate Wendy as well."

Richard turned and motioned for Wendy to join him. Taking both her hands, he studied her face, cheeks streaked with tears. "I am sorry you had to witness this so soon after joining with your mate."

Wendy nodded, her eyes flickering briefly to Arthur who stood, eyes fixed down, by Alex's side and then back to Richard. Her face glowed with hope.

"Do you, Wendy Taylor, wish to accept the invitation to join the Onondaga Pack?"

"I do, my lord. I wish to be with my mate."

Richard took her hands and placed them in Alex's. "I entrust the well being of this *lowell* to your care."

Alex bowed his head to Richard, demonstrating his acceptance of the honor. Turning to face Wendy, he pulled her hands to his chest just as she turned her face to the side, aiming her eyes at the ground, baring her neck.

"I put my life and well-being in your hands and pledge to do all I can for the benefit of the pack," she vowed, waiting to feel the rasp of Alex's teeth on her neck before raising her face.

Arthur shifted uneasily, obviously uncomfortable with the alpha being so close to his mate. A new bond was a volatile time. Alex stepped away from Wendy and motioned for her to return to her spot next to Will. He performed the same series of actions with Arthur, carefully searching the other man's eyes for any sign of deceit. He had no desire to adopt a pack member prone to machinations. When he appeared satisfied that Arthur wanted nothing more than to be with Wendy, Alex released him to sit with his mate.

Richard returned to his seat, exchanging a meaningful look with his father. Randolf rose to his feet. He was slightly thinner than his sons after Sienna's treatment, but the force of his presence had returned. The pack held complete silence as they waited for him to speak.

"My children, tonight I ask for your blessing. Not only to add a member to our pack, but to enable my son and heir to complete his bonding with his rightful mate." The king's eyes turned to Will and he held out his hand.

Having been prepared for this moment, Will followed the protocol as Richard and Raul had explained it. Standing in a fluid movement, using nothing but the muscles in his legs to lift and balance his body, he walked toward the king and bowed. He was dressed in a simple robe made from homespun cotton. "Gentle ruler, how may I be of service?" Will asked, sinking to his knees, head down.

"Rise and face the pack," Randolf instructed.

Will unfastened the clasp at the neck of the robe, allowing it to puddle at his feet as he stood and turned. Randolf and Raul had prepared him for the ritual, bathing him in the river and rubbing a sweet oil into his skin until he seemed to glow in the light of the full moon. Hammered copper bands that matched Richard's circled his biceps, and his grandmother's gold bracelet glinted from his ankle.

He heard a gasp from behind him and knew instinctively that it was Richard. Raul had commented on the powerful reaction a werewolf has to seeing his mate marked with his symbol as he fastened the copper bands to Will's arms. Will felt his power surge, feeling it channel up from the earth. Pushing his feelings of love back into the stream of energy, he projected it toward his lover, hearing Richard gasp again as a link formed between them.

Placing his hands on Will's shoulders, the king projected his voice, the deep timbre making Will shiver. "I, Randolf Carlisle, petition the Cayuga Pack to accept William Northland to be changed by ritual and accepted into the pack as one of our own."

The king paused, as much for effect as to give the pack a chance to consider his petition. "What say you?"

"Aye!" the pack chorused.

Will shivered at the raw power being raised by the pack bordering the circle. Their confirmation of his acceptance reflected that power directly at him, making his skin dance with pinpricks like an electrical charge. He immediately knelt, placing his hands on the earth to complete the circuit, a low hum of gratitude and blessing for the pack and the earth flowing from between his lips.

"And you, William Northland. Do you wish to become a member of this pack? Do you pledge to honor and support her in all you do?"

Will didn't think he could speak and was surprised when his voice rang out clear and true. "Always and forever."

Randolf motioned for the elders to rise. Raul joined them as they closed their circle around Will, Randolf at the north, Raul at the south. As one, they began a harmonious chant. With each step they took forward, the circle tightened and the chanting grew louder. When they were shoulder to shoulder, Will completely blocked from sight of the pack, each opened their hand to reveal a small object. Raul pulled the cork from a glass vial, pouring the clear contents onto Will's head. His voice alone rose above the chant. "Lady of the River. She who captures and directs the energy of the moon on a cloudless night. Grant this child your purpose."

The chant peaked as Will felt the cool water touch his skin and run in rivulets down his neck and back. The vibrations of the combined voices resonated to Will's core. He could feel himself reacting on a primal level, like his cells were being vibrated into a different configuration. He had a brief flash of rice jumping on the stretched skin of a drum before the earth began to spin. Closing his eyes, he dug his fingers into the damp grass in an attempt to anchor himself. Something touched his shoulder, and the voices rose again. He could no longer distinguish them as separate sounds.

Another touch and a matching surge of volume. Unstable even on his knees, Will rolled onto his side, muscles twitching and cramping. Time extended until Will lost all sense of how long it had been since he had turned to face the pack—to accept this decision to alter his very being. From a distance, he heard the king's voice separate from the others and call to him. Every part of him wanted to respond, but he seemed incapable of voluntary control of his muscles. An equally strong force anchored him and prevented him from moving toward the beckoning notes. He tried to open his eyes, speak, reach out his hand, but his body remained rooted to the earth.

The call came again. This time Will felt it within his body instead of registering the sound with his ears. It felt like his bones were being pulled from his flesh by a giant magnet. The night had fallen silent except for the hum of earth energy that swirled around him, but the pull of the call continued. If he wasn't able to break free soon, it was going to turn him inside out. Reaching out to the swirling energy, he pulled it to him and managed to lift his head. With great effort, he struggled to rise to his hands and knees. Like a newborn colt, he was wobbly and unstable but determined, rising halfway only to fall again.

The call rose—urgent—the feeling more familiar this time and Will quit trying to fight or even understand the forces pulling him in opposite directions. He allowed his mind to float with the sound until he hit an invisible barrier. A second voice joined the first.

Richard.

Will surrendered himself to the flow, consciously trying to move in the direction of the voices again, desperately wanting to reach his mate. The barrier stretched but didn't break. It continued to separate him from his lover. His frustration increased until he threw his head back and screamed... the anguished sound issuing from his throat as a howl.

A third voice crystallized from among the power-filled chant.

Benjamin?

Benjamin hadn't been part of the circle, had he? Something wasn't right. Confused, Will reacted instinctively, pulling back, digging in his heels and fighting the call.

A solid body molded itself to his back, warm arms coming around his chest. Will felt himself being propelled forward gently. A familiar smell soothed him.

Tristan.

Will turned his head to face his twin. "What—?"

"Time to go, little brother." Tristan smiled, pushing them forward again.

"Go? But you aren't supposed to be here."

"We can't go back and we can't stay here. We've got to go forward—through the barrier."

"I tried."

Tristan nodded. "I know. We can do it together. We can do anything together. Can't you hear them? Benjamin. Richard. They are calling us."

Will shivered, opening his hand and clasping Tristan's where it rested on his chest. "Let's go."

The brothers surrendered to the flow of energy surging around them together. Will felt himself dissolve into the energy. His sense of separation disappeared. He'd come close to feeling at one with nature while meditating, but it was nothing compared to this. His body ceased to exist as a separate entity—as did Tristan's. He could sense his brother's energy, but couldn't see or feel him. In fact, none of his senses worked. He was part of the river of energy, part of the earth, part of Tristan. Broken into their molecular components, they swirled freely together, free of form and intent.

The flow of power controlled by the elders continued to pull them. No longer solid beings, they moved easily through the barrier. Becoming part of the substance of creation for a moment and then breaking free on the opposite side. The chant resonated around them, reorganizing their cells, separating him from Tristan and the raw energy.

Just as he began to reclaim the familiar feeling of his body, Will sensed the new presence. A distinct set of thoughts different from his own. *The delicious smell of his mate. Comfort. Strength. Safety. Pack.* Will took a deep breath, but his senses still weren't registering. His body reacted to Richard's scent based on the thoughts flowing through his mind.

Richard called again, his mate's voice one distinct part of the harmony pulling him closer. Beyond the call was the soft and steady song of the pack. Without warning, Will threw his head back and howled. An excited chorus of howls, barks, and yips answered him. He jumped as the sound registered in his ears, the feedback interpreted two distinct ways within him—one startled, one excited.

The king's call. Will didn't understand the words but knew what he had to do. Tensing his muscles, he rolled to his feet and shook, feeling the dense fur tug at his skin as it was flung back and forth. His eyes opened to a completely different world. Smells swamped him: wolf, human, moist earth, green leaves, and emotions. He could smell excitement, fear, love… death! Swinging his head around, he spotted Benjamin's black wolf crouched and snarling between a prone body and Raul.

Tristan!

Will leapt in their direction, pleased with how fast and agile he was, but frustrated with the lack of hands and a voice when he reached them. Whining, he nuzzled and nudged Tristan's unconscious body. Benjamin growled a low warning, but Will met his eyes with a steady stare until the black wolf quieted, not relaxing his stance but allowing Will to approach his twin.

Will could feel Tristan's energy waning and his outrage burst from his mouth in a mournful howl. *Help!* He needed to communicate. He needed his voice.

The king. Richard. He'd no more than thought the name and he felt his mate's touch on his shoulder. Jumping frantically, he pushed against Richard's legs, trying to convey his need... his urgency. Richard crouched beside him, whispering words in his ear. At first, Will was too agitated to hear them, but his mate's voice slowly soothed him. When his body was calm, he could sense the dual presence in his head. Sense what was wolf and what was human and pull the human parts closer. His wolf's desire to help Tristan was equally strong and the powerful animal retreated. The feeling of being turned inside out started again and Will dove straight into the middle of the whirlpool. He shook for the second time in as many minutes and opened his eyes to find his human form sitting naked in the grass.

"Tristan!" he yelled, crawling on his hands and knees to his brother's side. Cradling his twin's head in his lap, he tugged at Benjamin's fur to get his attention. The black wolf seemed intent on keeping everyone away from his mate and snapped at Richard until he took three steps back. Randolf and Raul stood at a respectful distance, Alex hovering behind Raul.

Will pulled on Benjamin's fur again. "Benjamin!" He shoved against the muscular shoulder. The black wolf turned, snapping at Will's hand. Without thinking, Will swatted him across the nose.

"Stop that!" Will barked. "He needs you to call to him. He's lost and he needs to follow your voice."

The black wolf shimmered into human form with a grief-stricken look on his face. "I tried calling to him when he collapsed. He didn't hear me."

Will thought for a moment, trying to remember what he had felt. Like a dream, it was disappearing quickly now that he was awake.

"Well I heard you so I assume he heard you too. Were you calling to Tristan... or his wolf?"

Everyone, including Benjamin, looked perplexed. "Wolf?"

"We were changing together." Will's words tripped over each other, tangling in his head before he could get them out of his mouth. He didn't have time for details. "I couldn't change without him. Our souls are bound too tightly together. He was changing with me. The chant put me back together and the call led me here. He needs the same guidance!"

Randolf's voice boomed from behind him. "Form a circle," he snapped at the elders. "Alex at the north. Benjamin at the south. Raul in the east. I'll take the west. We aren't all of his pack, but it will have to do."

"Can I—?" Will looked up at the king as everyone fell into place.

Randolf reached forward and put a comforting hand on Will's head. "Stay by his side. He is bound to you by magic and blood. You call his soul; we'll call his wolf."

Will nodded, scooting to the opposite side of his twin so he could press his back against Richard's legs as his mate stood in the circle. He needed the strength of Richard's physical presence. The moment their skin connected, Will's wolf settled and a feeling of security and peace flowed through him, allowing him to focus on Tristan.

Do what you do best, Will told himself as he ran through the steps he used to establish the connection with his twin. It scared him how scattered Tristan's energy signature was. *Scattered... scattered... there is something important I'm forgetting.* The more Will tried to grasp the illusive thought, the farther out of reach it moved. Taking a deep breath, he cast a net of power to keep Tristan's energy from spreading any farther. He could hear the chant building around them and the energy pulsed in time with it, but Will could feel no reaction from Tristan.

Scattered! All of a sudden, Will had a flash of the experience of crossing through the barrier. Moving deeper into the stillness, he slowed his breathing and heartbeat until he began to feel anxiety flowing from his mate. Projecting a quick flash of well-being to reassure Richard, he opened himself to the vibrations of the chant, allowing it to work on him in reverse. He dissolved back into the energy flow, surrendering himself to the One.

He could feel Tristan all around and through him, as he had the first time. This is where they had taken different paths. The elders were creating the flow. Will heard Alex's voice and then Raul's until they blended into a single tone. Benjamin's voice joined the call, and Will could feel his twin's energy coalescing and strengthening. Relief flooded him at the first conscious touch of Tristan's mind.

Will?

I'm here, Tris. Go to Benjamin. Follow his voice. I'm right beside you.

Pulling some of his energy back, Will opened the power shield he had raised and followed Tristan, allowing the chant to draw them home to the pack.

WILL opened his eyes, expecting to find himself in the circle. Instead he was curled comfortably on his bed in Raul's suite. Bolting to his feet, he jumped to the floor. When four feet connected, he realized that he was in wolf form. He considered calming down enough to be able to change, but he was too worried about Tristan. Happy that Richard hadn't closed the door completely, he wedged it open with his nose. He had laughed at Benjamin's dog doors, but now he understood the convenience they provided. He would have been incredibly frustrated if the door had been latched, and precious time would have been lost as he changed.

The living room was empty, but he could smell Tristan, Benjamin, and Alex, along with the fainter scent of Richard and Raul, who were absent from the suite. Following his nose, he sniffed at the crack under Tristan's bedroom door. His twin was on the other side, but knowing that he was alive and here wasn't enough. He needed to see him. With a whine, he lifted his paw and scratched at the door. He sensed Alex's presence a second before hearing a deep chuckle.

"Look who's awake."

Will looked up at the alpha, feeling Alex's power skitter along his skin, raising his fur. He could even smell a unique edge to the man's scent. He had so much to explore with his new senses, but first his need was to see his twin. He pawed at the corner of the closed door and looked up at Alex.

"Yeah, I get it. Benjamin may not be thrilled with you joining them, but I'm guessing he's too happy that you saved his mate to do any real damage." Reaching over Will, Alex turned the knob and opened the door.

Will leaned his weight against Alex's legs to express his thanks and pushed into the bedroom.

Two wolves slept curled tightly together in the middle of the bed: one black, one the dark brown of fresh-ground coffee. Will looked down at his paws, wondering if he and Tristan were identical in wolf form as they were in human form. Judging from the parts of himself he could see, they were. He approached the bed slowly, willing Benjamin to wake so he wouldn't startle him. He whined softly—the wolf equivalent of clearing your throat apparently.

Benjamin's eyes opened, crystal blue against coal black, but he didn't move. Will took a step forward and paused. Benjamin's expression didn't change, but he didn't growl or move to intercept his lover's twin. Will lowered his head submissively and slowly walked to the edge of the bed, pausing and waiting for some sign from Benjamin that he could proceed.

Benjamin nudged Tristan until the other wolf opened sleepy, amber eyes. Standing, the black wolf circled twice and laid down facing the opposite direction, giving the brothers some privacy. Tristan stretched out his neck until his nose touched Will's, turning his face to the side and rubbing his face against Will's neck. Will crawled onto the bed, noticing that Benjamin's head turned to watch his progress but he didn't interfere. Will stretched out next to his twin, feeling the familiar peace of being physically close. They had shared a bed until they were teenagers, the steady beat of the other's heart getting them through long nights after their mother's death.

As his mind and body stilled, Will found it easy to change back to his human form. He had labeled it flipping in his head because he felt like a coin being flipped from heads to tails and back. Tristan whined and nudged his chest.

"You want to change too?" Will whispered, rubbing the dense fur behind Tristan's ears. Tristan's wolf nudged his chest again, making a low rumble of what Will figured was approval. "You have to relax. Use the countdown you use before you reach out to contact me over a distance, but when you get to that still, silent place, focus on the things that make you human: your hands, your voice, walking down the hot sand of the beach." Before he knew it, Tristan was shaking and lying next to him naked.

Will pulled him into a bear hug. "Fuck! You scared me."

Benjamin looked over his shoulder again, scooting over on the bed so that his fur was once again pressed along Tristan's back.

Tristan reached behind himself without seeming to be aware of what he was doing, winding his fingers into the dark fur. "I know. I'm sorry. I'm even sorrier that we didn't talk last night. Benjamin was so upset and all I could think about was calming him down."

"It's okay. You have to take care of your mate. No matter how close we are, he is your first priority now. Do you remember anything that happened?" Will asked.

"I remembered some last night, but most of it is gone now. A memory of remembering instead of the actual thing," Tristan admitted.

"I got halfway through the changing and was blocked. There was a barrier that I couldn't cross. You showed up and showed me the way, but when I arrived, you weren't with me. We set up the circle and I went in after you while Benjamin, Raul, Alex, and Randolf called to you. Could you hear them?"

"Yeah, I remember that now that you describe it." Tristan nodded his head slowly. "After you showed up, I could hear them again. Little brother to the rescue." He grinned, rubbing their foreheads together.

"Not sure about that," Will muttered. "You wouldn't have been in trouble in the first place if I had thought this through."

"Oh? So if you'd known that you couldn't change without changing both of us, you'd have just given up on being Richard's consort?"

"Well… no. I guess not, but it would have been nice to be prepared instead of blindsided. Are you okay with this? You never talked about petitioning the pack to be changed."

Tristan continued to stroke Benjamin's fur, both obviously comforted by the contact. "I really hadn't let myself think about it. Benjamin didn't care if I was human or lycan, and knowing Raul's feelings about changing witches, I wasn't sure it was an issue I wanted to bring up. Benjamin is so happy being part of a pack, but he'd leave them if they rejected me."

"Are you feeling okay? Physically?" Will stroked Tristan's arm.

Tristan stretched. "Tired and a little sore."

"Yeah, tell me about it. I feel like I swam over from London."

Tristan sighed. "I don't think either of us will go home again."

"Probably not to live, but we'll visit. I want to move Gram's stuff here. Officially make Davie and Scott partners in the store."

Tristan nodded and Will could feel him falling back to sleep. "Sleep, brother," he whispered, stroking the dark curls back from his face. Rolling over, he stood to leave the room, looking back from the door. Tristan was in wolf form again curled tightly to Benjamin's side. Will smiled and turned the knob.

Richard.

The familiar scent filled the room. His mate was perched on the side of a chair, talking with Alex but watching the bedroom door. Will's wolf jumped, but again they were in complete accord. Will ran to Richard and was met halfway. He buried his nose in the warm crook of Richard's neck, both arms and legs wrapped tightly around his mate. Supporting Will's weight, Richard shifted them to sit on the couch, Will straddling his lap.

"'Bout time you got up," Richard teased, his hands moving in soothing arcs over Will's back.

"And you weren't there," Will shot back.

"You've been asleep for almost twenty-four hours. I was helping Raul. He and Alex are leaving in the morning."

Will frowned. "But Tris—"

"—is staying. We've seen the consequences of separating the two of you and don't need a repeat of last night. Tristan and Benjamin are going to hang out for a while so we can explore your bond as lycans. Your wolves look just alike, you know." Richard cradled Will's face. "You are as beautiful as a wolf as you are as a man, and the blending of your powers is so incredible that it's a little bit scary."

Will pulled back to look at his lover. "What do you mean?"

"He means that the control and ability you showed during your turning outclasses even our most experienced shamans. Ian's going to hate not having you closer."

Alex's voice surprised him. Will had seen the Rajan when he entered the room, but he had been so focused on Richard that his presence really hadn't registered. "What ability? I couldn't even switch form without the king calling to me."

Richard and Alex laughed. "You don't understand," Richard explained. "Newly changed lycans have *no* control. They can't switch form at will for months. They are at the mercy of their instinctual drives, living to hunt and couple. You not only mastered switching, you seem to have completely normal drives, and you actually reversed the changing process—a ritual we follow but don't understand. You were able to go back and lead Tristan out."

"Oh...." Will rested his head on Richard's shoulder, thinking about what had happened the day before. "I can explain the process to you. I remember it pretty clearly now."

"Ian is definitely going to cry, and I'm going to have to live without a shaman for months while he comes down here to visit," Alex sighed.

Richard chuckled at the alpha's theatrics. "You'll both live."

"I couldn't have passed through the barrier without Tristan's help. We were both conscious during the process. Maybe Tris can train with Ian," Will suggested.

Richard smoothed Will's hair, wrapping a curl around his finger. "One more thing to explore before Tristan returns north. No one has ever remained conscious during their changing. Frequently they don't remember things for weeks on either side of the ceremony. What you have is very special. It will be interesting to see if you both have the skill. We haven't talked much about your role here with the pack, but we would be honored if you would be our shaman. Alex over there may be moaning, but he has already agreed to have Ian come down and mentor you, though it appears you may have abilities no one has ever exhibited."

"I... I don't...." Will frowned.

Richard pulled him closer, nuzzling the dark curls behind his ear. "You don't have to do this. You don't have to do anything but be my—"

"That's exactly what I want to do," Will interrupted. "Be yours." He laughed. "The shaman is the spiritual leader—healer—of the pack, right?"

Alex and Richard nodded.

"Then I would be honored. I know your father said that your pack hadn't had a shaman for years. Are you sure you want one now?"

"We recognize the will of the Mother when we see it," Richard answered. "You are a blessed gift in so many ways."

Will couldn't resist kissing his mate when he said things like that. Tilting his head to more firmly join their lips, he tugged at the buttons preventing him from touching Richard's chest. Richard covered his hands. "Not here. The cave. Raul and Alex don't leave 'til morning. We'll have time to say good-bye then. Come run with me."

Will scooted back off Richard's knees. Richard stood and shimmered into wolf form in one fluid motion that Will envied. Standing awkwardly, he shifted from foot to foot. He had changed several times from wolf to human, but hadn't changed from human to wolf without the help of the king's call. Then he heard Richard's voice. No, it wasn't his voice. It was more his… sound. Whatever it was, Will's wolf was more than ready to respond, a bundle of barely contained energy. Richard called again. Will's wolf jumped and Will stepped out of the way, concentrating on the feel of stretching, strong muscles as the wolf leapt. Landing slightly out of control, he slid into Richard's side, colliding with the solid strength of his mate.

Richard nuzzled him, the heat of their bodies increasing the smell that Will was beginning to identify as "them." Nipping playfully at Will's haunches, Richard barked, dashing out onto the balcony and then returning to nip again. Will jumped after him with an excited yip. An easy leap took them over the balcony and out onto the moon-soaked grass. Their race to the cave was much like the night Will had lured Richard's wolf there the first time—full of tumbles, tackles, and chases—but far more fun in wolf form.

Will slid into the cave first, colliding with the far wall and collapsing in the pile of furs, panting. Richard flopped down at his side, tongue lolling. Will nuzzled the soft fur of his mate's belly, covering himself with Richard's delightful scent. All of a sudden the soft fur changed to tan skin, but Will continued to rub.

Richard laughed, delighted. "Goddess, you feel good." His hands roamed through the soft, chocolate-colored fur, mapping and massaging the hidden muscles with his fingers. Will rolled onto his back, legs splayed. Richard laughed again, rubbing the pale pink skin with his hands and then his face, kissing the tender skin.

Will whimpered and squirmed. Richard's touch made it impossible to focus his mind enough to change. It had been fun to be in wolf form with Richard, but he wanted to touch with his hands, to have a voice to say, *I love you.* His wolf was aroused and reluctant to step back from the attention and Will was getting frustrated. He didn't realize he was growling until Richard laughed again, rolling him to his side and holding him close. Strong arms pinned him until he stilled.

"Shh… *conchure*… shh… Deep breaths. It is hard at first, but you are in charge. If you want to change, calm yourself, control your wolf. Hold him like I'm holding you." Richard's hands held him firm, no longer moving or increasing his arousal. "I'll help. As your mate and your alpha, I can call to you. Concentrate on me."

Will focused on his breath, sank his hands deep into the fur of his wolf and flipped, his mind following the pull of Richard's call. Feeling slightly disoriented and dizzy, he opened his eyes, looking down to see Richard's hand splayed open on his bare abdomen. "I did it!"

The chest behind him vibrated with more laughter and Will stabbed his elbow back into his mate's side. "Fuck you! You find all this very funny, don't you?" He spun in the tight embrace and smiled up at his lover.

Richard pressed his lips to Will's, feeling his mate's wolf rise up to meet his with an equal desire. "No," he growled, "I find it very arousing." Having Will as a werewolf was almost like having two of him—each part of him the perfect match for each part of Richard. His hands slipped lower to cup Will's ass and fit him tight to his body. "There are definite advantages to being naked when we change."

"Why do I have the feeling that you would keep us naked all the time if it was up to you?"

"Probably," Richard murmured against his lips. With an unexpected push, he tumbled Will onto his back and crawled over his body. He slowly ran his hand up the smooth, lean thigh and skimmed over the growing bulge between Will's legs. Settling himself across his mate's legs, he leaned forward and brushed a soft kiss over Will's stomach, grinning as the muscles twitched and quivered. Licking his lips, Richard moved them delicately around Will's belly button, scattering kisses that barely brushed the fine hairs, making Will tremble harder. When he heard Will's first moan, he nuzzled the trail of fine hair, his tongue tasting the salty sheen of perspiration, his teeth tugging gently. The musk of arousal hung thick in the air.

"I can't believe how intense this feels. I can feel your touch on my skin, but I can feel it in my head too. More. Please." Will panted, guiding Richard's hand over his erection and pushing down hard in an effort to ease the ache.

"Oh, there will be much more, but you can wait a little longer. For the first time, I feel like we are together with nothing hanging over our heads. I want to love you my way." Richard's feral grin raised bumps across Will's skin. He softly ran his fingers up and down his mate's torso before leaning forward and pressing a soft kiss to his lips. "Complaints?" he asked cockily, knowing Will wouldn't complain about a surfeit of pleasure.

Will caught Richard's hand and brought it to his lips. Kissing each one of the fingertips, he rasped, "As long as you are touching me, I'm happy." Will rolled his hips off the furs to emphasize his statement with a hard press of his erection against Richard's thigh.

Richard's hands stroked Will's chest, arms, and back. "I'm going to show you exactly how much I love you. I'm going to touch and mark every inch of you as I make you mine."

"Goddess, yes! I wasn't sure we'd ever get he—"

Richard cut off Will's words with his mouth. As the kiss deepened, he poured all his love, need and desire into it. He wanted to show Will how deep their bond ran. As their desire grew, Richard's wolf rammed against his mental barriers, desperate to be free to join with his mate. Slowly and with great difficulty, he pulled himself back from the point of completely losing himself. He had a purpose— teaching his lover the joy of mating with the passion of a wolf. "I want you to try and contain your wolf," Richard requested. "Picture him behind an invisible barrier. The more aroused we get, the more our wolves will want to participate, but if we hold them back until the very end...."

Will nodded. He didn't completely understand Richard's request, but he trusted his mate implicitly and got the gist of it. Controlling their wolves now would intensify the moment when they finally let them free.

Richard smoothed his hands over Will's chest, reluctantly pulling his lips away. Without opening his eyes, Will followed Richard's mouth, nipping and sucking at his lips, trying to tempt him into returning to the kiss. Chuckling, Richard pressed a final hard kiss to Will's mouth, pushing him back into the pile of furs and then quickly retreating before Will could react.

Looking up, his eyes locked with Will's as he settled between his legs. Starting at the ankles, he ran his hands up the muscled limbs, teasing the sensitive skin on his inner thighs with a light grazing of his fingernails. Every time his hands moved close to Will's cock, it jumped and the muscles under his fingers tensed. Pleased with the reaction, Richard moved his fingers closer in ever-narrowing circles. He touched every inch of skin below Will's chest and above his knees with the glaring exception of where his mate wanted to be touched most.

Will's wolf whimpered, the sound reproduced in his throat as he squirmed. He was not above begging, but knowing Richard, he didn't think it would influence his mate's pace. He couldn't completely control his body's reaction, however. His breath caught and gasped. His hips arched, and his hands twisted themselves in the furs until his knuckles were white. Finally Richard placed his hands open on either side of Will's cock, rubbing softly with his thumbs in the creases that separated his legs from his body. Closing the circle of his hands, he grasped Will's cock in both fists and moved them slowly up and down.

"Great Goddess!" Will cried, his body bowing as he thrust up into the joined hands.

"Hold on, lover." Richard chuckled and lowered his mouth to the leaking head. Still moving his hands, he began to lick at the silky skin, moaning at the musky taste of his mate's seed. The vibrations of Richard's moan set off another stream of expletives from Will. Opening his mouth, Richard allowed Will to thrust just past his lips while he teased the sensitive slit and foreskin with his tongue.

"Oh, fuck, Richard.... Stop! I'm going to come," Will pleaded, pulling at Richard's hair. "I can't hold onto my wolf if you make me come."

Richard pulled back long enough to shake his head. "I want your taste in my mouth while I fuck you. You can do it. You've shown more control of your wolf than most lycans from birth have. Use your strength. Come for me, *conchure*." Bending his head, Richard sucked strongly, pulling Will's cock completely inside his mouth.

"But.... Fuck! But I want to come with you inside me."

"Oh, you will. I'm just going to get you hard again," Richard rasped between strokes.

"Fu-uck...." Will groaned again. He knew it was over the second he felt Richard's finger pushing gently against his tight opening. Richard's finger slipped inside, seeking and finding Will's prostate. His hips bucked violently. Richard sucked harder, applying pressure from the inside in time with Will's thrusts.

Will thrust once, twice, and then three times, his hands twisting in Richard's hair. "Oh.... Oh.... Goddess! Help me!" Small explosions went off all over Will's body, building as they concentrated at his core. His legs pulled up as he thrust up one last time into Richard's warm, wet mouth. "Richard!" he screamed, his come shooting down his lover's throat, his wolf straining against the barrier. He could feel it yielding and used some of the power flow from his orgasm to reinforce it.

Richard just smiled around the semi-hard cock still in his mouth and hummed, causing Will to shudder and intensifying his aftershocks. When Will's cock finally quit pulsing, he let it slide from between his lips, nuzzling into the musky curls around the base, coating himself in the scent of his mate, sated from his loving.

Will's arms and legs felt like wet noodles as he tried to pull Richard up for a kiss. His wolf still paced restlessly, irritated at being caged while Will succumbed to pleasure.

Ignoring his halfhearted tugs, Richard shook his head, brushing his nose through the moist curls. "Nope, not done yet," he murmured against the soft skin between Will's balls and thigh.

"But Richard, you don't…. You can't…." Will protested, wriggling to try to get free of the firm grip Richard had on his body.

Richard growled, shooting a ferocious look up at his mate. Will immediately fell limp to his back, whimpering softly as Richard gently nipped with his teeth and soothed with his tongue. Richard explored the area between Will's still-soft cock and opening until he had him squirming against the bed. He bunched up the furs under Will's hips and stretched out on his stomach between the spread thighs to reach the opening he wanted to taste. Extending his tongue, he circled the sensitive pucker. Will groaned and tilted his hips forward, offering himself to Richard.

Richard couldn't resist completely claiming his mate. "That's it, *conchure*. Open for me." Will's thighs fell apart farther. "You taste so good." A small thrust from Will's hips made Richard's tongue penetrate the opening.

"You want that, Will? You want my tongue inside you?" Will was completely beyond words, and Richard knew it. Making one last broad swipe with his tongue, he thrust it in his lover's furled opening. Again and again, he tongue-fucked Will until both of them were thrashing, Will trying to get Richard's tongue farther inside, and Richard humping his own aching cock against the soft furs.

Knowing that if he continued much longer they were both going to lose control of their wolves, Richard pulled his tongue out and easily slid three fingers deep inside his mate. Wanting to continue the sensual spiral for Will, he twisted and stretched the tight opening with his fingers as he sat up and reached for the lube.

Will whined when Richard withdrew his fingers to coat himself with the slippery liquid. He opened his eyes just as Richard positioned himself and sank completely into the warm, wet passage with one stroke. His eyelashes fluttered, his head lolling to the side.

"Look at me, Will," Richard ordered. Will forced his eyes open and watched Richard's face as he pumped slowly in and out of him. "You are my mate, my chosen. I love you, Will. I love you. I love you," Richard chanted, his eyes shifting to gold as they locked with Will's. The words became part of the motion, which became part of the feeling, which became a part of them.

"Let go for me, *conchure*," Richard ordered. "Show me you are mine." Leaning forward to capture his mate's lips, Richard released his wolf. The two animals collided at full force in their effort to devour each other, to join, to meld. They were no longer two beings making love; they merged into two halves of one mated whole.

Richard could feel Will beginning to tighten around him. "You are mine," Richard growled. "Every part of you, and nothing will ever keep us apart again."

The raspy tenor of Richard's voice pushed Will over the edge. Crying out his mate's name, he came again, clawing at Richard's shoulders, unable to keep his eyes from closing as waves of pleasure rushed through his body.

The scent of Will's seed, shooting in long ropes over the tan skin of his chest, triggered Richard's climax. Leaning down, he licked at a long trail. As he'd said earlier, he wanted the taste of Will's seed on his tongue. He locked his arms and thrust forward into his lover again and again as his body exploded. With long, languorous laps, he cleaned every inch of his lover's body, a steady rumble of pleasure sounding from deep in his throat. With a final shuddering breath, he collapsed into Will's arms, almost instantly following his sated wolf into sleep.

Richard had no idea how long he had been lying on top of Will when he awoke. His back and butt felt cold. Will's arms were still tight around him. He shifted to the side to relieve Will of his weight. Will made grumpy noises of protest and turned toward him without truly waking up. Richard pulled him close with one arm, tugging a fur up to cover them with the other. He looked down lovingly at the man asleep in his arms. Softly he kissed the top of his head. "I love you, Will."

"Love you too," Will whispered against his chest, glad that everyone was safe. Tristan was staying. The king was fully recovered. They all had time. Time to learn their new roles. Time to learn each other. Time for love.

DON'T MISS

Upon their grandmother's death, Tristan Northland and his twin, Will, inherit her Book of Shadows and discover that one of their ancestors, a spurned witch, is responsible for dark magic that has affected the Sterling family for generations: *Your firstborn son shall know the lure of the night and the lust of the moon... he will become a creature of nightmares... until the true love that should have been, finally is.* Determined to right the ancient wrong, Tristan sets off across the ocean to reverse the centuries-old curse.

Benjamin Sterling might not be happy alone—not quite human, nor accepted by true werewolves—but his life is predictable, at least until Tristan Northland shows up in his office, unannounced and with nowhere to stay. Because of the curse he carries, Benjamin has plenty of reason to distrust witches and Northlands as well as the werewolf tribe that has always treated him as an outcast. But with Tristan at his side, Benjamin finds himself and his future transformed by two unexpected emotions: blooming hope and enduring love.

RHIANNE AILE has an unhealthy relationship with her computer, iced tea, and chocolate. Growing up, she split her time between Oklahoma and Chicago, making her equally fond of horses, skyscrapers, cowboys, and men in well-tailored suits. Facilitating retreats for women and authors keeps her traveling enough to stay happy.

Visit her Web site at http://www.rhianneaile.com/ and her blog at http://rhianne-aile.livejournal.com/.

Other Titles by RHIANNE AILE

http://www.dreamspinnerpress.com

Other Fantasy/Paranormal Romances From DREAMSPINNER PRESS

http://www.dreamspinnerpress.com

LaVergne, TN USA
07 May 2010
181890LV00001B/11/P